Praise for Aimée and David Thurlo

"Aimée and David Thurlo surely deserve to be called the successors to Tony Hillerman."   —Tess Gerritsen,
New York Times bestselling author,
on *A Time of Change*

"Ella Clah, a Navajo Tribal Police officer, is always good company, on and off the reservation."   —*The New York Times Book Review* on *Coyote's Wife*

"The skinwalker angle is especially creepy here. The Thurlos mix in a great deal of knowledge about trafficking in Native American antiquities with a well-constructed investigation steered by a believable and admirable heroine."
—*Booklist* on *Ghost Medicine*

"The resolution of this compelling story leads to one of the most difficult decisions Ella has ever made."
—*Mystery Scene* on *Ghost Medicine*

"*Ghost Medicine* is full of suspense, and the writing is topnotch. It can be read and enjoyed as a stand-alone novel."
—*Guardian Liberty Voice*

"An entertaining story; we also learn much about Navajo culture. Ella Clah books continue to entertain the reader with legend and mystery. This makes for another superior tale from the Thurlos."   —*Shelf Life* on *Ghost Medicine*

GHOST MEDICINE

✕ ✕ ✕ ✕ ✕

AN ELLA CLAH NOVEL

AIMÉE & DAVID THURLO

A Tom Doherty Associates Book
New York

GHOST MEDICINE

Copyright © 2013 by Aimée Thurlo and David Thurlo

A Forge Book
Published by Tom Doherty Associates, LLC
175 Fifth Avenue
New York, NY 10010

www.tor-forge.com

Forge® is a registered trademark of Tom Doherty Associates, LLC.

The Library of Congress has cataloged the
hardcover edition as follows:

Thurlo, Aimée.
    Ghost medicine / Aimée Thurlo, David Thurlo.—First Edition.
        p. cm.
    "A Tom Doherty Associates book."
    ISBN 978-0-7653-3403-9 (hardcover)
    ISBN 978-1-4668-0785-3 (e-book)
    1. Navajo Indians—Fiction. 2. Spirits—Fiction. 3. Paranormal
fiction. 4. Murder—Investigation—Fiction. I. Thurlo, David.
II. Title.
PS3570.H82G46 2013
813'.54—dc23

                                                                    2013022085

ISBN 978-0-7653-3405-3 (trade paperback)

Forge books may be purchased for educational, business, or promotional use. For information on bulk purchases, please contact Macmillan Corporate and Premium Sales Department at 1-800-221-7945, extension 5442, or write specialmarkets@macmillan.com.

First Edition: November 2013
First Trade Paperback Edition: September 2014

Printed in the United States of America

0 9 8 7 6 5 4 3 2 1

To Diana Norwood and Lilly Norwood,
two of our favorite people

ACKNOWLEDGMENTS

With special thanks to Steve Henry, attorney-at-law, for sharing his expertise, and Sergeant Ryan Tafoya, who's always there for us. You guys are terrific.

GHOST MEDICINE

ONE

✖ ✖ ✖

hange is in the air, part-
ner." Ella Clah, Special Investigator for the Navajo Tribal
Police, gazed at the steep, pastel layered walls of the sandstone mesa north of the valley. She and her partner were
10-7, out of service, having lunch, and she was staring out
the window of the Totah Café, her favorite restaurant. Even
the land itself changed. New arroyos appeared, and old
ones faded away under clouds of dust and sand, leaving fans
of washed-out gravel, and sometimes even petrified shark
teeth from an ancient sea.

"Every time we get a new politician out to make his
bones, it's the same thing," Justine said. "The department
gets screwed. From what I've heard, Safety Director Bidtah
plans to get rid of nonessential officers and what his speech-
writers called the 'deadwood.' Rumor has it that includes
Police Chief Atcitty."

"Bidtah is all flash and dash. He's racing up the ladder,
walking over anyone who gets in the way. Nothing good

ever comes from that kind of ambition," Ella said. "I understand he plans to cut costs by closing down our special investigations unit, and reducing the number of detectives at our station."

"Big Ed was responsible for creating our unit, so by phasing us out, he takes away one of Big Ed's most successful operations."

Ella took a bite of her red chile enchilada. The wonderful spicy taste improved her mood instantly.

"If Bidtah wants to disband something, I wish he'd cut those mandatory departmental training workshops," Justine said. "They're essentially useless. The last one I suffered through was on how to manage nonviolent confrontations. The only new thing it offered was a segment on the impact of cell phones."

"Instant communications can mean even more people involved in altercations, like a family dispute. Fortunately, officers also have that technology. Now, if we just had the manpower," Ella said.

"I'm scheduled for a session on Saturday. This one is on utilizing nonlethal weapons. Nelson Natani, Bidtah's right-hand man, is teaching that one himself. Shall I take notes?"

Ella was about to answer when her cell phone rang. She spoke hurriedly, then looked at her partner. "We've got to roll. Finish up fast or get a doggie bag."

Having already paid when they were served, a necessity when on call, they were out the door in minutes. As they crossed the parking lot, Ella filled Justine in. "We've got a possible 10-27 several miles southwest of Rattlesnake," Ella said, using the code for a homicide.

"I wish I hadn't just wolfed down that enchilada. After all these years, I still get queasy around dead people." Justine kept her eyes glued on the road as she raced off the old steel-trestle San Juan bridge and took the curve at sixty, emergency lights flashing. "Any details on the body?"

"A girl out horseback riding found a gold pickup on a hill beside the road. She reported seeing a bloody man inside, slumped over the seat, not moving. That's all we have except for the general location. If it checks out, we'll bring in the crime scene team."

"That poor kid," Justine said. "Bet she remembers this for the rest of her life."

"Images like that stay with you, no matter how many Sings you have done," Ella said in a quiet voice. "When my kid closes her eyes, she dreams of horses. Me? I get corpses. Good thing I'm not a Traditionalist or I'd have to hire a full-time *hataalii*," she said, referring to their tribe's medicine men.

"Maybe your brother, Clifford, could give you a 'friends and family' discount," Justine teased.

"If my brother knew how often I have nightmares, he'd conduct a month's worth of Sings, but it still wouldn't help. It's just something that goes with the job," Ella said.

Justine nodded as she turned right, continuing on Highway 64 west, passing Shiprock High, then the Phil, the performing arts center.

There were a few cars in the parking lot, probably belonging to kids and staff involved in the summer recreation program. At least today there was no school zone to slow Justine down.

The route was familiar, rising west into the dry desert

hills past the river valley and bosque on the north. Down to their right, farms lined both sides of the river. Water gave life, but except for a heavy rain the other day, there had been almost no moisture so far this year, and it was already mid-June. With so little snowpack last winter, the irrigation ditches were barely flowing. When droughts came, life became even tougher on the Rez.

"Earth to Ella."

Justine's voice brought her back to the present. "Sorry. What did you say?"

"I was thinking of taking the old turnoff west of Rattlesnake," Justine said. "The road's rougher there, but I think we'll reach the scene a few minutes faster. What do you think?"

"You're driving, go for it," Ella said, sitting up straight and clearing her mind. As she tried to focus on the job ahead, her cell phone rang. The caller ID told her it was her fourteen-year-old daughter. "Hey, sweetie, what's going on?"

"Bitsy just called, Mom. She was out riding her mare a while ago and found a dead man in a pickup less than ten minutes from her front door! She said his body was really messed up. Did you know?"

Dawn's voice was an octave too high and it reminded Ella of the little girl her daughter had once been. She missed those days more than she'd ever admit.

"Yes, daughter, I heard the news. I didn't realize until now it was your BFF who found the body. My partner and I are on the way to the site right now. It's our case."

"I thought so. I told her you'd probably have to stop by and talk to her."

"How much did she tell you about what she saw?" Ella asked, hoping the teen hadn't been busy calling or texting her friends with the news. Details often changed with the telling, and the notion of a body being "messed up" could be interpreted a hundred ways.

"Just what I told you. She would have told me more, but her mom made her get off the phone," Dawn said. "So what's going to happen to her now? Will she have to go to the police station and everything?"

"Probably not, but don't talk about this to anyone else. It's a police matter now," she said. "Just get on with your day. You have your riding lesson with Tonya this afternoon, right?"

"Yeah. I really hope someday I can barrel race like her, Mom. You should see all her trophies."

"You're learning from the best. Just be careful." Ella put her cell phone back in her pocket and looked around, trying to figure out exactly where they were.

As Justine turned off the highway, Ella had to grab on to the door handle. The road here was a jumble of ruts and potholes more suitable for an obstacle course than for their vehicle. It ran south, paralleling the foothills of the Carrizo Mountains beyond.

"Maybe it'll just be a drunk sleeping it off after taking a beating," Justine said.

"Yeah. When a fight gets out of hand, blood makes it look a lot worse. I hope you're right."

Ella looked around cautiously as they topped the third in a series of low hills in the undulating terrain. "Nothing up ahead," she said.

Justine gripped the wheel tightly. "It's muddy in this stretch. It looks like they got a lot more rain here yesterday than we did over at my place."

They topped the next hill, and clearly visible in the road cut of the next ridge over was a dark gold pickup with the hood raised. Another, an older green pickup, was parked alongside it, and there were two men working on something in the gold pickup's engine compartment.

"We've got company," Justine said.

"Speed up," Ella said. "Those aren't our people and they have no business going near that truck."

Justine raced down the slope, siren and emergency lights on. The two men, both in jeans and straw Western hats, turned at the sound. The tallest one had what looked to be the pickup's battery in his arms. He stared at them for a second, dropped his load, and raced around to the driver's side. The other man jumped into the truck, barely making it inside before the vehicle spun around in a tight turn.

"They're making a run for it," Ella said.

The green truck sped away, bouncing on the uneven ground as Justine remained in close pursuit, racing uphill.

"There's nowhere to go, so just keep them in sight," Ella said, holding on to her seat and trying to keep her balance. "I'll call for backup."

She reached down for the radio mike twice, and each time got bounced away as Justine had to swerve to miss a pothole or encountered a stretch of washboard road that rattled their teeth.

Ella finally made a successful grab, and called it in. After several seconds of hurried conversation, she racked the mike. "Get that?"

Justine nodded, her eyes still on the green pickup, which

was fishtailing back and forth across a dry, sandy wash, raising clouds of dust. "Highway east and west will be covered. Meanwhile, we want to drive them south and cut them off. There's no outlet south, right?"

"Right," Ella said.

"Hang on!" Justine shouted as they hit another series of ripples in the hard dirt and gravel. The perps ahead had made it through, though their pickup was veering to the right, and slowing rapidly.

"He's got tire trouble," Ella said. "Get ready for a foot chase."

"You think they killed the driver?"

"Until we know otherwise . . . yes."

The green pickup swung to the left, trying to spin around, do a 180, then slip past them as they entered a deep arroyo. The laws of physics, however, refused to cooperate with their tactics. Instead, their right front tire, flat as could be now, hugged the ground and the vehicle skidded, lifting the driver's side off the ground.

"They're going to roll if they keep this up!" Justine yelled.

The pickup flew up another foot, then dropped back down hard, sliding to a stop, the rear end coming to rest against the steep side of the wash.

"Gotcha now." Justine hit the brakes, trapping the truck between the canyon wall and the department SUV.

Ella jumped out the passenger-side door, drew her Glock, and leaned across the hood, barrel pointed at the driver. "Police officers! Stay in the vehicle and show me your hands—both of you."

Justine's door was blocked by the front of the green

pickup, so she ducked low and slid out Ella's side. Running to the back of the Suburban, she aimed her weapon at the men.

"Stay *in* the vehicle," Justine called out to them, exposing only her head, left arm, and handgun.

"We're not armed, officers!" the passenger yelled back. "Don't shoot."

"Driver, keep your hands up and come out slowly," Ella ordered, moving around the engine compartment, her sights on the young Navajo man's head.

The driver slid out of the vehicle, but suddenly ducked below the door and ran down the arroyo, losing his hat in the process.

"Hold your man. I've got this idiot," Ella said, holstering her pistol as she raced toward the driver, who was trying to claw his way up a twenty-foot-high, forty-five-degree embankment.

Ella stood her ground and waited, watching as the man cursed, grabbed at the dirt and rocks, dug in his toes, and basically got nowhere trying to climb the embankment.

"Crap," the man groaned, then gave up and slid down the five feet he'd managed to climb. Raising his hands high, he turned and faced Ella, a sheepish expression on his face. "Okay, you got me. Now what?"

She brought out her yellow Taser and pointed it at the young Navajo's torso. "You been drinking, *hosteen*?" she said, using the Navajo term for "mister."

"No, ma'am. We just stopped to check out the pickup back there. The driver's dead, blown away. He got shot in the head but we didn't do it—honest!" He coughed, and tried to take shorter breaths.

The subject's clothing reeked with the odor of decaying flesh. "You got real close to the body, didn't you?" Ella said, fighting not to gag.

"Too close. I'll have to throw away this shirt. It really stinks but it's nothing compared to what it's like near the cab of that truck. It almost made me hurl. The guy's all covered with flies, even on his hands."

"Turn around slowly, then go back to the center of the road, kneel down on the ground, and lock your hands behind your head."

"Okay, okay." The barrel-chested man followed her instructions to the letter.

Ella nodded to Justine, who'd already handcuffed the skinny passenger. He appeared to be somewhere around eighteen.

"We'll secure them inside the SUV, take a look in their vehicle for any weapons or possible evidence, then drive back to the scene and check things out," Ella said.

"What about my truck?" the driver protested.

"I've got the keys, bro," Justine said, "and you've got a flat tire. It's not going anywhere."

Once they'd placed both men in the rear of the cruiser, Justine drove back, much more slowly this time. Ella used the men's driver's licenses to run a check through the MDT, the mobile data terminal.

"Petty crimes, but no outstanding warrants," Ella said.

"See? I told you we were clean," Ernest Cohoe, the younger man, said.

"So why'd you run?" Ella asked.

"Hello? We were stealing the battery," Ernest said. "Well, technically, Andrew was."

"Thanks, idiot," the driver whispered.

Five minutes later, they pulled in about twenty feet behind the gold pickup. As Ella stepped out of the vehicle, the unbearable stench of spoiled meat engulfed her, a reminder of what was waiting for them inside the truck.

Justine climbed out, looking around at the scene, one hand over her mouth. "This is going to be . . . really bad."

"Yeah, but there's no avoiding it," Ella said, rubbing Mentholatum around her nose to mask the scent, then handing the jar to Justine. "Let's go check out the body."

"Take short breaths, it'll help. And watch out for the *chindi*," Ernest said.

"Wise up, bro, they're cops. They don't believe in that BS," Andrew said.

"It's not BS. When we die, the evil side of us stays close to the body and will try to hurt the living. That's why I stayed clear of the truck. The *chindi* can make you nuts—or worse," Ernest said.

"You're already nuts, so don't worry about it," Andrew answered.

"You're the idiot, bro. You already had a good battery in your pickup. Now we're both going to jail."

"Just shut up, man," Andrew replied.

"Both of you shut up!" Justine yelled back to them as she and Ella continued walking toward the pickup.

As Ella drew near, she swatted away the big blowflies that circled the open cab.

Ella stopped a few feet from the driver's-side door and

checked the ground. There was one set of footprints in the damp roadbed, probably a match for Andrew's, the driver of the green truck who didn't believe in the *chindi*.

"Partner, I'm sick," Justine mumbled, then suddenly covered her mouth with one hand and ran back across the road.

Ella breathed through her mouth as much as possible. They were both seasoned homicide detectives, but the rain and the heat had done their usual job on the body. It was difficult even to take a breath without triggering a gag reflex.

With a burst of self-discipline, Ella forced herself to focus. The tall, slender Navajo man with the military-style haircut was slumped over, partially resting on the passenger's side. The position wasn't natural. It was more likely that someone had pushed the body aside.

There was a bloody hole about the size of a dime in the left side of his skull two inches above the top of his ear. The right side of his head was splattered all over the passenger's inside door panel—which accounted for most of the flies.

Ella tore her gaze from the victim's head and, swatting away the flies, glanced down again. The tips of the man's fingers and thumbs on both hands had been chopped off at the top joints, probably with something like bolt cutters. He'd undoubtedly been dead at the time because there was no evidence of a struggle, but the mutilations had been immediate. Blood had oozed from each wound, creating a real mess on the seat and floorboard.

Ella swallowed hard. This was a skinwalker's MO. She'd seen it before but usually at perverted ceremonial sites where Navajo witches had mutilated bodies stolen from their graves. This time, however, the skinwalker had also done the killing, which meant that trouble was only beginning.

These secretive people distorted Navajo beliefs to generate fear among their targets, usually to intimidate and control members of the community. They were also skilled tricksters and often created illusions or magic tricks to demonstrate their "power."

Ella tried to focus on the physical evidence. Theories would wait till later. Despite the swelling and discoloration from maybe two days' exposure to the elements, something about the man looked vaguely familiar to her.

Silently giving thanks that the last couple of days had been a little cooler due to the cloudy weather, she climbed up on the running board, canted her head, and looked into the dead man's face. The little mole above his left eyebrow and the tiny scar along his jawline . . .

A sudden chill enveloped her, and her heart began to race. She staggered back a step or two, nearly fell, but somehow caught herself in time.

"I know who the victim is," she said in a strangled voice as Justine returned. "We both knew him."

Justine stood beside Ella, looking pale but ready to work. "Who is it?"

"Harry Ute," Ella said, her voice a tight whisper.

"*Our* Harry, the officer who was part of our team for years?" Seeing Ella nod, Justine shook her head. "No way. Ralph and I took him out for coffee and apple pie just a few days ago. He came to the station to catch up with old friends."

Though the temperature was in the high seventies, Ella felt ice cold. She crossed her arms in front of her chest, trying to warm up. Harry was more than a friend. They'd dated exclusively for almost a year, and before leaving to join the U.S. Marshals Service, he'd asked her to be his wife. Though it had broken her heart to say no, she just hadn't been ready to make that kind of a commitment, so they'd parted ways. That was almost ten years ago, she realized, when Dawn was starting first grade.

The connection they'd shared once and faded memories of another time lingered in her mind along with an overwhelming sense of loss. A shudder ripped through her.

"Are you thinking what I'm thinking? I saw his hands," Justine said. "Stealing the whorls, the fingerprints, that's the mark of . . . the evil ones."

"I know, but I'm still hoping it's just some sicko thinking we won't be able to ID the body now," Ella said.

"I suppose so, but that would mean he's not particularly bright," Justine said. "We could trace the pickup from the plate."

"I better call this in," Ella said. She moved around the area, holding up the phone in hopes of getting a signal. "No luck. I better use the radio," she said at last, and went back to the SUV.

TWO

—— ✖ ✖ ✖ ——

While waiting for the crime scene unit and the tribe's own medical examiner to arrive, Ella and Justine separated the men and questioned them thoroughly. Both had records for shoplifting and, when employed, usually worked construction, often for the same contractor.

The men claimed to have been on their way to Shiprock to look for work when they saw what they'd thought was an abandoned truck. Short on cash and knowing the battery would be easy to sell, Andrew had stood on the running board, reached inside through the open window, and pulled the hood release.

"So, Andrew, did you intend on reporting the body?" Ella asked.

"Yeah, sure. As soon as I got to Shiprock, I would have stopped at a pay phone and called it in. Ernie probably wouldn't have. He thinks he'll call the *chindi* if he even talks about the body. He really believes in all that traditional stuff. He's already talking about going to a *hataalii* for a blessing—once he scrapes up enough money, that is."

"Did you look at the body?"

"Me? No, not after I knew the guy was dead. Why would I? That's too gross even for me."

Ella questioned him for several minutes, and once assured he had no more information to share, placed him back in the SUV, still handcuffed. Moments later, Justine followed, securing Cohoe there as well.

With their prisoners put away, Ella and Justine moved out of the men's hearing range to discuss what they'd learned.

"Our friend wasn't killed today, and maybe not even yesterday," Justine said.

"Unless those two morons decided to return to the scene just to see what else they could find, there's no way we can link them to the homicide," Ella said. "They don't have anything on them or in their vehicle that ties them directly to the shooting. No rifle, no bolt cutters, no . . . trophies."

"All we can prove is that they were about to take the battery and that they fled the scene," Justine said. "They also weren't planning on stealing the truck, though the keys are still in the ignition, or they wouldn't have removed the battery."

"My guess is that they wouldn't have wanted to touch anything that had been in direct contact with the dead, not even Andrew, who's clearly a Modernist," Ella said. "These two will probably lawyer up once they're at the station, but I'm going to hold them for twenty-four hours. Once the ME establishes a time of death, we'll question them again and verify their alibis."

Justine glanced off at the mountains, purposely avoiding looking back at Harry's truck. "Our friend was as thin as a rail when I first met him. Then he bulked up, started with the bodybuilding, and his face filled out. For an old guy—no offense—he was pretty good looking. And a fine investigator, too," she added quickly, looking back at Ella. "I know you two were real close for a while. Are you sure you'll be okay working the scene?"

"I'll be fine. What we had ended a long, long time ago," Ella said, for her own benefit as well.

"Do you have any idea what he might have been doing out here?" Justine asked.

"No, but that's only one of the many questions we'll need answered," Ella said.

As she waited for the crime scene team, Ella glanced back at the tribal SUV, checking on their prisoners. They both appeared to be fine but bored. That would end soon enough. A patrol car was en route and they'd be taken to the station and processed within the hour.

Ella took another look at Harry's truck, then the surrounding terrain. Her old friend had been ambushed, and from the angle of the wound, he'd never even seen it coming. In a way, that was a mercy. The mutilations had been performed postmortem, and he never suffered. She'd take all the comfort she could from that.

"I'm going to start taking photos," Justine called out.

"Yeah, do. In particular, I'd like you to document what the evidence has already told us."

"Like what, specifically?"

"His head had been facing forward, so he'd been looking out the front windshield when the bullet struck him high above his left ear. It passed through him completely, then continued through the passenger's door and into the exposed road cut. From the angle, I'm guessing the shooter was on the top of the opposite slope."

Justine nodded. "Yeah. A drive-by shooter would have been at about the same level as him, and the bullet would have passed out the open passenger's-side window instead. Hopefully the round won't be too badly deformed when we find it and we'll be able to match it to a specific weapon eventually." She paused for a moment. "I know he was doing PI work, but do you happen to know what kind? Background checks, business thefts, security?"

Ella shook her head. She'd noticed that, like her, Justine was avoiding using Harry's name. That was said to call a man's *chindi,* and though neither of them were Traditionalists, some habits were too deeply ingrained to ignore.

"All I know is that he was working for Teeny," Ella said. Bruce Little, an old friend and former cop, had his own PI agency. Despite his name, Teeny stood just shy of seven feet and was shaped like a barrel with arms. "Stay sharp out here, partner. We've already seen that there's a lot more to this murder than just being in the wrong place at the wrong time."

Ella was marking off the area by setting out orange cones and Justine was taking photos when the tribe's crime scene vehicle roared up the incline.

Sergeant Benny Pete was at the wheel of the modified RV and Officer Ralph Tache was in the passenger's seat next to him. Sergeant Joe Neskahi, also part of their team, had been off duty but, according to dispatch, would be arriving soon. A half mile farther down the road, Ella could see the much smaller medical examiner's van following in their wake.

Tache, limping from injuries he'd suffered years back while trying to disarm a pipe bomb, stepped down out of the van first. "Okay to pull in close?" he called out to Ella.

"Yeah, go ahead. We've already checked the ground inside the markers." She pointed to the Day-Glo orange cones.

Benny, the driver, looked at Tache, who then guided him in closer using hand signals. The taller vehicle would provide them some shade for the next few hours, at least, and there was an awning they could extend, if needed.

Once the vehicle was in position, Ella met Officer Tache halfway. "I'm sorry you have to see this, too, Ralph," she said. "You were his partner for years, it won't be easy."

Tache nodded and cleared his throat before speaking. "He thought the world of you, Ella," he said, looking down the road and not making eye contact with her.

She swallowed hard, but kept her voice steady. "Let's get to work. Our friend deserves our best efforts. I'd like you to take over the camera work. Justine and Benny can complete a perimeter search and I'll see if I can narrow down the shooter's location. Also be on the lookout for anything odd, like Navajo ceremonial items or displays. Once you see the body, you'll know what I'm talking about."

As Ralph turned toward the van to get his gear, Benny came up, catching the last of her words. A heavily tattooed city Navajo with an army buzz cut, the thirty-five-year-old had spent years with the LAPD and was a master at spotting details and finding trace.

"Benny, once the ME removes the victim, I want you to

help me examine the interior of the vehicle. It looks like a one-shot kill, but it's also clear that someone, probably the shooter, moved the body, and not just to give easy access to the fingers."

"What about the fingers?" Benny asked.

"The tips have been chopped off at the joint."

"Sorry I asked."

"Besides the missing body parts, I suspect that there are personal items that have been taken, like the victim's weapon," Ella said. "Nothing ever gets past you, so I want you to go over the crime scene with me."

"Okay, boss. I know this guy worked with the team, so he's one of ours. The mutilations . . . are you thinking, skin-walkers?" He whispered the last word.

"Yeah, maybe." Ella also lowered her voice. "You might also keep an eye on Ralph. He was the victim's partner. If he needs some space, or a kind word . . ."

Benny nodded. "I've got it covered."

As Ella looked up at the top of the road, where evidence indicated the shooter must have been, she heard Carolyn pull up in the van. "I have to go meet the ME."

Not needing a response, Ella went to greet Dr. Carolyn Roanhorse. Her friend had never looked better. Losing sixty pounds over the past two years had changed her inside and out. These days, their ME turned heads wherever she went.

Carolyn worked exclusively on the Navajo Nation, though officially she was an employee of the Office of the Medical Investigator based in Albuquerque. Unfortunately, her job as ME had made Carolyn almost an outcast on the Rez. Traditionalist Navajos believed that her work with the bodies of the dead meant she was contaminated with their essence. Modernists avoided her, too, but with them it wasn't out of fear. It was a culturally enhanced, natural aversion to someone who spent their day working on corpses.

Despite the odds against it, Ella and Carolyn had hit it off from the first day they'd met. Never one to run with the pack or bow to public opinion, Ella had understood Carolyn in a way few ever could have. Over the years their friendship had grown even stronger.

"You made good time," Ella said, and smiled. "Hot date tonight? That's your new blouse, and you did your nails, too. Let me guess. You're meeting Dr. Sheldon for dinner?"

"No, that didn't work out. He was too much in love with himself."

"So who are you seeing? Anyone I know?"

"Maybe," Carolyn muttered, not looking directly at her.

"You're being awfully cryptic." Ella was trying to maintain the small talk they always used to take the edge off at crime scenes. It was a survival skill they'd all learned to help them cope with the brutality they often faced. Yet today for some reason Carolyn wasn't in a talkative mood and Ella was running out of things to say. After a moment she gave up. "I guess I better let you get started. The body's been mutilated in a way you'll need to check more closely. We've seen stuff like this before."

Carolyn nodded somberly, then untied the colorful scarf she'd been wearing and placed it into her pocket. As Ella started to move away, Carolyn touched her forearm gently. "You sure about the ID?" she asked.

Ella nodded.

"All right, then. I'll give this top priority."

A few minutes later, digital recorder on, Carolyn began

recording her findings. With more light and an open driver's door, Ella was able to look over Carolyn's shoulder and verify that there were no objects under the seats except for a candy wrapper.

The floorboards showed evidence of heavy rain splatter that had since dried. The absence of any marks on the now dusty interior, except for the scuff mark left when Andrew had leaned inside, suggested that nothing else had been disturbed recently. Ella made a mental note to ask the locals about the timing of the rain itself. A review of Doppler radar images would also help them establish the time line—at least of the rain.

Carolyn's voice was clinical and her comments precise as she examined the body. Ella moved away. Normally she liked listening in on Carolyn's observations as she made them, but the identity of the victim changed things. She decided she'd rather face the news all at once than piecemeal.

Ella was busy searching the ground when Carolyn finally called her over.

"What do you have for me?" Ella said.

"Today's Thursday, so I'd say he died about forty-eight hours ago. I'd place the TOD Tuesday, between noon and four, judging from the condition of his skin, his eyes, and a few other indicators," she said. "The finger joints were removed with something like bolt cutters or metal snips, but after his death. No sign of torture. The only thing I found in the victim's clothing was this." She held up a paper bag and Ella looked inside. There was an inexpensive ballpoint pen, a tube of mostly melted lip balm, and a pack of mint chewing gum with two remaining sticks.

"No wallet, handgun, extra clip, or cell phone?" Ella asked. "He always carried a pocket spiral notebook, too."

Carolyn shook her head. "They weren't on him. Maybe you'll find those under his seat, or in the glove compartment."

"Okay, we'll go over the interior once you release it to us," Ella said, handing the bag back to Carolyn, who added her name, date, and the location of the found items.

"Anything you can tell me about the gunshot?" Ella asked.

"Only that it was probably fired from a high-velocity rifle, considering it went through and out the passenger's-side door." Carolyn said. "Until you recover the slug, we won't know for sure, but it looks like a hunting round that mushroomed on impact."

"He was parked here, maybe waiting for someone or watching down the road." Ella looked at the intersection a quarter mile away, then glanced up at the top of the road cut. "The way I see it, the sniper took the shot from up there," she said, pointing to the rise on the left. "That's what, fifty yards?"

"If that," Carolyn said. "I've already taken tissue samples, so I'm ready to move the body and turn the scene over to you. Anybody on your B-list today? I can use a strong back or two to help get the victim into my van."

Ella thought about volunteering, but this wasn't an ordinary scene and she just didn't have it in her. Right now her priority was keeping it together. Hearing a new voice, she glanced around and saw that Sergeant Joe Neskahi had arrived. The bulky former wrestler caught her eye and nodded, sympathy evident in his soft expression. No words were needed.

"Need some help, Doctor?" Joe asked, stepping up and giving Carolyn a smile.

Ten minutes after the two would-be thieves were transported to the station, Carolyn drove away with the body.

Benny came up and joined Ella. "Photos, then a closer look?" he asked, holding up a camera and motioning toward the open door of the pickup.

"Yeah, go ahead," Ella said.

After Benny had taken a dozen photos from various angles, they both put on a second set of latex gloves, a habit of most tribal homicide cops. The outer layer would touch the dead and the things that had been left by the victim. The other would protect the wearer from contamination with the first pair when the gloves were removed.

"See that outline on the passenger seat?" Benny pointed to a rectangle not marked with blood spray and gore. "It's about the size of a cell phone."

"He probably set it there, and his killer removed it before the body was tipped away from the steering wheel. The shooter seems to have taken almost everything the victim had on him. If you happen to find a small spiral notebook anywhere, let me know."

Ella heard digging sounds on the opposite side of the pickup. "Anything yet, Justine?"

"Just a second . . . ," she said. "Gotcha," she added a second later.

Justine stood and held up a round. "Found the bullet. It's a mushroomed rifle slug, but it's in pretty bad shape. Some of the copper jacket is probably still in the ground or the door panel." Justine came around the front of the pickup and handed the evidence bag to Ella. "There's not much hope for a match. The rifling is barely there."

"Yeah, but at least we should be able to identify the caliber and the manufacturer." Ella handed it back. "Get whatever you can from around the area the bullet impacted, but hold back on checking the door panel until we're done with the interior."

"Okay."

Ella and Benny processed the cab slowly and methodically. The stench had dissipated some now that the body had been removed, but much of it continued to cling to the upholstery and the interior of the truck.

Forcing themselves to ignore distractions, they went over every square inch. By the time they were done, Ella's patience had been stretched to the limit. The flies were an ever-present nuisance and even mentholatum in her nose hadn't been able to successfully mask the odor of decaying flesh.

Ella stood well back for a moment, swallowing hard. She'd lost a friend, and though sorrow—and anger at the way he'd died—filled her in equal measure, there was no time to grieve. She had a job to do and Harry deserved nothing less than 100 percent from her.

"I can process the exterior myself, if you'd like," Benny said.

"Yeah, go ahead. That smudge on the driver's side was supposedly made by one of the thieves when he reached in to pop the hood."

Ella walked over to meet Joe Neskahi, who was coming down the hill, camera in hand. "Any luck up there?" she asked.

"I found a depressed area in the sand where the shooter

lay in a prone position, but there wasn't much else to go on. The rain pretty much obliterated everything except the gross outline. From the angle, I'd say he had an easy shot, especially if the vehicle was stationary. Is that your theory?"

"Yeah, that's the way it looks. The engine was off, the brake set, and the transmission in park, judging from the blood splatter pattern. Besides, if he'd been moving, the pickup would have rolled downhill and off the road," Ella said. "Did you find any shell casings?"

"No, but Ralph's going up there in a few minutes with the metal detector. I was about to check this side of the road cut in case it had rolled off the edge," he said. "I did find one thing you need to know about right away. Tracks were deliberately left up there to mess with our minds."

"What do you mean, Joe?" Ella asked.

"First of all, they weren't made until after the rain. I figure they were left there yesterday or last night, and they go backwards from the shooting site."

"Backwards?"

"Yeah. The shooter—who else would know where he'd been the day before—walked backwards from a section of hard ground to the spot where he took the shot. Then he carefully walked back in those same tracks. It gives the impression that he beamed down from above, took the shot, then walked off. Weird, huh? Something a Navajo witch would do?" he added, his voice lower now.

"You took photos?" Ella asked.

"From every angle," he said.

"Good work," Ella said. "Another thing, Joe. You volunteered to help Dr. Roanhorse before being asked. Thanks for stepping up like that."

"Glad to help. I know this one's not easy for you," he said, "and the doc's always hard-pressed to find an extra pair of hands."

It was the slight gentling in his voice when he spoke of Carolyn that let Ella know what she'd somehow missed. Joe was interested in her longtime friend.

"Are you two getting together later?" she asked, curious.

"I wish. We've had coffee a few times, but she's more into medicine, science, and tribal politics than baseball, rodeo, and cars," he said, and shrugged.

"So what are you saying, that she's dating a politician?"

"No, more like a lawyer." Joe shifted uneasily. "I'd better go look for that shell casing." He nodded toward the slope in the road cut.

"Wait a sec. You know something. What's going on?" she pressed.

"Don't kill the messenger, okay?" He looked at the ground for a second or two, then spoke slowly. "Carolyn's dating a guy pretty close to home these days—your home."

Ella stared at him in confusion. All she could think of was Herman, her mom's husband, who was pushing eighty. Then it hit her. "You mean like a lawyer—close to home?"

Joe nodded. "Yeah. She's been seeing Kevin Tolino."

The news left her speechless. Although she and Kevin hadn't been intimate in years, and had never lived together either, he was her daughter's father and played a large role in their lives. Getting used to this was going to take time.

Justine, who'd apparently been standing behind her, cleared her throat and stepped forward. "I'm done, boss. We need to send an officer to our friend's residence to preserve any evidence there, but the system doesn't have a current address for him. I figured that since he worked for Bruce Little, maybe you could get the address?"

"Yeah, but I want to tell him what's happened in person. Have Benny check area cell phone carriers and see if he can get our friend's address through them—just in case. Also have him tell everyone on our team that the skinwalker angle has to stay under wraps at least for now. Something like this can create a panic."

"Okay. Afterwards, do you want to start questioning area residents?" Justine pointed to a lone house perhaps a mile in the distance.

"Yeah, let's do that," Ella said, glad to be able to focus on police procedures again. "Our friend's death is connected to whatever business he had here and to skinwalkers. The sooner we figure out what that link is, the faster we'll be able to put his murderer behind bars."

Justine spoke to Benny, then met Ella back at their tribal SUV. Ella got into the passenger's seat while Justine took the wheel.

"Does it bother you, about Kevin and Carolyn, I mean," Justine asked her as they got under way.

"It just feels . . . strange," Ella said.

"It's going to be interesting, though probably not in a good way, once your family finds out. How do you think Rose will react, knowing Kevin is spending time with Carolyn and also with Dawn?"

Ella stared at Justine and sucked in her breath. "Oh, wow. I hadn't considered that. I think my brain's about to explode."

THREE

—— ✖ ✖ ✖ ——

Twenty minutes later, Ella and Justine had finished conducting their first interview and were walking back to the SUV. "Well, that got us nowhere," Justine said, opening her door as Ella climbed in the other side.

"Harris Largo's in his nineties and very hard of hearing, so it wasn't a surprise that he never heard the gunshot," Ella said.

"It also makes sense that he seldom goes past the area where our friend died. From his residence, Rattlesnake Road, to the east, is the best and quickest route to the highway."

"At least we got some intel on the other area residents, like who might have been at home during the day," Ella said. "Let's go back by the crime scene so I can leave that list with our people. Once they finish processing the area and the pickup is hauled to impound, Ralph can drive the van back to the station. That'll free up Benny and Joe, and they can interview the other locals. You and I are going to drop by Teeny's. I need to give him the news and find out what our friend was working on at the time of his death."

"Teeny probably already knows what happened. He monitors police calls, or at least he used to," Justine said, pulling back onto the graveled road.

"No, I really don't think he's found out yet," Ella said. "He would have called me by now if he did. Remember that we got the initial call over the cell phone, not the radio."

"Our friend had an ex-wife and a daughter. They'll also need to be notified," Justine said.

"We never met—that was after his time here—but last I heard, they were living in the Albuquerque area. I'll arrange to have an officer go by their home and give them the news as soon as Teeny gives me their address."

Ten minutes later, they passed through the small community of Rattlesnake and Ella was finally able to use her cell phone. She got Teeny on the second ring.

"Hey, Ella, good to hear your voice," Teeny said, his tone mellow and upbeat. "Howsit? I've picked up some carefully worded department transmissions this afternoon and news that the crime scene unit was deployed. You have a hush-hush case you want to talk about?"

Justine, who could hear the penetrating voice of the mostly gentle giant, turned, eyebrows raised. "He's good," she whispered.

"Naw, great. Hi, Justine," Teeny said distinctively.

"Hi, Bruce," she mumbled, then turned back to focus on her driving.

"We need to talk, Teeny. See you in—say, a half hour?"

"Of course," he answered, suddenly serious. "Can you tell me more?"

"Not over the phone. See you in a bit." Ella ended the call. Teeny and she had shared a special connection all the way back to high school. He could pick up even the most subtle changes in her voice. If she'd kept talking, he would have put things together, and that wasn't the way she wanted him to get the news.

Teeny and Harry had been friends for years. They'd both started out as tribal officers working out of the Shiprock station. That was one of the reasons Teeny had been so quick to hire him when Harry returned to the Rez.

Delivering the news of Harry's death would be difficult, but she owed it to Harry and Teeny, too.

They arrived at Teeny's compound, a combination home and business located in a small warehouse several miles east of Shiprock. Stopping in front of the camera lens by the electronic gate, Justine pushed the intercom button.

A moment later they heard Teeny's deep voice. "Come on in, Officers."

The gate opened, and within a few minutes they were met at the front door of the metal building by a nearly seven-foot, three-hundred-pound Navajo man with dark, intelligent eyes.

"It's good to see you two," Bruce said, motioning to the interior, a big room filled with tables and cabinets containing electronic gear of all kinds.

Teeny had been a tribal cop and the department's IT expert until budget cuts took away his job several years ago.

Yet it hadn't taken Teeny long to turn loss into opportunity. These days, Bruce Little—only Ella could call him Teeny—was a highly paid consultant and the sole owner of a well-known and successful private investigations agency. Though he still worked with the department on special cases, his services were much more expensive now that he was in business for himself.

"Is this about Harry?" Teeny asked abruptly, leading them to a central patio with a view of the blue skies overhead. "I tried to reach him, but couldn't even get an e-mail to his cell phone. The GPS on his cell phone is no longer broadcasting, too. What's going on?"

The tile floor was cool, shaded by the rows of weather-treated beams that broke up the skyline, leaving a sun-shadow pattern. Ella came up behind one of the four chairs that surrounded the round mosaic-tiled table, but remained standing.

There was no good way to break news like this.

"I'm sorry to have to tell you this, but we found Harry's body a few hours ago," Ella said. "He was shot in the head with a high-powered rifle while sitting in his pickup."

"Where was he at the time?" Teeny asked, his voice taut.

"Parked on an isolated road southwest of Rattlesnake. According to the ME, the time of death was approximately forty-eight hours ago."

Teeny looked down at his feet, uttered something that sounded like an oath, then pulled back a chair and took a seat. Ella nodded to Justine, and they both sat as well.

"There's more," Ella said, then told him about the signs they'd found of skinwalker involvement.

He stared at the wall for a minute or two, then finally

spoke. "Dammit. He was a good man and my friend. He was also a top-notch investigator, though he had an independent streak a mile long." Teeny ran a hand through his close-cropped hair. "I should have insisted that he file more updates and keep me in the loop. Then I would have had a clearer idea of what went wrong."

"His pockets had been emptied, Bruce," Justine said. "His wallet, cell phone, weapon, almost everything was taken. We caught a couple of men ripping off his truck's battery, too, but that was maybe a day after the shooting. We have no reason to believe that those men had anything to do with the homicide."

"He was parked beside a road that had been cut through a ridge, which meant he was pretty much hidden from view. It was the perfect position to watch the road to the north, toward the highway. It's possible he was waiting to meet someone," Ella said, leaning forward and resting her elbows on the table. "His killer left our friend's truck behind, though the keys were still in the ignition, but took everything else. That's what makes me think the murder was job related. I need you to tell me what Harry was working on and if there's any connection between that and skinwalkers."

"Don't use his name," Teeny said, his jaw clenched.

"I'm sorry. I wasn't thinking," Ella said.

"It normally wouldn't bother me, but he died hard and he worked here. I'm not worried about the *chindi*. I just want to . . ." He paused, searching for the right words. "I don't know," he said at last.

"I think I understand," Ella said. They were both Modernists who didn't believe in ghosts or evil spirits, but they were also Navajo. That part of them never stopped whispering urgent warnings, assuring them that there was more to life than what was easily seen.

"I can't tell you the exact nature of the case H was working on, not without permission from my client. I also can't tell you why he was at that location, but that's because I don't know the answer to that myself. You knew H. He was an old pro. I gave him a long leash."

"Come on, Teeny. Give me something," Ella pressed. "Anything to set us on the right track."

"I can tell you this much. He was investigating a series of thefts my client had discovered, but H hadn't nailed down a suspect yet," he said, then after a beat continued. "The curious thing is that the killer took our friend's notebook. That makes me think he'd finally come up with some names, but having that suspect turn out to be a skinwalker"—he shook his head—"that makes no sense to me. As far as I know, H's investigation centered on Anglo suspects."

"But he was on the Rez," Ella said. "Watching or waiting for someone."

"I got that, but I can't give you a reason why. Maybe his murder is unrelated to his work here."

"The reason he was there might be on his computer in a daily log or report he'd yet to file," Justine said. "We'd like to take a look."

"He usually left his laptop at his apartment. Have you checked out his place?" Teeny asked.

Ella shook her head. "Do you have his current address? The killer has his apartment keys and a two-day lead. We may already be too late, but I need to check it out."

"Let's go," Teeny said, picking up his keys as he gave

them the address. "His apartment is off the main highway between Farmington and Bloomfield. Follow me and I'll save you some time trying to find it."

A few minutes later, they were racing east, following Teeny in his dark gray pickup. It was at least a half hour drive, so Ella phoned the sheriff's department, asking that a deputy be sent to secure the scene. They'd be well off the Navajo Nation, and she needed someone with jurisdiction on hand.

Next, she called Special Agent Dwayne Blalock, their local FBI liaison. "I'm going to need a warrant to search for computers, memory devices, notebooks, and papers that might contain information on Harry's investigations."

"I'll phone in a request to the district judge. You should have it shortly, since the need to put a rush on it is there. I'm just leaving Albuquerque. As soon as I'm back in the area, I'll let you know."

Ten minutes later, as Justine pulled up in front of an apartment complex west of Bloomfield, Ella reached for the copy of the search warrant. It had just been relayed electronically to her mobile data terminal's printer, and she'd been given the go-ahead to serve it on behalf of Blalock.

A SJC deputy walked over to meet them seconds after Justine parked next to Teeny's pickup. The deputy, his name tag read WALKER, waited as Ella and Justine stepped out of the cruiser.

"Investigator Clah?" Seeing Ella nod, he continued. "The apartment's locked, and there are no signs of any break-in. There's also no one hanging around, except for a few kids on skateboards."

Ella noted that Teeny had remained in his pickup.

Knowing he had no jurisdiction at all, he hadn't wanted to complicate matters.

"The perp has a key. Did you try the knob?" Ella asked Walker.

"No, ma'am, but I tried knocking and there was no answer. I also listened and it was quiet inside."

"Thanks," Ella said, walking over to the first-floor apartment door and taking a look around for herself. The curtains were drawn across the front room and bedroom windows and the lights were out, making it impossible for her to see inside.

"Would you like me to get a key from the manager?" Justine asked.

Ella nodded and handed her the warrant in response. As Justine left, Ella waved to Teeny. It was time to introduce him to Deputy Walker, who'd kept looking at him, clearly uneasy.

Five minutes later, Justine returned with a man in his late forties. He looked ex-military, judging from his bearing, stride, and short-cropped hair. Ella identified herself, took the key he offered, and unlocked the door.

She held up a hand, signaling the others, Teeny included, to wait. She stepped inside, hand on her Glock .40-caliber handgun, and took a look around the small, simply furnished apartment.

After several moments, Ella gave them the all-clear. Justine, Teeny, and the county deputy were still at the door, though Teeny was taking up twice the space.

Justine began to search in the bedroom, and Teeny went to Harry's desk, looking inside the drawers for the laptop.

Another uniformed deputy soon appeared at the door, and Ella went to meet him.

"I'm Deputy Schutz. I was sent to provide additional backup here. What do you need?"

The blue-eyed, sunburned deputy in his late forties filled out his tan uniform almost to the bursting point, but he wasn't overweight, just muscular. "Join Deputy Walker and talk to the nearby tenants. I want to know if anyone, besides the resident, was seen entering or leaving this apartment this past week."

"Yes, ma'am."

Lost in thought, Ella watched him go. Sooner or later, she'd have to meet with Sheriff Taylor and discuss the case. She'd coordinated many investigations with county over the years, and had found the sheriff an exceptionally good ally, even under the most trying circumstances.

"No luck," Teeny said, catching Ella's eye. "There's a clear spot free of dust on the desk that indicates where his laptop was at one point. The charger's on the floor, unplugged, but no computer."

"Maybe he moved it elsewhere," Ella said. "Let's search the place from top to bottom."

Ella worked alongside Teeny and Justine, opening drawers, searching the closet, even looking under the bed and mattress, and behind the furniture. She'd just finished searching the kitchen area when Deputy Schutz came back into the room.

"Walker's going back to recheck the apartments that didn't answer our knock the first time, but I've got a hit from the man in apartment 107. He just came home from work."

Schutz handed her a piece of paper. "This is the witness's name and phone number. Below that is a description of the woman he saw with the victim the night before last, at about 2100. Mr. Alan Sanchez knew the victim well enough to be on a first-name basis with him, and according to him, they'd gone out for a beer several times."

Ella read the neat script describing a "tipsy," leggy Navajo woman in her twenties, with a shapely figure and short reddish hair. She'd been wearing ultra-tight jeans and a halter top.

"The neighbor, Mr. Sanchez, suggested from their coziness and age difference that Mr. Ute had picked her up at the bar just down the highway—the Horny Toad."

"Did he think the woman was a hooker?" Ella asked.

"Not his exact words, but that was the implication, yes," the deputy said.

"Do you have a full list of the people you spoke to?" Ella asked.

Schutz handed her two small sheets of paper neatly torn from his notebook. "Names and numbers."

She looked at her watch, noting it was nearly seven. "Okay, thanks for your help. If Deputy Walker finds anyone else home on his second try, let us know, otherwise you're free to go. Thanks for your help."

Schulz nodded, said good night, then left.

Ella shut the door, then briefed Teeny and Justine. "If our friend had a woman guest here the night before last, her fingerprints are probably around. I'll ask Big Ed to put in a request for the county's crime scene unit. We need them to go over this place. There are bound to be prints around the bathroom and the bed, and maybe on one of the beer bottles in the trash. Once we ID the woman, I'd like to question her." Ella looked over at Teeny. "You wouldn't happen to know if he was seeing someone regularly, would you?"

"He wouldn't have spoken to me about something like that," Teeny said. "We were friends, but he also worked for me. There was a line there he didn't like to cross."

"A Navajo woman with red hair? It was either a wig or a dye job," Justine said.

"I'll see if I can get a lead from the county's vice unit. I'd also like to bring in one of their detectives to help us work the case whenever we're on this side of the Rez border," Ella said. "Dan Nez might be willing to give us a hand."

She'd been dating Detective Nez for months. Dan had served for several years as a Winslow, Arizona, cop, but recently relocated to the Four Corners.

The attraction between them had been fast and strong, maybe too much so. Dan wasn't relationship shy, but Ella was, after her breakup with Reverend Bilford Tome. Sensing it, Dan had suggested that they shouldn't take things too fast, and she'd agreed, grateful that he was willing to give them the time to really get to know each other.

"Justine, if Officer Walker is still out there, ask him to place a crime scene notice on the door before he goes and thank him for his cooperation."

After leaving the key with the manager, Teeny and Ella found Justine waiting in the courtyard. Together, they walked back toward the parking lot.

"So what's going on with you lately, Ella? I've heard some talk about the Public Safety Director wanting to phase out the homicide division at Shiprock and have it based in Window Rock."

"Yeah, we'll see how that plays out. I can tell you this—I'm not moving to Window Rock and ending up behind a desk. If it comes to that. I'll retire first."

"If you finally get a bellyful of department politics, come work for me," he said. "The job will pay better than what you're earning now and you can work full- or part-time. Whatever you decide."

"Is this a serious job offer?" she asked, interested.

"Of course. I could really use someone with your experience."

"Thanks," she said. "I'll give it some thought. I don't like the direction the department has taken on a whole range of issues lately. Politics and law enforcement are a bad mix."

"Then go while the going's good. That's what I did, and I've never regretted it."

"I hear you, but before I can do anything else, I've got a murder to solve," she said. "Talk to your client, explain the situation, and then tell me what I need to know."

"I'll see what I can do," Teeny said.

"Keep the skinwalker angle between us, at least for now, okay? I want to talk to Big Ed about that first," Ella said. "And remember that the clock's working against us. If a skinwalker's involved, there's no telling what lies ahead."

FOUR

——— ✖ ✖ ✖ ———

Teeny walked with Ella and Justine back to the tribal SUV. "Before we start heading back, there's something I want you to know, Ella. I'm going to be working this case, too—H was one of *my* people. The only open question is who'll catch the killer first," Teeny said.

"Whatever it takes," Ella said. "Is there anything you can give me right now that wouldn't break your client's confidentiality agreement?"

Teeny stared at an indeterminate spot just beyond the tribal SUV, then after a long moment, spoke. "H has handled several cases for me this past month, including one where our client's ex-boyfriend was threatening her."

"Was that solved?" Ella asked.

"Supposedly settled to our client's satisfaction," Teeny said with a nod, then after a pause, continued. "Currently, H was on the trail of a thief." He looked around carefully— with his eyes, not turning his head—and made sure that they were still alone. "I shouldn't be telling you this, but the circumstances warrant it. H was on the trail of someone selling stolen San Juan County property on the Internet. The thefts haven't been reported yet, because we don't want to tip off the thief, who's believed to be a county employee. My guess is that H was there to meet an informant, or maybe following a lead."

"Give me a little more to work on, Teeny, like what was being sold and who first discovered the losses," Ella pressed.

"Not without talking to my client. For what it's worth, you probably would have had all that information if you'd been able to retrieve H's notebook or find his laptop. I'd be willing to bet it's all in there."

"Which explains the theft of the computer, his notes, and even his cell phone," Justine said. "It looks like our friend was getting too close and someone decided to take him out."

"Who's your client, Teeny? It has to be a county worker, someone who doesn't want publicity of any kind," Ella said.

"Reach your own conclusions, Ella. I can't tell you anything more. If the investigation reaches a critical point, I'll insist my client tell you his or her identity. Until then, walk carefully and run with what you know."

"Which isn't much."

"I can't give you the name of my client unless you can prove that the case H was working on is directly linked to his murder, and at this point, I still have my doubts, especially with that skinwalker angle."

"Okay, but I still want you to ask your client for permission to disclose his identity," Ella said, then nodded to Justine. "Let's get back. Maybe Ralph and the others have found a witness who knows or has seen something that'll be useful to us."

They arrived at the station around 8 P.M. Justine, who was their on-site tech as well as Ella's partner, went straight to her lab to process the evidence collected at the crime scene.

Ella didn't make it past the lobby before being directed to the chief's office. Big Ed Atcitty, whose name said it all, rose from his swivel chair as she arrived at his open door.

"Come in, Shorty, and tell me what your team's got so far," he said, using the nickname he'd given her years ago, though at five foot ten, she was taller than he was. "I'm behind you one hundred percent, so if you need more manpower, or whatever, just say so."

"Thank you. I will." She took a seat and gave him a rundown of what they'd learned. "I think that the murder's related to one of his current investigations, but I can't rule out the possibility that his past caught up to him. He made enemies as an officer for the tribe, and later as a U.S. Marshal."

"How long had he been working for Bruce Little?"

"A little under a year, but it's his latest case that concerns me most. His pocket notebook and laptop have both gone missing, so I'm guessing that's the motive behind his murder. Why else take them, especially the notebook?"

"Do you have anything more on that skinwalker connection?"

"Other than the corpse mutilation, no. I intend to talk to my brother and see if he can help me come up with a list of possible suspects."

"Keep that part of the case under wraps for as long as you can."

"That's not going to be easy, but we'll try," Ella said.

"Tell me more about the woman he was with Monday night," Big Ed said.

"She was the last person known to have seen him alive," Ella said. Sensing someone behind her, she stopped speaking and turned her head.

The stocky duty officer was accompanied by a tall, good-looking Hispanic woman in her late thirties wearing a visitor's pass.

"Sorry to interrupt, Chief Atcitty," he said. "This is Mrs. Selina Ute, the former wife of the deceased. She's asked for a moment of your time."

Big Ed walked around the desk as Ella stood. "Of course. Please, come in," he said. "Your former husband has some very good friends in this department, Mrs. Ute. We'll do all we can to find his killer."

Selina Ute nodded to Big Ed, but as she glanced at Ella, her expression hardened in an instant. "I've seen you on TV. You're Ella Clah," she said, her voice filled with contempt. "Surely this woman isn't leading the investigation into Harry's murder," Selina added, looking back at Big Ed.

Ella studied the unfamiliar face, wondering if her attitude came from grief or anger, or if that even mattered right now. Clearly she wasn't the Navajo woman who'd been with Harry the night before his death. The description was way off.

"This woman had a relationship with my ex-husband," Selina stated. "She ruined my marriage and is the last person on this earth who should be working on his case."

Stunned, all Ella could do for a moment was stare. Finally she got her voice back again. "My relationship with him ended ten years ago, ma'am, months before your marriage."

"It was never over for him, and you know it," Selina said, then looked back at Big Ed. "This woman was personally involved with my ex-husband, and I insist that another investigator take charge."

"Not going to happen. Investigator Clah is the head of our homicide division, and investigating this crime is her responsibility," he said coldly.

Selina stared at Ella with narrowed eyes. "You messed up his life, then lured him back here to his death. Haven't you done enough?"

Ella was unsure of how to handle such irrational behavior. Grief often distorted people's perceptions, and in a situation like this, she knew it was better to remain calm. "I'll do whatever's necessary to find the person who killed him, Mrs. Ute, you can count on that."

"I'm not interested in your assurances." Still standing, Selina looked at Big Ed. "I know my husband was murdered. My daughter and I are visiting relatives in Farmington and right now my five-year-old child is with my sister, less than thirty miles away. Are we in any danger?"

"We have no reason to believe that." Big Ed sat down, and finally, Selina did the same.

"No one with personal ties to my husband, past or present, should be involved in the investigation," Selina said, more calmly now, though she avoided looking at Ella.

"Investigator Clah is the leader of our major crimes team, and I stand behind her," Big Ed said. "She's your best hope if you're really here to find justice and closure."

As it always had been, Big Ed's loyalty to his people was unwavering. Ella smiled.

Selina rose to her feet. "Then I'll have to take this up with someone in a position to force the issue. My cousin Nelson Natani works with Gerald Bidtah. Gerald's in charge of all the police agencies on the Navajo Nation, and I'm sure he'll be interested in how you've chosen to handle this matter."

"You're free to discuss my professional judgment with whomever you wish. But my decision stands," Big Ed said, crossing his arms and leaning back to signal he was done talking.

As Mrs. Ute spun on her heels and stormed out, Big Ed's gaze returned to Ella. "Is there something I should know?"

"Harry and I broke up when he left the force to join the U.S. Marshals, about ten years ago. Several months later, he married Selina and that was the last I heard from him until he moved back to the Four Corners. I doubt I've said more than a dozen words to him since he came back."

"She believes that he still had feelings for you."

"If he did, I never heard him say so, and he never acted on them. It's more likely that Harry mentioned me from time to time and that made her jealous. It's also possible I may have become a convenient scapegoat for the failure of their marriage. I don't know."

"Sounds like Mrs. Ute isn't ready to let this go," Big Ed said, his voice somber.

"I could try to talk to her, but if her mind's already made up, that might make things worse."

"Leave it to me," he said. "Concentrate on your job. Skin-walkers . . ." He shook his head. "That's going to frighten people, and nothing good ever comes from fear."

"I'll keep you updated every step of the way, Chief." Ella hurried down the hall to her own office, thinking about Harry's ex, trying to see the situation through her eyes. Coping with grief was never easy, and maybe lashing out was the only way Selina could deal with it.

As Ella sat in front of her computer, she pushed Selina Ute from her mind. It was time for her to get to work.

The paperwork was overwhelming and it was nearly midnight by the time Ella got home. As she climbed out of the truck, she saw a light on in the kitchen and a familiar dark shape close to the ground, waiting for her on the porch.

"Hey, Two," Ella whispered, greeting the sixty-pound mutt. The dog came up, tail wagging, and Ella gave him a hug. The elderly stray was protective of all of them, and he usually didn't go to sleep until she was home safe.

Two followed her inside, then went to his own bed in the kitchen.

As Ella opened the fridge door, Rose came in.

"I was wondering if you'd make it back tonight at all, daughter," she said, braiding her silver hair. "I stayed up, thinking you might need someone to talk to." Rose tried to tie a rubber band around her hair, but her rheumatoid arthritis was making the motion painful.

"Let me help, Mom," Ella said, then fastened the band for her. "You don't braid your hair much anymore. When was the last time?"

"I can't remember, but it got pretty hot this evening and I need some way of cooling off," Rose answered. "You want some herbal tea?"

Seeing Ella nod, she walked to the refrigerator and brought out a gallon jar half full of her special blend.

Ella found two glasses in the drain rack, and her mom poured.

They sat down at the table and sipped their tea for a full five minutes before either of them spoke.

"Your daughter spent hours talking to her friends on the phone. They all seemed to know what was going on," Rose said. "I made her hang up and go to bed around ten."

"Then you probably already know what kept me," Ella said, avoiding mentioning Harry specifically. Rose was a Traditionalist, and they all respected Navajo ways in the house in deference to her.

"You lost an old friend today. I'm sorry about that," Rose said, looking into her eyes.

"I seem to have a problem with men, don't I?" Ella said with a thin smile.

"To Anglos, romantic love is everything, but we're Navajos. We're taught to value lasting things like compatibility and shared goals. Romantic love is all too often a cheat."

Ella smiled. "Maybe so, but I'd rather keep looking than settle."

Rose sighed. "What happened to that county detective? I've seen the way you look at him when he isn't watching, but it's been a while since you had him over for dinner. Did you two have a fight?"

"No, it's nothing like that, Mom. I like him, and he likes me, too, and we've been dating. I just want to take things slow, and he supports me on that."

"The Navajo Way teaches that a man and a woman need

each other to be complete," Rose said. "Don't keep finding excuses until it's too late—for you and for him."

"I'll be seeing him again soon, Mom. The county will be helping me investigate my old friend's death." Detective Dan Nez, who spoke Navajo as well as he did English, usually acted as liaison between tribal and county operations.

Rose finished the last of her tea, walked to the sink, washed out her glass, then put it in the drain rack.

"You know you don't have to wait up for me, Mom," Ella said, joining her at the sink.

"I sleep better once I know you're home safe," she said, and gave Ella a worried glance. "I've heard what you're up against. Make sure you have protection at all times."

Though she hadn't mentioned it specifically, Ella knew Rose had somehow found out about the skinwalkers. It shouldn't have surprised her. Her mother had more connections than anyone else she knew.

"Good night, daughter," she said, and walked down the hallway that separated the new and old wings of the house. They'd added on several years ago to accommodate Rose and her husband, Herman.

A few minutes later, with only the hall night-light to show her the way, Ella silently opened Dawn's door and looked inside.

Her daughter's eyes were closed, her breathing deep, but she still had the earphone of her smartphone attached. The expensive phone, with dozens of apps, had been Kevin's birthday gift, something Ella would never have been able to afford. As an attorney working for the tribe, Kevin was very well compensated.

Wondering if there was a sleep mode app on the device,

Ella shook her head and closed the door. Kids could sleep through anything, especially fourteen-year-olds. At least it was summer, so Dawn didn't have to be up every day at six thirty.

Thankful for the peace that encircled her family, Ella continued down the hall to her room.

She was up early and out of the shower before seven. When she walked into the kitchen, Herman and Rose were making breakfast together. As usual, her mom was wearing a shapeless flowerprint housedress with big pockets and her fluffy green slippers. Her freshly brushed silver hair hung down loosely around her shoulders.

Herman had on a long-sleeved, plaid flannel shirt, faded jeans, and his blue suspenders. His cowboy boots were so old and scuffed, they looked like tan velvet, but he bragged that they were as soft as gloves. For years he'd worn his gray hair long, with a headband, but for the past several months he'd adapted the buzz cut of a soldier. That alone had made him look years younger, which seemed to please him much more than it did Rose.

"Good morning, you two," Ella said, holding back the impulse to ask if hell had frozen over. Having married in their seventies, Herman and Rose had very different habits, particularly when it came to breakfast. It was rare to see them together this time of day.

"Oatmeal?" Herman asked Ella.

"No thanks, just coffee," Ella said.

Herman had slowed a step or two the last few years, fighting a heart ailment that still worried her mom. Rose had read up on it, and after learning about oatmeal's supposedly beneficial effects, she insisted Herman have a serving each morning.

"Mom!" Dawn came into the kitchen, still brushing her long black hair.

Ella smiled. Her daughter was already taller than Herman and Rose, and would probably exceed Ella's five-foot-ten-inch frame by the time she graduated high school.

Dawn gave Ella a big hug—a welcome contrast from the usual mumbles and groans that went with the school months. Nothing made her child happier than a carefree summer and lots of time to spend with their horses.

"I love you, Mom. Make sure you wear your vest today, okay?" she said, tightening the hug before releasing her. "I know it's hot, but it's better to be safe."

"Of course, dear. It's with my handgun, and I usually put it on before I get in the pickup," Ella said, squeezing Dawn's hand and noting that her daughter wasn't making eye contact.

"Okay, well, gotta go check on the horses," Dawn said, heading for the kitchen door.

"Where did that come from?" Ella asked, watching her daughter walking across the yard.

"We're all worried, after yesterday," Rose said, "but she's at an age when admitting something like that to you isn't . . . cool?"

Ella looked over at Herman, who nodded. "Listen to your daughter. Stay safe."

———

It was seven thirty by the time Ella arrived at the station. She parked her Ford 150 pickup beside the main entrance and went inside. These days, with budgetary considerations, few of them ever got to take the tribal SUVs home.

At her desk minutes later, Ella checked her in-basket first. Nothing new had come in since last night, and several residents in the general area of the murder scene had yet to be interviewed.

As she skimmed through her team's reports, Ella found a Post-it note on Sergeant Neskahi's report. His message, "Call me," got her immediate attention.

She picked up the phone, dialed his cell number, and got him on the first ring. "What's going on, Joe?"

"I'm on my way to the station right now. Could you assemble our team? I ran into a problem, and I'd like everyone to hear this firsthand."

"You've got it."

Ella left voice mail for FBI Agent Blalock, then word at the front for Benny and Ralph to come to her office as soon as they reported in. After that, she went to the lab to touch base with Justine.

The improvised facility wasn't much bigger than a storeroom, with work counters around the perimeter and a big island in the middle that usually held the instruments needed for a rudimentary examination of evidence.

Justine was measuring the recovered slug when Ella came in.

"Morning, boss," Justine said without looking up. "New perfume?"

Ella shook her head. "Dawn found this cucumber herbal

shampoo and I tried it this morning. Supposed to be great for my hair, but I smell like a salad, don't I?"

"Nah, more like a bushel of cucumbers. Nice, but if you want to attract a man, try Coors."

Ella smiled. "How much longer you going to be with that slug?"

"Pretty much done. I've identified the manufacturer and caliber, it's a .308 Hornady 165-grain Spire Point, Boat Tail, I think. The brand and boat tail are for sure, but there was so much damage, I can't be sure about the weight. I'm sending it to the FBI lab in Albuquerque via Agent Blalock. They've got all the instruments and technology needed to confirm."

"No rifling marks you can use?"

"Not enough to get a match in court, but at least we have a rifle caliber and manufacturer," Justine said, then looked at her. "What's going on? Are you calling a meeting this morning?"

She nodded. "Joe wanted to share something he didn't want to put in his report for some reason. I'd planned on us going over to finish up the interviews—to talk to people who weren't around when Benny and Joe were working the area—but let's wait and see what Joe has to say first."

"Do I have time to pick up another coffee?" Justine asked, holding up her empty cup.

"Yeah, and grab one for me, too. I need to get back. Joe should be here by now." Ella reached into her pocket and brought out a couple of dollars. "I'm buying."

As Ella went around the corner of the hall, she saw Sergeant Neskahi standing outside her office door, talking to Agent Dwayne Blalock.

FB-Eyes, the nickname he'd been given by local Navajos

because he had one blue eye and one brown, was close to the Bureau's mandatory retirement age of fifty-seven now. Despite that, the six-foot-plus agent looked as fit as any of the younger men in the department. He had a barely detectable limp due to a bullet he'd taken while working with her in the field years back, but it hadn't slowed him down.

A pain in the butt at first, Blalock had mellowed over time, and these days received more respect than disdain in their community.

Blalock turned as she walked up, and gave her a nod. "My condolences, Ella."

"Thanks, Dwayne," she said, motioning both men to her office. "So fill us in, Joe. What's going on?"

"If it's okay, I'd like to wait until we're all behind closed doors," he said.

Hearing footsteps, Ella saw Ralph Tache walking down the hall just ahead of Benny Pete and Justine.

"Pull up a chair, guys," she said, waving her hand. The office wasn't the smallest one she'd had, but with all these officers, they were cramped for space. Justine, the last one in, closed the door behind her and handed Ella her coffee.

"Before we get started, let me say that we all lost a friend, and although it hurts, we have to stay focused on the job at hand. Until his killer is caught, consider this case top priority," Ella said, noting the heads nodding in approval.

"Joe? You had something you wanted to share with us?" Ella added.

Neskahi stood. "When I went to speak with Sarah Willie, aka Bitsy, the teen who discovered the body, I picked up some strange vibes. They're Modernists, but the father was on the phone, making arrangements for a local *hataalii* to come do a Sing over his kid. That surprised me, so I asked Mr. Willie about it. He told me that he knew the murder was the work of skinwalkers. Exactly how word got out, I don't know, but it's no longer a secret. The only question is how far it's spread."

"What made him so sure it was skinwalkers? Did he go back to the site and take a look after his kid told him about it? Bitsy didn't get that close a look," Ella said. The very situation they'd hoped to avoid was now a reality.

"I wanted to know that, too," Joe said. "When I asked, he said that he'd been hearing strange howling sounds at night—nothing that came from any animal he recognized. Something had also been scaring his horses all week. He hadn't personally seen anything, but he said that most of his neighbors were convinced that skinwalkers were active in the area, especially after sundown, out to make trouble."

"Crap," Ella said, rubbing her neck with one hand. "That means people will shoot first and ask questions later. If accusations begin flying around about who's responsible, we may end up with more than one body."

"Fear, murder, and a gun in every home. A recipe for disaster if I ever heard one," Blalock said.

Seeing the others nod, Ella continued the briefing. To emphasize the point that they were all law enforcement professionals with a clear job ahead, she used the deceased's name. "Harry was working for Bruce Little, but his death may not have been linked to his current case. We need to dig hard without tipping our hand, and see why a skinwalker went after him."

"Maybe he saw something he wasn't supposed to," Benny said.

"That's one possibility," Ella said.

"What about Harry's laptop and notebook?" Tache said. "Have those been found?"

"No, they're still missing. The killer undoubtedly used the key to Harry's home, let himself in, and took the laptop along with any flash drives and hard drive backup systems."

"What about the woman he brought home with him? Could she have taken his laptop?" Benny asked.

"No way. Harry would have noticed. It was sitting in plain sight on his desk," Ella said.

"So, bottom line. Ute may have been killed for what he knew or was about to find out, which may explain why the killer took the laptop later after the shooting. Also, any answer has to include the apparent skinwalker connection," Blalock said, recapping.

"That's the way it looks so far," Ella said. "Ralph, go over the cases Harry handled while he was with our department and see if he had any run-ins with skinwalkers or suspected skinwalkers. Dwayne, I'd like you to search and see if any of the enemies he made while in the marshals service are from this area or have voiced credible threats. Although it appears likely that his murder is related to something currently happening on the Rez, we can't afford to overlook anything."

Benny stood. The former L.A. sergeant was the most recent addition to their team. Like Ella, he'd returned to the Navajo Nation after a long absence to serve his tribe. "I'd like to bring up another possible motive—the victim's personal life. I understand he was divorced and had a daughter. Maybe there's a custody battle in the works. Also, he seems to have retired from the marshals service long before retirement age. We need to find out what happened there."

Ella turned to Officer Tache. "When he dropped by the station last month to visit, did he share anything about that, Ralph?"

"He said that his job with the marshals service had cost him his marriage and he was tired of never being anyplace for long. He'd come back, where his roots were, to start over, but there were no current job openings with the tribe," Ralph said. "When Bruce Little offered him work, he jumped at it. From here, it's only a two-and-a-half-hour drive to visit his kid on weekends."

"Did he ever mention anything about his ex-wife having a boyfriend, or did he have another woman in his life that you know about?" Blalock asked, glancing very briefly at Ella.

Justine and Neskahi also turned her way for a second.

"Okay, guys, for the record, I dated Harry for several months back in the day," Ella said, "but that was before he met Selina—*never* after. What we had was over a long time ago, and, no, we didn't see each other after he returned."

"How about the Navajo woman who was at his apartment the night before last? She may not have been a one-night stand," Justine said. "Maybe she had a jealous boyfriend, or it's possible she was upset because Harry wasn't moving things along more quickly. She could have learned Harry's schedule and set him up to be ambushed."

Blalock eased back in his chair. "Or maybe she was just a few hours of company for a lonely man. Until we track her down, there's no way for us to know."

"Agreed," Ella said. "County has a description, and both our departments are actively searching for her now."

"Are you *sure* you want county deputies looking for a woman who might be connected to thefts of county property?" Blalock said. "I trust Sheriff Taylor and the few county deputies I've worked with personally, but I've also been burned by bad cops and bad ex-cops."

"Sheriff Taylor's people have been told that she's a person of interest because she was seen with Harry before he was killed, nothing more. If they find the woman, we'll conduct the interview."

"Make sure I'm in on that," Blalock said.

"You've got it," Ella said. "Watch yourselves out there, people, and if anyone hears anything more specific about skinwalker activity, come to me right away."

FIVE
———— ✖ ✖ ✖ ————

As they headed back into the remote community west of Shiprock where Harry's body had been found, Ella noted how tightly Justine was gripping the wheel.

"The one advantage the rumor about skinwalkers will give us is that most of the People will stay away from the area—Modernists and Traditionalists alike," Ella said. "We all grew up hearing about Navajo witches, but even those of us who don't believe in that will still try to steer clear."

Justine nodded. "You're right. Though logic tells me there's nothing to those stories, a part of me still feels uncomfortable when I have to deal with stuff like this."

"On the Rez we grow up listening to whispers about skinwalkers digging up bodies for corpse powder, and using bits of bone for ammunition. That's creepy and not something you just forget."

Justine nodded. "Yeah, that's for sure."

Ella glanced around, getting her bearings. They'd turned

off the mail route to a smaller, thinly graveled road. Ahead was a gray stucco pitched-roof frame house. Two narrow ruts led from the road to a pair of vehicles parked twenty feet from the front door.

"This is the teacher's place. Truman John wasn't there when Benny and Joe stopped by yesterday, but maybe we'll catch him today," Ella said.

"Truman John's got to be a Modernist, and not just because he's got a college degree. He's not only got electricity and a phone line, he's got satellite," Justine said, gesturing.

A line of telephone poles running alongside the road continued north to Rattlesnake, and then to the large community of Shiprock to the east. Two lines split off the closest pole and led to the roof of the house.

"Looks like we lucked out," Ella said. "With tracks leading to the Dodge pickup and that old VW Bug, somebody's got to be home. Wonder where the man's working these days? According to what Tache got from the tribal records, Truman was laid off from his teaching job at Kirtland Middle School last fall when the district budget got the axe."

"What'd he teach?"

"Social studies and Navajo culture."

"We had New Mexico history, but no courses on Navajo ways when I went to school. I had to learn that on my own at home," Justine said, coming to a stop behind the VW.

"Write down the vehicle tags. We'll run them later," Ella said, looking toward the front window. A man was standing beside the curtain, looking out at them. Considering the rumors, it wasn't unexpected.

"Got the plate," Justine said, jamming the small spiral

notebook back into her pocket, then rolling down the electric window with a touch of the button. "It's going to get hot today. The temperature's climbing fast."

"Although Truman's not a Traditionalist, try to avoid mentioning skinwalkers directly, partner," Ella said, opening her own window. "Even Modernists sometimes feel uncomfortable hearing the word spoken out loud. Our culture says that's enough to draw the evil ones to you."

Ella got out, deciding not to wait to be invited since Truman clearly wasn't a Traditionalist. As she walked to the front door, Justine right behind her, she saw a corral in the back. It appeared to be in good shape and clear of weeds, although there were no animals currently in it. A big, new-looking metal loafing shed open on one side held at least fifty bales of either really bad hay, or straw.

As they walked to the front of the house, Ella's attention was drawn to the well-laid-out and landscaped yard with its colorful desert plants, some of them mulched with straw. Most locals saved their precious water resources for crops and fruit trees. Landscaping was considered a luxury in this community.

They'd just stepped up onto the shaded, weathered, wood-plank porch when the front door opened a crack, letting out a stream of cool air and the scent of something cooking.

"Ah, air-conditioning," Justine said happily. "And fry bread!"

A well dressed, clean-cut Navajo man in his mid-twenties waved them inside. "I was wondering how long it would take the tribal police to pay me a visit."

"I'm Investigator Clah, and this is my partner, Officer Goodluck. Are you the homeowner?" Ella asked, checking to see if anyone else was in the front room. Seeing no one, she focused back on the man.

"Renter, actually, Officers. I'm Truman John. I heard on the news that the police found a body inside a truck parked just north of here on the old road. He'd been shot, right?"

Ella nodded. "That's why we're here. We were hoping you might have spotted something that seemed out of place or noticed someone you didn't recognize hanging around," she said, studying the man. He was reasonably good looking and neatly dressed in a short-sleeved oxford shirt and sharply creased tan cargo pants. His leather sandals were a smart concession to the weather.

"I don't know how much help we can be, Officers, because we always take the east road through Rattlesnake and missed seeing that truck. But please come in and sit down." He led them into a small but well-furnished living room. At the back of the room was the entrance to the kitchen, where the pleasant scent of fresh fry bread originated.

Ella took a seat on the comfortable-looking sofa while Truman chose the matching love seat across from a large flatscreen TV.

"Nice place—entertainment and education at your fingertips," Ella said, glancing at the bookcase below the window. It held at least a hundred reference books and novels, based on their titles, and a plastic rack of DVD and CDs.

"You probably already know I'm a social studies teacher," he said. "I'm not employed right now, but I'm trying to keep up in my field. I hope to return to the classroom once the district starts rehiring."

An attractive barefooted Navajo woman in her midtwenties wearing a flowery, shapeless sundress appeared at the kitchen door. She wore only a trace of lipstick, and her long black hair was fastened at the nape of her neck with a silver barrette.

"Hi," she said with a hesitant smile. "I'm Eileen. I don't mean to interrupt, but I've just made some fry bread. I'm going to bring it in so we can all eat while you ask your questions, okay?"

As Ella nodded, the woman stepped back out of view.

Justine smiled. "The nose knows."

Ella looked back at Truman.

"Eileen Tahoe is my girlfriend," he said. "She works at the Little Bear Café up in Beclabito. Unfortunately, her boss is my idiot neighbor, Norman Yazzie, who also owns the café. As soon as she can, Eileen's going to find another job, but at the moment she's stuck. Work's hard to find."

Ella made a mental note to find out some more about the neighbor he'd mentioned. "Did you see or hear anything unusual last Tuesday? I know it's several miles, but maybe a gunshot?"

"No, and I was here all day, working on future lesson plans and tweaking my résumé," Truman said. "I never went outside, but I heard Mrs. Yazzie's old pickup go by once or twice. Norman Yazzie's grandmother lives down the road about a mile west from here."

"You're not currently employed so you're usually here at home?" Ella recalled reading in one of the reports that no vehicles had been parked by the house yesterday when Benny and Joe had come by.

"Right now I'm actively looking for a job so, no, I'm not usually home. I spent most of the earlier part of the week in Shiprock and Kirtland, talking to some of my former coworkers. Networking, you might say. I may have to apply for an out-of-state job, so I've been picking up some hand-written recommendations."

Just then, Eileen came into the room holding a big plate of golden, puffy fry bread. "Anyone hungry?" She set the tray down on a glass-topped coffee table. I don't have nap-kins, but will paper towels do?"

Truman looked at Justine and Ella, who nodded.

After Eileen returned, they began eating. Although she wasn't particularly hungry, Ella had learned over the years that sharing food was a great way to set people at ease. Once they relaxed, it became much easier for them to re-member important details.

"Eileen, you work in Beclabito, right?" Justine asked off-handedly. "What are your hours?"

The woman took a bite of fry bread, then held up her hand, not answering until she'd chewed and swallowed. "I work the seven-to-three shift, Monday through Wednesday, then I have Thursdays and Fridays off. Saturdays and Sun-days are our busiest days."

"What route do you take from here to Rattlesnake and the main highway?" Justine asked.

"The east road, always. The old way is too rough on my poor VW," Eileen said.

"During your drives to and from work," Ella said, "have you ever noticed anything strange or unusual going on around here? We've heard some talk." Ella purposely didn't elaborate.

Truman spoke first. "Ah, I get it. You've heard about all that skinwalker nonsense. It's just mumbo jumbo, someone out to scare others," he said, and shrugged.

"Wait—are you saying that a witch killed that guy?" Eileen asked, staring wide-eyed at Ella.

"We don't know who the killer was yet," Ella said, "but since we're on the subject, have either of you seen any evidence of skinwalkers in this area?"

"When people get spooked, they talk themselves into believing a lot of crazy things," Truman said, his tone somber. "Norman Yazzie once accused *me* of being a skinwalker, but I don't think he really believes it. He was just angry because I refuse to let him take a shortcut through my property to get to his grandmother's house. He's already destroyed some plants in Eileen's vegetable garden with that truck of his, and he's created deep ruts that'll become flood channels next time we get a hard rain. I've told him all that, but he doesn't listen."

"Norman's a real jerk," Eileen added.

"I put up some rabbit-proof fencing around Eileen's garden to protect it, and the very next morning, I found what looked like a coyote skin on the fence. I'm thinking Norman got angry because I blocked him off, so he decided to make me look like a skinwalker."

"Are you sure it was him?" Ella asked.

"Well, I didn't actually catch him leaving it there, but who else would have done something like that?" Truman said.

"Do you still have the animal skin?" Ella asked.

"No, I put it in a trash bag and took it to the landfill. That way it couldn't turn up again," Truman said.

Silence stretched out, but Ella didn't interrupt. Long pauses were common among the *Diné*. To try to speed up a conversation was seen as rude at best, and in her case, it was counterproductive.

Eventually, Eileen spoke, her voice low. "This area has changed a lot. It's not peaceful like it used to be. Evil's close by and likes to leave bad things for others to find."

"Like what?" Ella pressed.

"Charcoal sandpaintings," she said in a near whisper. "Real medicine men make those with colored sand and use them to heal. Sandpaintings, well, some call them drypaintings, are sacred. To make them with charcoal defiles everything they stand for, which is why witches do that."

"Of course, I've destroyed the three we've seen beside the road between here and the highway," Truman said. "I've also come across dead animals strung up on fences. When I find crap like that, I get rid of it. Someone's out to scare people, and there's no sense in creating a panic."

"How long ago has it been since you saw either of those things?" Ella asked.

"Let me think," Truman said, then stared at the floor for several seconds. "Two weeks ago, maybe less."

"One of those charcoal drypaintings was left right in front of our drive," Eileen said, and shuddered.

After everyone had eaten another piece of fry bread in silence, Ella wiped her lips with one of the paper towels and stood. "All right. Thank you both," she said. "We've got to get going. Maybe Mrs. Yazzie will be able to add to what you've already told us."

"If we hear or see anything that might help, we'll give you a call, Investigator Clah. Do you have a card?" Truman asked.

Ella gave him hers, then walked with Justine to the door.

"One last thing," Truman said, "that is, if you don't mind a little advice."

Ella stopped. "Go ahead."

"Mrs. Yazzie is a hard-core Traditionalist, and if you start talking about skinwalkers, she'll probably throw you out."

"Good to know, thanks," Ella said.

"Not too long ago, I noticed that she'd brought in a *hataalii* and had a Sing done," Eileen said. "I don't know for sure, but I have a feeling she found something on her property that scared her."

"Thanks," Ella said, stepping outside.

"And for the fry bread, too," Justine added.

They walked back to the car in silence. Soon they were on their way up the road, which now ran west toward the Chuskas.

"Those two are in serious danger if there's one or more Navajo witches working this area. You don't disrespect crazies and get away with it, not for long, anyway," Ella said.

"Do you suppose that's the real reason our friend was killed—he came across a ritual he wasn't supposed to see?"

"Maybe." Ella remembered her own father, who, like Harry, had fallen prey to skinwalkers. But with her dad, it had been a lot worse. They'd carved him up like some horrific art exhibit. It had been over fifteen years, but the memories were still as sharp and clear in her mind as if it were yesterday. She'd carry those images to her own grave.

She brushed the memory aside and focused on the present. "Let's keep pushing for answers and see what we get."

"Maybe Mrs. Yazzie saw something we can use, particularly if Truman's right, and she was driving around that day," Justine said.

"I hope so, but the odds are against it. A Traditionalist worried about skinwalkers would probably keep to herself and avoid looking at strangers."

Ella accessed the MDT to check out the tags on the vehicles at Truman John's place. "No police record for either. Let's see what else I can get." A moment later, she continued. "John has a BA in secondary education from NAU in Flagstaff. Eileen Tahoe graduated from Chinle High. Both are Arizona Navajos. Truman was riffed last year from Kirtland Central. Eileen has been working full-time at the Little Bear Café for the past two years."

Justine smiled. "Bet she's a cook. That fry bread was yummy."

"Yeah." Ella smiled. "If you weren't such a bundle of energy, cuz, you'd be rolling instead of walking. I have to run my butt off, literally, just to stay even." Ella almost sighed as she thought of how it had been for her when she was in her twenties and thirties. She'd eaten like a horse back then and never put on any weight.

Time . . . it wasn't always a friend.

The Yazzie residence was about a half mile farther down a rutted dirt road, and consisted of a rectangular wood frame structure with unpainted, weathered wooden trim and a roof that was missing a few shingles. A small medicine hogan stood in the back, about a hundred feet away.

Ella pointed to a double stack of plastic water barrels in the meager shade of the roof overhang. "She doesn't have a well, so she has to haul water in. That means she can't afford a garden."

Justine parked within view of the front of the house, about twenty feet from a red Ford pickup. "How long do you think we'll have to wait?"

Ella shrugged. "Give it some time. If Mrs. Yazzie is home and worried about skinwalkers, she'll have to decide whether or not to trust us."

Minutes passed slowly. At long last, they saw a gray-haired woman and a dog herding about twenty sheep down the long slope of a hill west of the residence. After the livestock was gathered into a sturdy pen cut from cottonwood branches, she waved them toward the house.

Ella opened her car door. "Let's go, partner."

Three minutes later, they were standing in the center of a small living room. Mrs. Yazzie was in her late sixties, wearing a long-sleeved blouse and floor-length pleated skirt. Her home was simply furnished, with woven rugs on the floor and simple wooden chairs around what was clearly an old picnic table. Instead of a sofa, a wooden bench had been placed beneath the window. Despite two open windows, it was warm inside.

"Did you see any strangers or unfamiliar vehicles around here this past Tuesday, aunt?" Ella asked, using the term to show respect for a woman of the tribe who was her senior.

Mrs. Yazzie gripped a deerskin medicine bag in the palm of her hand so tightly that her knuckles turned a pearly white. "I heard about the shooting on my radio, but I didn't hear or see anyone Tuesday. My grandson and I went shopping in Farmington, then stopped on the way back at the new grocery store in Shiprock. They had a sale on bread and Spam," she said. "My grandson enjoys these day trips as much as I do now. He's been lonely since his wife left to help her mother over by Window Rock. The woman had a stroke and needs extra help right now."

"Your grandson, you mean the one who lives close by?" Ella asked, trying to avoid saying his name aloud.

She nodded. "He runs a café in Beclabito, so he usually isn't home until late except on Tuesday, his day off. He's a good boy, always watching out for his *shimasáni*," she said, using the Navajo word for "grandmother."

"I've been told that he's had some problems with your neighbor to the north," Ella said. "The teacher."

"If you ask me, that young man's just looking for trouble to give himself something to do. I told my grandson to stay away from him," she said, neither confirming nor denying.

"Have you or your grandson had any problems with your other neighbors?" Justine asked.

"No, but everyone's scared. It's very dangerous here now," she said in a whisper.

Ella could see the .30-.30 Winchester standing in the corner of the room behind the door. It was probably loaded. "Dangerous how? Tell me," Ella said, and reached into her jacket pocket, bringing out her beaded medicine pouch. The sight of it seemed to allay the woman's fears somewhat. "It's okay to talk about it, aunt. We've got the right medicine." Ella gave Justine a nod, and her partner brought out her own bag.

"Deerskin, with beaded trim, just like mine," Mrs. Yazzie observed. "You must know the *hataalii* who lives just west of the Gallup highway."

"He's my brother," Ella said, and smiled.

"And my second cousin," Justine added.

"Tell us about the troublemakers in this area," Ella insisted gently. "Do you think they might be responsible for what happened to the man in the pickup?"

She expelled her breath in a soft hiss. "The evil ones cause problems for everyone. That's why I tried to contact the *hataalii* again today. I want him to give my home some extra protection."

"My brother took his family to their sheep camp up by Red Rock, so his son can learn how to care for their livestock. He should be back in a day or two."

"I don't want to wait that long. I'll try to get the Singer from Cudei to come over," Mrs. Yazzie said, then looked toward the kitchen. "I have to tend to my stew. Do you need something else?"

Ella sensed that finding out Clifford wouldn't be readily available had frightened her. Pressing Mrs. Yazzie now wouldn't get them anywhere. She was too on edge already. "I'll leave my phone number here on the table," Ella said, placing a business card by the base of the lamp. "Call if you have any problems we can help you with, or if you remember anything that might help us solve the crime."

The woman nodded, but didn't speak.

Ella glanced at Justine, who recognized the signal and walked toward the door. Ella followed.

Mrs. Yazzie remained silent, but accompanied them to the porch, then closed and locked the door as soon as they were outside.

"She's really frightened," Justine said as they reached the SUV. "Do you think she knows more than she's telling us?"

"Maybe." As Justine drove back toward the road, Ella

looked in the rearview mirror. Mrs. Yazzie was still watching them from the window. "My gut tells me that she's convinced skinwalkers are responsible, but she's afraid to point fingers and have them chopped off—or worse."

"She's an old school Navajo," Justine said. "If someone tries to give her a hard time, or she thinks she's being witched, she'll take her rifle to them."

"That's what worries me," Ella said. "We need to speak to her grandson, Norman Yazzie, but if the schedule we got is right, he won't be home now. Let's go visit another one of the neighbors instead," she said, checking her notepad.

"Okay," Justine said.

"While you drive, I'm going to try to reach Clifford on the phone. I may not get him right away, but I know he'll be checking his messages as often as possible. If a skinwalker's really in this area, he'll have more details."

SIX

✖ ✖ ✖

They'd driven about a mile when Ella, looking up after leaving a message for her brother, noticed a dead crow dangling from the wire fence that paralleled the road.

"Stop," she said, and pointed.

"Birds sometimes collide with windows, but they don't get hung up on fences like that," Justine said, pulling over to one side of the road.

"Let's take a closer look." Ella got out of the SUV and walked over to the fence. "Decapitated and left hanging upside down by a string."

"The kind of thing a skinwalker would do," Justine said.

"Yeah, he's advertising his presence. He wants people to be afraid," Ella said. "We need to remove this. Like it is with graffiti or tagging, by getting rid of it you show him he's wasting his time."

Ella glanced around, taking in the area carefully to see

if they were being watched. Except for the house they'd just left, barely visible now, there was no sign of life.

"Looks like the bird was shot." Justine cut the string with her pocketknife and lowered the dead bird onto a bed of black ants. "Not worth collecting as evidence. Might as well let the body serve as a meal to something."

"And at the same time piss off a nut job," Ella said with a mirthless grin. "Let's get going, but keep your eye out for any more not-so-subtle messages. It looks like it's going to be a long day, cuz."

They soon drove past the home of Dawn's friend, Bitsy, the girl who'd found the body. An old Navajo man with a white headband was lifting a cardboard box out of his pickup, and as they went past, he looked up, and nodded to Ella.

"That's Samuel Henderson," Ella said.

"The *hataalii* from Cudei?"

"Right. Looks like Joe's observation was right on target. Bitsy's family are Modernists but they'd decided to have a Sing done."

"Bitsy saw way too much for a girl her age," Justine said. "They're probably hoping that'll help their daughter deal with things."

"It'll also keep her Traditionalist friends from avoiding her altogether. I'd do the same for Dawn."

"Which reminds me," Justine said. "What's your daughter think of her dad dating Carolyn?"

"We haven't spoken about it," Ella said.

"Do you think Rose knows?" Justine looked over at Ella.

"I doubt it. Otherwise, she'd be making the mother of all

medicine bags for my daughter. To her, the *chindi* is as real as you and I are to each other."

Following Ella's directions, Justine continued down the slope of one of the low ridges running perpendicular to the foothills to the west.

"We're here," Justine said at last, pointing with a fingertip raised from the steering wheel.

"This is the home of Delbert Sells, his wife, and their two elementary school children," Ella said as Justine pulled over to the side of the road. "He's a mechanic and she works at the Sixty-four Laundry in Shiprock."

A well-maintained pickup with a metal storage compartment in the bed was parked halfway down the narrow driveway. The hood was up and a big red toolbox was on the ground beside the vehicle.

Beyond that stood a lone mobile home beside a cluster of four very well established fruit trees. "Like the teacher's rental home and the Willie residence, these people have a well," Ella said, pointing toward a low shedlike structure at the rear of the trailer. "Nice to be able to have a garden or a small orchard."

A man in a dark green shirt with a label above the pocket opened the door of the home and came out onto the small wooden porch.

"Good morning," Ella called out. "We're police officers. Can we speak to you for a moment?"

"Yes, we've been expecting a visit. Come inside," the slender man in his late twenties said.

Mr. Sells, who introduced himself on the porch but declined to shake hands with strangers, motioned Ella and Justine inside. He then introduced them to his wife, Marcie

Sells, a short, stout Navajo woman with two young kids beside her. The first- or second-graders, judging from their size, fixated on Ella's badge at first, then her holstered handgun.

"Cori, Lexy, take your books and go read in your room while the adults talk," Mrs. Sells said.

"Have a seat, Officer Clah, Officer Goodluck," Mr. Sells said as his wife urged the kids down the narrow center aisle of the mobile home.

Ella motioned for Justine to take the inside seat of a padded bench and table attached to the floor, then slipped in beside her. From where she was, Ella could see out of the mobile home's large window. As she watched, a nondescript pickup in the distance made its way up the long stretch of road.

Mr. Sells took a seat across from Ella. When his wife returned, she remained standing by the small stove in the kitchen area.

"Would you like some coffee, Officers?" Mrs. Sells asked, then, hearing someone driving up, glanced out the window. "Who's that?"

Ella saw the pickup come to a stop beside the tribal SUV. The driver, wearing sunglasses and a baseball cap, was looking straight ahead, his hand up, blocking his face. Catching a glimpse of movement, Ella shifted her gaze and saw the passenger door on the opposite side open and someone hurry out.

Suddenly alert, Ella stood, bumping the table as she moved out from the bench. "Are they messing with our unit?"

Seconds later, the passenger, also wearing a cap, jumped back into the cab, and the driver took off, still hiding his face.

Ella raced for the door. "Hurry, Justine. I think those guys did something to our SUV."

Justine followed her out onto the porch just as a loud pop and an ominous whooshing sounded. An instant later, they saw a cloud of black smoke, and flames came billowing out from beneath the SUV's engine compartment.

Ella looked around for something to put out the fire with, but Mr. Sells had already grabbed a large fire extinguisher from a shelf in the wall.

"Here. I've got another in my truck. Go!" he said.

With a quick thanks, she took the heavy cylinder and ran down the driveway toward the SUV.

In the distance, Ella heard the pickup's driver honking his horn as he raced away. She almost expected to hear a war whoop.

The second she reached the SUV, Ella pulled the safety pin on the extinguisher. She aimed the nozzle in front of the burning object on the ground—a broken glass jug full of some kind of oil—and squeezed the trigger.

A dense cloud of creamy white powder from the extinguisher enveloped the underside of the vehicle as Ella swept the hose back and forth at the base of the burning container.

The scent was familiar, like that of cooking oil that had ignited into a kitchen-style grease fire. At home, she would have smothered it with a metal lid or wet towel, but this required a different solution.

Ella tried not to inhale any fumes or breathe in the noxious smoke. Hopefully, she could put out the burning oil before the chemical spray ran out, or the gas or brake line of the Suburban ignited.

"I'm going to bury the bottom of the car in the sand,

Ella. That should smother the flames!" Justine shouted, circling to the driver's side. "Try to keep the undercarriage from catching for a few more seconds."

Justine slipped behind the wheel as Mr. Sells ran up and added the chemical spray of a second extinguisher to her efforts.

The SUV started instantly and Justine hit the gas, driving across a shallow drainage ditch and up on to a three-foot-high mound of sand. High centered now, the wheels spun for a second before Justine killed the engine and scrambled out of the vehicle.

Ella and Mr. Sells ran over to the stranded SUV, fire extinguishers in hand, and circled it slowly, looking for any flames still needing attention.

Standing closer than before, Ella checked the bogged-down vehicle's undercarriage closest to where the oil had been spilled. She could see a section of scorched paint below the driver's-side door panel. It was still smoking.

She hit it with a sweep of the spray, then stepped back, looking for other hot spots as she continued to inch around the vehicle.

"Looks like we've got it now," Mr. Sells said, still circling around the SUV, looking underneath.

Ella glanced back at the road where the amber liquid, probably cooking oil judging from the smell, still smoked amid the broken glass. Mrs. Sells was walking toward the origin point, pulling a garden hose with a spray nozzle and a slight drip. The children were inside, watching out the window.

"Shall I hose everything down, Delbert?" Mrs. Sells asked her husband.

"Not the oil, just the SUV, okay?" Justine said, looking at Sells, who nodded.

With everything under control now, Ella glared at Justine. "*Are you crazy?* That was a really dangerous thing to do."

Justine cringed. "I took that fire department training last spring, remember? I removed the SUV from the heat source, then cut off the oxygen," she said, then with a sheepish smile, added, "And I saved us both from days of paperwork while we tried to get another car from the motor pool."

Ella didn't know whether to hug her or slug her. "Vehicles are expendable—you're not. If anything like this ever happens again—"

"Yeah, let it burn," Justine said.

"Exactly. Now, take the hose from Mrs. Sells and soak down the undercarriage of the car and the engine compartment, just in case. I've got to call this in." Ella looked in the direction the pickup had fled. All she could see now was a faint trail of dust.

"Think they'll get stopped?" Justine said, following her gaze.

"If they took off for Shiprock, maybe. If they headed west, we're probably screwed, at least for now. That was a Ford 150, right?"

"Yes, a 2004 or '05," Mr. Sells answered, coming up beside her with the other fire extinguisher. "Two-wheel drive, mineral gray finish."

Ella looked at him in surprise.

"Delbert knows his pickups," Mrs. Sells confirmed.

———

Ella decided not to drive the SUV in case there were damaged components that would create a hazard. While they were waiting for a tow truck from Shiprock, they spoke at length with the Sellses, but neither had seen anything the day of Harry's murder nor any sign of skinwalkers. Having heard the gossip, however, they were now keeping their children under close watch.

Two hours later, with nothing but frustration to show for their efforts, they headed east toward Shiprock in another tribal cruiser. The patrolman who'd brought over the vehicle had ridden back in the tow truck.

They'd just passed the high school and were approaching the intersection of Highway 491 and 64 when Ella's cell phone rang. The number was blocked, which usually meant it was one of her officers.

"Investigator Clah, it's Detective Dan Nez," said the familiar voice.

He was all business, which meant he wasn't alone, but she knew him well enough to notice the slight gentling in his tone as he spoke to her.

"Detective Nez," Ella said, trying to ignore Justine's knowing smile. "What can I do for you?"

"I'm assisting county officers trying to locate the woman seen with your murder victim the night before his death. We've got a sketch to work with now, and we'll be showing it around the apartment building, local markets, and gas stations. After that, I'll start hitting area night spots. By then, I expect it'll be around eight P.M., so why don't we meet and work this as a joint undercover op, beginning at the bar closest to the vic's apartment? If this woman's a hooker, she'll be wary of cops, and I've got that look. With you on my arm, I become just another lucky cowboy."

"Love your sweet talk," Ella said, smiling. "So, shall we meet at the Horny Toad Bar around a quarter till eight?"

"Good enough. If I get any hits between now and then, I'll give you a call."

"Dan, one more thing. Mail me a copy of your sketch."

"Will do. The witness assured us it's a decent likeness," he said, then ended the call.

"You guys have been going out pretty regularly. Is it serious?" Justine asked her, slowing down as they crossed the concrete south-side bridge leading into old downtown Shiprock.

"No. Yes. Maybe. We're still getting to know each other, and I'm trying to be cautious. How about you and Benny?" Ella asked, wanting to change the subject.

"We're ahead of you two, I guess. In fact, lately I've been getting the impression he wants us to move in together."

"How do you feel about that?" Ella asked, picking up the undercurrent in her words.

"For me it's marriage or forget it. I'm through with test drives. I'm in my mid-thirties, Ella, and if I ever want to have a kid, I can't afford to keep wasting my time," Justine said. "Benny's a good man, and I think he'd be a terrific dad. If he wants to make things official, I'm ready."

"Seriously?" Ella asked, surprised. "You're ready to go for it?"

"Yeah, I am," Justine said.

As silence fell around them, Ella considered what Justine had said. She understood Justine's desire to have a child.

She couldn't even imagine her own life without Dawn. Her love for her daughter gave everything she did additional meaning. That love not only defined her, but it had also refocused her life, enriching it in ways she hadn't even thought possible.

As the quiet stretched out, Ella's thoughts soon returned to the case.

"You think those clowns today were connected to the murder?" Ella asked. "That firebombing attempt came across as an amateur job—more like harassment than anything else. Took balls, though, trying to cook a clearly marked police unit."

"I agree," Justine said. "The thing is, even an amateur could have shot Harry from ambush. He was a stationary target."

"What we still need is that one thread that'll tie things together," Ella said

"The makeshift bomb won't get us far," Justine answered. "All we were able to recover from it was leftover cooking oil, pieces of a gallon glass bottle, and the pickup's cigarette lighter, what they used to ignite the oil. Except for the lighter, which we already know belonged with the pickup, there's no way to track the rest."

"My gut tells me that the answer lies with Harry and whatever he was investigating," Ella said. "Let's go pay Teeny a visit again, but on the way, stop by the Totah Café. We'll pick up some takeout green chile burgers and bring lunch with us as a bribe. I want to push Teeny for more information on Harry's cases, and a couple of the New Mexico Beef Burners might improve his mood."

"One for me, one for you, and three for Teeny?" Justine asked, slowing down and pulling over to her right into the local café's parking lot.

"Yeah. That sounds about right, but be careful about using that nickname to his face," Ella said. "You're cute and female, but he might still dangle you by your boots if you call him anything but Bruce—gun or not."

"Yeah, you're right," Justine said as she braked to a stop. "Want me to place the order while you check to see if he's home?"

"Yeah." Ella reached for her wallet. "I'm buying. Make my chile mild—a no burner."

It was one fifteen in the afternoon when they arrived at Teeny's and, following his lead, walked into the kitchen. Big stainless steel appliances lined the wall, and a school cafeteria table, folding benches and all, was placed in the center of the room.

While Ella and Justine sat down, he whipped up three smoothies and brought them to the table.

"Looks like a great lunch." Teeny took a massive bite of the saucer-sized hamburger and chewed mightily. "Nice and hot—like Hatch chile and a couple of New Mexico's finest." He sipped his smoothie, then added, "And just so you know, although I appreciate the bribe, I'm still not giving you my client's name."

Ella looked up from her plate. "Didn't think you would, but tell me more about our friend's past cases, like the woman who was being stalked. Was the boyfriend dangerous or just posturing?"

"Both," Teeny said. "He liked pushing his weight around, so he was dangerous around the woman. H provided a hands-on demonstration of what violence against a weaker person actually felt like. He may also have mentioned that he was willing to come back as often as necessary to illustrate the point. There was no further problem after that."

"I'd like to check out the punk's alibi for the time of death," Ella said. "Can you give me his name?"

"Sure. It's Albert Shields. He works at the Super Rentals over in Kirtland. It's just south of the old Conoco station." Teeny picked up his iPad, tapped the screen a few times, then waited as the printer in the other room started. "His photo is printing out now."

"You know this place?" Ella asked Justine.

"Sure. I've got a cousin who lives just down the hill past the stop sign," Justine said. "We go to some of the Kirtland Central home games."

"You've got relatives everywhere," Ella said, laughing. Justine came from a large family of mostly girls, the majority of them now married with families of their own.

"Speaking of Justine's relatives, Teeny, you still dating Jayne?" Ella asked, referring to Justine's flakiest sister.

Justine gave her a dirty look.

"What? I'm just asking." Ella said, looking back at Teeny, who shrugged.

"We're between breakups right now," he said, then took another bite of his sandwich. "I forgot the eighteenth-month anniversary of our first date."

Ella nodded. "Maybe I should stick to business."

"Maybe so," Teeny said. After a moment, he spoke again. "I picked up something on the scanner a while ago. Someone tried to blow up your unit?" He sniffed the air. "What did they use, canola oil . . . or is that perfume?"

"Sorry, I didn't realize we were so pungent," Ella said. "It happened while we were interviewing a family not far from the site of the shooting. Two guys in a gray Ford pickup drove up and tried to set fire to our SUV. They put a bottle of vegetable oil underneath it, then threw a hot car lighter into the stuff. Went up like a kitchen grease fire."

"Fortunately, the mobile home owner kept a fire extinguisher handy. We were able to put it out before anything on the vehicle ignited," Justine said.

Teeny nodded. "It'll probably still need some time in the shop just to make sure it's safe to operate."

"That's why we had it towed, but we don't know the extent of the damage yet," Ella said. "So what else can you tell us about this Shields character?"

Teeny, who had an IQ that matched his bulk, pulled up another report and skimmed it. "Here's one important thing. You look a lot like my client, with your long hair and narrow cheekbones. You're a few inches taller, though, and a bit . . ." Teeny's voice trailed off.

"If you're about to say heavier, *don't* go there. I have a high kick, and I'm wearing my pointy boots," she said, looking up from her last bite of burger with narrowed eyes.

"Prettier. I was going to say prettier," he said with a smile. "The only reason I mentioned this is because Shields is into verbal and physical intimidation. He gets off pushing women around, the ones he finds attractive, that is, and you're his type. I'd offer backup, but if he sees the three of us together, he'll probably bail. Of course, I could wait outside," Teeny said, removing the straw and polishing off the last of his drink with a big glug.

"Thanks, but we can handle this," Ella said. She looked down at her watch. "We'd better get going, partner."

"Right, boss. Uh, Bruce, just how big is Albert Shields?" Justine asked.

"He's a real half-pint, about five-five—no offense. But he's got that bodybuilder frame—all muscle—and likes to use his fists. You two should be careful."

"Always," Ella replied, standing. "If we learn anything useful, even if it's only to rule him out, I'll let you know."

"Good. I'm rereading our friend's reports, and I'll call you if I find anything useful. Thanks for lunch, and make sure you grab that photo off the printer on your way out."

As they continued east on Highway 64, Ella looked across the San Juan River valley, noting how much the area had changed in just her lifetime.

"When I was a kid, this was mostly fields, orchards, and farmland. Now look at all the small businesses crowding both sides of the road. Do you remember when Flare Hill over there used to have a derrick, burning off waste gas night and day?"

"Before my time, cuz," Justine said, slowing at the red stoplight, the first since leaving Shiprock. They made the right turn, then drove into Kirtland proper.

"There's the place," Ella said, pointing toward an off-white block building on the left-hand side of the two-lane road. "Make a U, then come back and park just off the road. We'll walk up."

Ella liked to approach any possible confrontational

situation with as little fanfare as possible. Less forewarning, less forearming.

After taking another look at the photo of Albert Shields, they walked up the road and into the rental shop.

At a glance it looked like an old mercantile shop, with everything it offered for rental on display. There were chairs, tables, sofas, a wall of electronic devices that included big-screen TVs, and even gardening tools and equipment. Outside, on a covered patio, were party and wedding supplies ranging from tables and umbrellas to an inflatable slide.

A blond woman in her mid-fifties with big hair, jeans, and a country-western blouse came up to them almost instantly—a predictable move because the bell over the door had announced their presence. Sue Ann, according to her name tag, greeted them with sparkling blue eyes and a toothy smile.

"How can I help you ladies this fine afternoon?" she said with a hint of an Eastern New Mexico twang.

Ella pushed back her jacket, revealing the badge pinned to her belt. Knowing that technically she was out of her jurisdiction, she allowed her jacket to quickly cover it up again. "We're police officers," Ella said, identifying herself and Justine. "We'd like to speak to one of your coworkers, Albert Shields. Could you tell us where you can find him?"

"Aw, jeez. He's not in trouble again, is he?" she said with a scowl.

"We hope not," Justine said. "We just need to ask him a few questions. Where is Mr. Shields?"

The woman seemed to relax slightly. "Al's in the warehouse. It's right through that door." She pointed toward a large entryway leading into what looked to be a storeroom.

"Thanks." Ella went inside the combination workshop, warehouse, and garage. The walls were lined with rows of folding chairs and gardening equipment, and the big shelves were crammed with power tools.

Across the room at the far end, Ella spotted Shields working on a power carpet cleaner. "Hey, Al?" she called, walking toward him.

"That's me, darlin'," the man said, turning his head. His brown hair was cropped close, military style, and although he was smaller than Ella, it was clear he worked out with weights.

His smile quickly faded once his gaze dropped past their breasts to the gold badges on their belts. "What the hell do *you* want? I haven't seen Rachel in over a month, and if she or the goon she sent to try to intimidate me said differently, they're lying."

Ella glanced around, making sure he didn't have a gun or potential weapon within reach. Verifying that none was readily accessible, she relaxed. If the guy was hiding a weapon in his jeans, it was too small to matter, and all he had on the floor beside him was a cordless screwdriver and some kind of paper filter.

Shields took a step toward her, then stopped and crossed his arms across his chest, pumping up like a steroid-enhanced action figure.

Ella moved closer, forcing him to look up at her. She wanted to judge his temperament by deliberately pushing his buttons. "So tell us, what happened between you and that PI? Did he skin up your nose when he jammed your face into the ground?"

Ella watched him carefully. His face turned a little red, but he didn't react.

"He say that?" Shields said, and laughed. "Bull crap. I folded him up like a taco with a jab to the gut. Guy went off retching like a sick dog."

Ella said nothing. Instead she took another step forward, getting in his face.

"Back off, bitch," the man said, throwing out his palm to slam her in the chest.

Anticipating the move, Ella caught his open hand in a pinch grip, digging in her thumbnail below his index finger. He groaned and launched a left jab toward her jaw. She slipped the punch with a dodge to her right, pinching harder and twisting his arm painfully.

As he sagged to his knees, cursing, Justine brought out her Taser and aimed it at his chest. "Try anything else and I'm lighting you up like a tribal casino," she said. "Now, chill."

Suddenly they all heard a shrill voice behind them. "What in *the* hell are you doing, Albert Shields? I warned you what would happen if I ever caught you picking another fight with a woman!" Sue Ann stood in the doorway behind them, hands on her hips.

Ella wasn't quite ready to let go of Al. "What do you say, Mr. Shields? I let go, you step back, and then we can talk like normal people?"

"Fine," he whispered, his face contorted in pain, rage, or both.

Ella eased up on the pinch, then let go of his hand as he stood again.

Justine looked back at the clerk. "We're okay here, ma'am. If you could give us some privacy for a few minutes, we'd appreciate it."

"Whatever," Sue Ann answered. "And if you wanna

kick him in the tool bag, go right ahead. I'll never tell. By the way, Al, if they have to throw you in jail, don't bother coming back to work again, you hear?" She backed out of the room and shut the double doors.

"Bit—," Al began, then clamped his mouth shut and looked at Ella. "You got under my skin and I lost my cool. Let's start again." He attempted a smooth smile, but it never made it to his eyes, which remained cold and angry.

"You lose your cool with the PI, too?" Ella asked.

"Yeah, and if he ever gets into my face again, I'm going to drop him like the sack of shit he is. Let him file charges. It'll be his word against mine," Shields said, doing the arms-across-the-powerful-chest move again. His eyes went back and forth between her and Justine, who still had the Taser out. "No need for the cattle prod, cutie. I'm cool now."

"Glad to hear it," Ella snapped, forcing his attention back to her. "I just have one question—providing I get the right answer. Were you here at work all day Tuesday?"

He looked at her curiously. "Yeah. Eight to five thirty, an hour off for lunch. I ate across the road at the family diner."

"Can anyone verify that?" Ella said.

"Sue Ann, for one. I spent half a day cleaning and maintaining the carpet steamers that came back Monday and Tuesday mornings."

"What about during lunch?" Ella said.

"Hector, the owner of the diner, and I sat together and talked. Check it with him."

"Count on it," Ella said, then glanced at Justine. "Let's go, partner."

Ella reached the double doors when Shields spoke again. "Hey, what was that all about, anyway?"

"Read the papers or listen to the news. You'll find out soon enough," Ella said. Stepping into the front room, she glanced around, searching for Sue Ann, and found her with a customer.

Ella caught her attention, then nodded and held up a hand, signaling that she'd wait until the customer had been served.

As she sat on a concrete bench to wait, Al came out, ostensibly looking for his boss. Seeing them, he immediately went back into the workroom.

"Think he was about to coach his alibi?" Justine whispered.

"Or excuse his behavior. Abusers are usually great at coming up with reasons that'll explain their outbursts," Ella said quietly as Sue Ann came up.

"I'm sorry Al gave you a hard time. He's got anger issues, as you saw," the woman said, her eyes on the workroom entrance.

"We noticed," Ella said. "Before we go, I'd like to verify Al's work schedule this past week."

"He works from eight to five thirty Monday and Tuesday, is off Wednesday and Thursday, then comes back Friday and Saturday. We're closed on Sundays. He gets an hour off at lunch beginning at twelve thirty. There's no clock to punch, but he's supposed to let me know when he arrives or leaves."

"Does he do any deliveries?" Ella asked.

"Oh, yeah. Several per day, as a matter of fact. Would you like to see his schedule for last week?" Sue Ann asked, and saw Ella nod.

"We keep a paper copy, just in case the electricity goes

out," Sue Ellen explained as she picked up a large ledger beside the computer terminal behind the counter. Placing it on the counter, she turned the pages back to Monday. "Which days do you want to look at?"

"Monday to Wednesday, this week," Ella said, refusing to give her specifics in case the woman decided to protect Shields.

"Al had to deliver a wedding tent to Beclabito late Tuesday morning. He returned at around one thirty, took lunch, then came back to work around two thirty."

"Anyone go with him to make the delivery?" Justine asked.

Sue Ann shook her head. "Not Tuesday morning. We have a teenager who helps part-time from four to six in the afternoons and all day on Saturdays. During school hours, Al makes the deliveries by himself."

"Okay," Ella said, taking notes, including the Beclabito address and phone number.

They had what they needed now. Though Ella had looked over toward the workroom a few times, there was no indication Al had been eavesdropping. "Is that the delivery van parked out there?" Ella asked Sue Ann, gesturing to the white van with a business logo on the side parked to the left of the entrance.

"Yeah, that's it. Al drives the black Mustang parked beside it, in case you're interested," Sue Ann added.

"Thanks again for all your help, Sue Ann . . . ," Ella said, letting her words trail off as she waited for the woman's last name.

"Quigley," Sue Ann answered. "Glad to help. Could you tell me what this was all about, Detective Clah?"

"We're looking for possible witnesses to a crime, and someone suggested that Mr. Shields might have seen something."

"I hope Al isn't involved in some way. He's actually a very hard worker, but from what I can tell, his personal life is a disaster."

"We'll be in touch," Ella said, handing the woman her card.

They were back on the road within five minutes. "That guy has anger issues and ego issues, too. So what do you think? Is he a viable suspect?" Justine said as they headed north toward Highway 64.

"He's a bully and a coward and Harry bruised his ego. He also has no conclusive alibi to cover the time of death. It's possible he drove down the highway, took the turn off at Rattlesnake, tracked Harry down, shot him, then came back to Kirtland for lunch," Ella said, then paused before speaking again.

"I just thought of something else. Turn around and go back to the rental store. I want to take a closer look at that van. It rained around the time of the shooting. Maybe we can find mud on the vehicle that matches what's around the crime scene."

With a nod, Justine did a 180 and headed back down the road.

SEVEN
✖ ✖ ✖

The van turned out to be a disappointment. The vehicle had been recently washed. There was even a local car wash receipt in full view on the dashboard.

Halfway back to Shiprock, Ella started looking through her notes. "I'm thinking of crossing Albert off our list at least for now. We don't have much on him, but somehow I doubt he'd know enough about Navajo witches to effectively mislead us."

"And how would he know where Harry was going to be unless Al set him up somehow? On the other hand, the guy has access to plenty of tools," Justine said.

Ella nodded, knowing she meant heavy cutting tools, like bolt cutters. "My gut's still telling me he's not our guy. Al's personality suggests he'd be more likely to use his fists than a bullet. Let's dig deeper into this county theft investigation instead."

"That's going to be tricky," Justine said. "It's out of our

jurisdiction, so you're going to have to rely heavily on Dan. You'll be seeing him tonight, right?"

"Yeah, but I'll need to make things official, so I'm going to ask Big Ed to call Sheriff Taylor and request Dan," Ella said, weighing her strategy. "What makes this a risky proposition is that we don't know who's behind the thefts. Instinct tells me we should keep things as quiet as possible."

"What if Sheriff Taylor doesn't know about the missing stuff? He's a straight arrow, and I can't see him not taking immediate action on something like that," Justine said.

"If he does know, he may purposely be keeping it low profile. He wouldn't want to tip off the perp or perps. Then there's also the political angle to consider. He's an elected official, so he wouldn't want news of this to get out, not until he can make an arrest," Ella reminded.

"Guess you're right," Justine said. "While you're handling that, is there anything in particular you want me to be doing?"

"Yeah, get a warrant to look at all of Harry's phone calls. Maybe his 'date' has his number. We'll also want to seize any mail that arrives at his apartment. We need a solid lead."

"What about the skinwalker angle? Have you been able to talk to Clifford about possible suspects?"

"Not yet, but I'll keep trying to reach him," Ella said.

It was five thirty in the afternoon and still in the high eighties outside when Ella left work for the day and headed home. She drove at a leisurely pace, welcoming a little time to herself.

She passed the scattered houses and businesses lining

both sides of the long hill rising to the south. To the west, the volcanic cone of Ship Rock rose from its base in the dry sand. Off to her left, Cathedral Mesa stood alone, like an enormous bench rising in the desert.

She soon reached the turnoff that led to her home and, beyond that, her brother Clifford's place. After a five-minute drive down the dusty road, she pulled up by her large wooden frame house.

As Ella stepped out of the vehicle, the wonderful aroma of freshly baked pinto beans, fry bread, and roasted green chile filled the air. Rose's cooking was second to none.

Rose appeared at the kitchen screen door a moment later. "Daughter, you're just in time for dinner."

"Navajo tacos?" Ella said, suddenly very hungry.

"How did you—? Oh, of course," Rose replied with a wide smile, sniffing the air.

"Mom, I wouldn't be much of a detective if I couldn't pick up the trail of freshly cooked pinto beans." Ella held the screen open while her mother went inside. Dawn, still in her riding clothes, was already at the table eating. Her mouth full, she waved with a twittering of her fingers. Herman, seated at the end of the table, stood as they came in.

"It's good to have you home for dinner," he said. "You're planning to join us, right?"

"Yes, but I have to work later tonight, so I won't be able to stay for long." She still had to talk to Clifford, then meet Dan at that Farmington bar so they could try to track down Harry's mystery date. If they ended up having to go bar hopping in order to find her, she might not make it home until after the local bars closed.

"Here, eat," Herman said, offering her a serving. The large plate was filled with a saucer-sized piece of puffy fry bread, pinto beans, spicy salsa, shredded lettuce, green chile, and the whole thing was sprinkled with grated cheddar cheese.

"Thanks," she said, realizing suddenly how hungry she was. Ella took the plate.

"So, where are you going tonight, Mom? Do you already have a suspect?" Dawn said, then seeing Rose's stern look, cringed and stared at her plate.

Ella, knowing her mother didn't like that kind of talk at the table, lowered her voice and leaned closer to her daughter. "Let's not discuss that right now, okay, beanstalk?" Dawn was growing by leaps and bounds, and was nearly five foot seven and a half now. In another year, she'd be wearing Ella's jeans.

Dawn laughed. "You managed to find a nickname even worse than 'pumpkin.'"

"You're growing like a weed, but I thought you'd resent being called 'tumbleweed,'" Ella said, grabbing her fork and digging in to her meal.

Rose joined them at the table with her own plate and looked at Dawn. "I'm glad that you finally emptied the trash in your bathroom, but you haven't cleaned in there yet. No more excuses, granddaughter. It gets done before you go to bed tonight."

"But tonight's—," Dawn began.

"You heard your *shimasání*, daughter," Ella said firmly. "Now, eat your food while it's warm."

About twenty minutes later, while sipping the last of her iced tea with her family, Ella's cell phone rang. Seeing it was from Clifford, she excused herself and answered the call in the living room.

Ella spoke to her brother quickly and, in hushed tones, agreed to meet him at his home in a few minutes rather than talk over the phone. Though she hated to leave the family dinner early, she took her plate and utensils to the sink and said good-bye, giving Dawn's shoulder a quick squeeze.

Five minutes later, she was in her pickup driving west to Clifford's home. The drive was short and as she pulled up, she saw him attaching a windshield wiper blade to his pickup on the passenger side. He waved, then walked over to meet her.

"Hey, brother, how's your family doing up at the sheep camp?" Ella greeted.

"My son's a much better camper than my wife. She's supposed to be a Traditionalist, but she's lost without her gas stove. Cooking in a Dutch oven over an outdoor grill makes her nervous. She's too much of a perfectionist these days."

Ella smiled. She and Loretta had never gotten along. Though Loretta had turned out to be the perfect wife for her brother and a good mother to Julian, Ella felt no sympathy for her sister-in-law, who had a tendency to act superior at times.

"How is your son's *hataalii* training going these days?" Ella asked. Though only sixteen, Julian continued to express an interest in continuing his father's work.

"He's just now realizing how much time and work it's going to take to become a Singer. He also knows that in to-day's world, he's going to need a second job if he wants to be able to provide for a family. Not many Navajos are still following the Way. That means learning a trade or attending college, and probably leaving the reservation for some time at least. You walked the same path, sister."

"True, but your kid's more grounded than I was at his age. He knows what he wants. My primary goal back then was to get away from what I didn't want."

"Or thought you didn't want," he said. "Now, here you are, doing some of the tribe's most valuable work. I'm glad you came back when you did. The People needed you."

"Police work is never-ending," she said with a nod. "Did word reach you up at the sheep camp about my friend's murder?"

"Yes and I got your messages, too. The minute you mentioned where you'd found your friend's body, I knew why you needed to talk to me."

"So you've also heard stories about evil ones in that area? Is there any truth to those rumors?" Ella said, careful not to voice words like "skinwalkers" and "Navajo witches." Although Clifford was one of the most powerful Singers on the Navajo Nation, he still regarded them as highly dangerous and avoided doing anything that might call them to him.

"What kind of signs have you found?" Clifford asked.

Ella described the removal of Harry's fingertips, the backward footprints, the dead crow, and, lastly, the charcoal drypainting Truman John and his girlfriend claimed to have seen.

"Those backward steps aren't inconsistent with what I've seen or heard regarding their trickery. They want to generate confusion. As for the rest, that's certainly part of their MO, if you will. Do you have any suspects?"

"Two individuals tried to set fire to my department SUV, but there's no way I can link either to the evil ones. I've spoken to the area residents, too, but if anyone has actually seen the one or ones responsible, they aren't talking. What I can tell you is that most of the people our officers have interviewed so far are really frightened."

"You and your team need to carry protection at all times." He glanced down at the medicine bag Ella had fastened to her belt. "If you need more of those, let me know."

"I will, and thanks," she said. "There's another way you can help. I need a list of suspects, people you think might have been drawn to this evil. Word always gets around, even if it's only spoken in whispers, and people do talk to you about things like that."

"All right. I'll see what I can do."

"Thanks," Ella said. "Will you be staying for a while, or are you going back up to join your family?"

"Looks like I'll be sticking around for a few more days. I've had several calls from patients, and with this new danger, there'll be others who'll need me. I'll give you a call before I leave again."

"Good, I appreciate that. If I come across any more physical evidence like ritual items or ceremonial sites, would you be willing to come take a look for yourself? I'd like you to verify that it's legitimate and not just someone out to scare people."

"If I can, I'll come," he said. "Just be careful when you handle any artifacts. Keep your protection with you at all times."

"Okay. I'll be in touch," Ella said, and walked to her truck.

"Stay safe," Clifford called.

"You, too," she said, and waved.

As she climbed into the vehicle, she saw that Clifford had already disappeared into his medicine hogan. Though their careers were worlds—and centuries—apart, they were both Navajos who believed in the *Diné*. They still joined forces whenever necessary to protect their families and the tribe. She'd never have a more dependable or stronger ally than Clifford, especially when things got tough.

Seeing a cottontail dart out in front of her on the road, Ella slammed on the brakes. As she came to a stop, successfully avoiding the animal, she heard something tumbling in the bed of her truck. She looked back through the rear cab window, but didn't see a thing. Curious, she unfastened her seat belt, deciding to take a closer look. Normally, unless she was hauling hay, there was nothing back there.

Ella walked to the tailgate, wondering if something had come loose. A second later, she saw a white object several inches long resting on the truck bed close to the cab.

Rather than climb in, Ella went around to reach in. The second she picked it up, she realized what it was. The bleached-out animal jawbone still held a tooth—a canine. Scratched into the bone were two crude letters—"CE," her initials—written backward. There was something on the bone, too. She looked down at her hand. What she'd thought was sand was too finely ground. It was bits of gray ash.

The implied threat was clear. Cars and trucks could be witched. The skinwalker had meant for her to have a fatal accident.

Yet that didn't bother her nearly so much as the knowledge that her truck had been parked at home when this . . . thing . . . had been added to it.

Nothing had been sliding back there, or rolling around when she'd left the station. At Clifford's, both she and her brother had been in full view of her pickup the entire time.

Anger swelled inside her. The skinwalker had wanted her to know that she wasn't out of his reach, no matter where she was.

She tried to calm down and clear her thoughts. Although he'd hoped to scare her, what he'd actually done was really piss her off. The skinwalker probably didn't realize it yet, but he'd made a big mistake—and a bad enemy. By coming to her home, he'd made it personal. She wouldn't rest until the slimeball was behind bars.

Ella placed the jawbone into a school-lunch-sized paper bag. She always kept a few of these around to collect and contain evidence. Being on call virtually 24/7 meant that sometimes she'd arrive at a crime scene in her personal vehicle.

Ella headed to the station next and called Justine on the way, giving her a quick rundown. When she walked through the doors a short time later, Ella saw Justine waiting for her in the hall, Big Ed a few feet behind her. Like everyone else, he was working late today—no surprise, considering the publicity the murder had generated in the community.

"You told him?" Ella asked Justine quickly after Big Ed cocked his head toward his office and disappeared from view.

"It was the only way I could get a larger police presence around your house, effective immediately."

"You called for more units to actively patrol the area?" Ella asked.

"Yeah."

"Thanks, partner," Ella said, and handed Justine the paper bag. "See what you can get from this thing."

"You've got it."

"I'll catch you later." Ella went to the chief's office next.

"Tell me what happened," Big Ed said, and waved her to a chair.

Ella gave him the highlights. "Chief, if this crazy thinks I'm going to run away screaming, he's in for one helluva surprise. All he's done is guarantee that I'll go after him with everything I've got."

"He's trying to rattle you, to divert your focus away from the homicide investigation. Don't get sucked in," Big Ed said. "I've already arranged for Phillip and Michael Cloud to alternate patrols around your home and that of your brother's. One of them will be in the immediate area at all times."

When she heard him mention Herman's nephews, she nearly cringed. "Those guys are top-notch officers, but once they tell their uncle, my mother will find out. Knowing that a skinwalker was that close to our home is really going to scare her."

"Maybe so, but you can't keep your family in the dark about this. This perp left the jawbone in your truck, but how do you know there's not another surprise waiting around the house?"

"Good point."

"Do you still have a family dog?" Seeing Ella nod, he added, "So how come he didn't bark when a stranger approached?" Big Ed asked.

"Two's getting old. He can sleep through a thunder-storm. I think his hearing's nearly gone."

"Consider getting a second dog."

"Before I go, Chief, I'd like to request that you speak to Sheriff Taylor and ask for his cooperation. I think Harry's murder was linked to the theft of county property, a case he was investigating," she said, giving him the information. "I can really use an official liaison."

"I'll handle that for you, but keep me updated."

"I will," she said, and soon afterwards left the station.

By the time she pulled up to the house and parked, Herman was outside, waiting for her. Judging from the look on his face, he already knew, and that meant that the ones inside probably did, too.

Ella braced herself. As she walked up to the front door, Rose came out to the porch. "We've searched everywhere, daughter, but there are no hidden warnings or evils waiting for us here. Just to make sure, your brother came by immediately and offered prayers for our protection. He also added a few things to our medicine bundles."

Ella stared at her mother. She'd expected hysteria, or maybe anger, but not this calmness. She glanced at Herman, hoping for an explanation.

"My nephews phoned after dispatch called them with their new orders, and told me what you'd found in your truck," he said. "They promised to make sure we stayed safe."

"I was going to suggest that all of you pack up and go stay at my brother's sheep camp in the mountains. After this matter is settled, you can come back."

"No, daughter, no one's running us out of our home. My

husband's nephews will be close by if there's trouble. In the meantime, there's a way I can help you. I'll ask my friends and see if anyone knows who this evil one is," she said quietly. "They may not talk to the police, but people trust me."

Ella had no doubt about it. "All right, Mom, but be very careful. Does my daughter know what's going on?"

"No, but you can't keep this from her," Rose said, reading Ella's mind with alarming ease. "She needs to know, if only to be more careful herself."

"Yeah, you're right, Mom." Ella went inside to her daughter's room and found Dawn at her desk.

Dawn turned her head as Ella came in, her expression grave. "Mom, you're being careful, right? I've been reading about those . . . people."

Ella stood behind Dawn and looked down at her daughter's computer screen. Dawn was researching skinwalkers on the Internet.

"I'm being smart, like you suggested." Ella tugged her shirt open to show Dawn the ballistic T-shirt she often wore while working undercover. "So how much do you already know about recent events?"

"I heard *Shimasání* talking," Dawn said with a shrug. "It's okay, Mom. None of us are that scared. I just wish there was some way we could scare *him*."

Ella smiled. "I'll see what I can do."

EIGHT

—— ✖ ✖ ✖ ——

Ella was running late. As she pulled into the Horny Toad's parking lot, she spotted Dan Nez's pickup, a newer model Ford Silverado, just ahead. Dan was leaning against the cab of the big truck just aft of the driver's door, watching the bar entrance.

The Horny Toad had been easy to find, with its distinctive sign depicting an overweight, winking cartoon reptile standing with his "arms" around two big-breasted women wearing partially unbuttoned Western-cut blouses.

Ella had never been inside this particular bar, but it was a fairly safe bet that they served more beer and buffalo wings than chardonnay and Brie.

Dan came over just as she got out and locked her door. Tonight, he was dressed in blue jeans, a dark blue and white short-sleeved Western shirt open at the collar, and shiny brown boots—his favorite Tony Lamas. His belt sported a big silver buckle with a cowboy on horseback, a trophy from a rodeo event over in Arizona. He'd skipped wearing his

Stetson, probably not wanting it to get smashed up if they ran into trouble.

"I hope I didn't keep you waiting too long. Things got complicated," Ella said.

"You called ahead and let me know, so it was no problem. It also felt good to get a few minutes to unwind."

"Yeah, I'm with you on that. Things can get crazy." She smiled. Dan was sure nice to look at, but what made him stand out went beyond his physical attributes. Confidence gave him an undeniable presence. He looked like a man to be reckoned with, one who could handle any situation, no matter what the circumstances.

"You're looking fine, as usual," Dan said, giving her a quick hug.

As he stepped back, his gaze drifted over her in a thorough and appreciative way. She smiled. That was the thing about Dan. He made her feel like a desirable woman, not just a cop.

Tonight, her hair was loose and fell just past her shoulders. Though mostly black, there was a smattering of silver in it these days. Her dress jeans and formfitting Western-cut blue shirt completed the picture.

Her casual look, of course, was deceptive. She was carrying her undercover weapon—a SIG Sauer .380—at her waist, tucked beneath her blouse in an inside holster. She also had a small derringer in her boot—her backup weapon since her days with the FBI. Then there was the sleeveless ballistic T-shirt.

"When was the last time we actually went out on a date, Ella?" he said, taking her hand, staying true to tonight's undercover assignment.

"Two weeks ago—Saturday night." She looked at him, smiling. "Why do you ask me that every time we cross paths?"

Dan grinned. "Insecurity. I need to know you haven't forgotten me already."

Ella laughed. He was easy to be with and had a great sense of humor. She liked being around Dan a lot, but unfortunately, it was going to be strictly business tonight.

"Don't know if you've seen it yet, but I sent you a copy of the sketch we made of the victim's mystery date," he said, and unfolded a sheet of paper he'd carried in his breast pocket.

"Great sketch," she said, studying it as they approached the tavern door. "Attractive, high cheekbones, full lips. Short, layered crop, a little too perfect. Probably a wig."

"I hope it's close enough to the real deal to give us a solid lead," he said, reaching for the handle. "By the way, I spoke to Sheriff Taylor. Chief Atcitty has asked for county's continued help, so I've been told to remain available to you and help coordinate your murder investigation whenever it involves county. Just let me know what you need and I'll do my best to make it happen. That work for you?"

"Absolutely," Ella said, wondering if Taylor had told Dan about the thefts yet.

"So tell me, have you been here before?" Dan asked as they stepped inside the Horny Toad.

"No, but I gather you have," she said as one of the waitresses waved enthusiastically at Dan.

He grinned. "Now and then. After a long day of catching bad guys, a man's gotta have a cold one."

She smiled back at him. "I used to enjoy the nightlife, too, but having a daughter changed everything."

"Head over there." He gestured to a small, empty table in the far corner. From there, they'd be able to see the entire room and the entrance. "Do you miss it, your carefree days, that is?"

"No, can't say I do," she said loudly, trying to be heard over the country western ballad blaring out from hidden speakers.

The room was dimly lit, but Ella's eyes adjusted quickly. As she made her way past an enthusiastic cluster of line dancers stepping more or less to the music, she made a point of checking out the women's faces. No one matched the sketch.

A chemistry-enhanced redhead came over and greeted Dan seconds after they sat down. Wearing a thin T-shirt that left little to the imagination, the waitress beamed Dan a broad smile. "What can I get you, honey?"

"Hey, Ruby. Before we get to that, take a look at this, will you?" he said, angling the sketch toward the light. "Have you ever seen this customer?"

"So you're working tonight, Danny?"

Danny? Ella's eyebrows shot up. She might have been just a little jealous if Dan hadn't looked so uncomfortable. The waitress was barely in her twenties, and judging from Dan's reaction, he wasn't into May–December relationships.

"I'm off the clock," Dan said, "but as you probably know from some of the other cops who come in here, the line between on duty and off gets a little blurry sometimes."

She looked at the sketch again. "I haven't seen anyone who looks like her, but if I do, I'll let you know," she said. "So what can I get you two?"

"You got Coors on tap?" Dan asked.

"Sure do, hon. And you, ma'am?"

She bit back a groan. Dan was "hon," but she was "ma'am"? She suddenly felt ancient. "Bud Light," Ella said. "In the bottle, please."

As soon as the barmaid moved away, Dan looked at Ella. "I swear to you I've only met her once or twice, and there's no way we ever dated. We got talking one night when business was slow, that's all."

Ella laughed. "No explanations are necessary, and I'm not dating anyone else, either. But let's not get off track. Line of duty, blurry . . . remember?"

Before he could respond, the waitress came back with their drinks and bowls of chips and salsa. Ella took a tiny sip of her beer. The drink was mostly civilian cover and she'd ordered a light beer to keep up the image. What made it easy to keep her drinking to a bare minimum was that she *hated* beer. Sipping it came more naturally to her than an actual swallow, and the salsa and chips helped her keep it down.

"I'm thinking that we should look for a hooker working the customers rather than a single girl looking to hook up," Dan said. "I heard that the woman with Harry was all over him."

"Based on looks alone, Harry would have been a good target for a working girl—if she didn't let his body language get in her way," Ella said. "He was difficult to approach. Getting to know him was even harder."

"Yet you and him . . ."

"That was a long, long time ago," Ella said, finishing the line of thought she assumed he was following. "Things didn't work out, because what I saw in my future and what he wanted in his were too far apart."

"Your life is just how you like it?"

The question was innocent-sounding enough, but she knew there was more to it. "I like my life because I love the people in it. Family, both at home and at work, is important to me."

"I know, which is why I don't get what you're doing now. There's trouble ahead for your unit, and your job and that of your team's could be on the line. Yet you're not using your considerable influence to fight back."

"I've heard about Gerald Bidtah's plans, but that's Big Ed's fight, not mine."

"What if they insist on having all homicide investigations run out of Window Rock and disband your unit, sticking you in some office at tribal headquarters? Will you take a stand then?"

"It hasn't come to that yet," she said, then shook her head, signaling him to drop it. "Stay focused. Our objective is to find the woman in the sketch."

He nodded, his gaze taking in the room. "Tell me about Ute's work. What was he investigating that may have given someone a motive for taking him out?"

"He was working for Bruce Little, and Bruce won't divulge specifics unless we can prove it has a direct link to the murder. All I know is that Harry was looking into thefts of county property. Do you know, or have you heard anything about that?"

He shook his head. "News to me. Does Sheriff Taylor know?"

"I don't know for sure, but I suspect he does and is keeping a lid on it and his investigation."

"Makes sense. So who's Little's client?"

"I have no idea, but I'm fairly sure that it's someone of influence, maybe a county official."

"You're telling me that there's corruption inside county government, but you're not really giving me anything to go on." Dan's tone held an edge. "What division of county has the problem with thefts? Are we talking the sheriff's department?"

"I don't know."

"You don't know, or won't say?" Dan pressed.

"I'm giving it to you straight. I don't know." Ella's gaze remained on the women around them, but there were no Navajo women in the bar that matched the description. "Concentrate on the women, Dan."

"First time my date's ever suggested something like that, but if you insist," he said, then forced a slow grin. "Hey, I recognize one of the bartenders working tonight. Let me show her the sketch. If she doesn't know the girl, maybe she can pass the sketch around to her coworkers."

"Good idea."

Dan had been gone only a few minutes before Ruby came over. "Everything still okay here?"

"Yes, thank you," Ella said, her gaze still on the room.

"Do you two have a thing?"

Ella, who'd been studying the room, glanced back at her in surprise. "Say again?"

"You know, are you officers just working together, or are you hooking up?"

Before she could answer, Dan came back. "Hey, Ruby."

Ella bit back a smile. "Ruby wants me to clarify our status."

"Just askin' in case I decide to make a move of my own," Ruby said, winking at Dan.

Dan gave Ella a sad smile, then looked back at Ruby. "Ella keeps me guessing, but I'm not giving up, not yet."

To her credit, Ella didn't choke.

"Well, sweetie, if you ever get tired of the chase, I'll be around," Ruby said, then walked off.

Ella looked at Dan in surprise. "Why the heck did you tell her that?"

"She went away without feeling rejected. What's the harm?" He gave her a slow grin. "It's the truth, isn't it?"

Ella rolled her eyes. "Getting back to business. Did you get anything from the bartender?"

"Yeah, Nadine remembers Harry. She said that the woman was seriously groping him, even nibbling at his ear. They left together right before she had to ask them to get a room."

"Interesting. For a guy, I guess that beats the heck out of nachos and salsa."

"More than you realize. Nadine said the woman was hot. She knows most of the working girls on West Main, but she'd never seen this one before," Dan said. "Nadine also told me that it surprised the heck out of her when she targeted Harry. Several suits were here that night, high roller oilmen sitting on fat wallets, but this girl set her sights on Harry right from the start."

"Could be a Navajo girl looking for another Navajo, or maybe she likes men who have that dangerous edge about them. Or more likely, she had an agenda—scouting out his apartment. Harry was missing his laptop, remember? We've got to find this lady, so what do you say we go to the Bucking Bronco Lounge next?"

Dan left several bills on the table and winked at Ruby as they walked out.

Seeing it, Ella laughed. "So, do you like her or not?"

"I won't rob the cradle, but every man appreciates an ego boost."

"You need that?"

"It's nice to get a little attention once in a while," he said.

"Here I thought I was enough for you," Ella teased with a labored sigh.

He met her gaze. "You would be, if that's what *you* wanted."

The intensity of that look took her by surprise. "Focus, focus. Later, when we're off the clock, we'll see if I can think of a way or two to make you smile."

"Looking forward to it."

His voice, low and deep, gave added meaning to his words. There were no dull moments with Dan. As they stopped by her truck, he leaned back against it and hooked his thumb into his pocket.

Following his movements, Ella glanced down, her eyes lingering for a second over his belt buckle, remembering the last time she'd unbuckled it. Dan was an excellent lover who knew when to be tender and when to get rough. Maybe he was the man for her after all.

She pushed the thought back instantly and focused on business. "There's something I need to follow up on. I'm going to call Justine while we're on our way to the Bucking Bronco. Harry's date was messing with him, so it's possible her prints are on his belt buckle."

"Good idea," he said, smiling slowly. "So tell me, where did that belt buckle idea come from?"

"I'm taking the fifth," she said, chuckling. She was physically attracted to him, but even more important, she really liked Dan. "I'll follow you out. I don't want to leave my truck parked here."

"Don't blame you."

Ella climbed into her truck and started the engine while Dan continued walking to his. She was looking forward to the next time she and Dan met off the clock. Justine dreamed of babies. Ella's dream was simpler. She wanted to have time on her hands to just relax and enjoy herself.

She tried to picture herself without the badge—a civilian with leisure time at her disposal, going on dates where "strapped" meant too little cash instead of referring to the weapon she carried.

Change . . . maybe it wasn't a bad thing after all.

Ella waited at the parking lot exit for an opening in traffic as vehicles whizzed by. She'd be going with the flow, so all she needed was an opening in the outside lane.

As she pulled out onto the street, the right front end of her truck suddenly wobbled, pulling her sharply back toward the curb.

She compensated instantly, but not before a horn blasted and she heard squealing tires. A sporty Mustang raced by her on the inside lane and the guy flipped her off.

Ella touched the brakes, trying to track a straight line, but it was hard to maintain control of the steering as the wobble grew worse. She didn't think she'd had a flat, but something was definitely wrong. She looked in the rearview mirror just as Dan moved into position behind her and flicked on his high beams.

"Crap." Ella searched for a place to pull over, but there

was nothing but sidewalk and curb for another half a block. Knowing she couldn't risk veering out into traffic, she pulled to a stop.

Ella saw Dan, his emergency blinkers on, stop right behind her to block the lane. Grabbing the key from the ignition, she climbed out the passenger's side, her gaze on oncoming traffic. With the nearest streetlight fifty yards away and the business beside her closed and darkened at this hour, walking around to check her tire was risky business.

As she took a closer look, Ella saw the wheel and tire were canted inward and hanging on to the axle by a single lug nut. Another few seconds and the tire would have come completely off. The other lug nuts were probably somewhere back down the street or in the parking lot.

"Want me to arrange for a tow truck?" Dan called as he came up the sidewalk, waving his phone.

"Yeah. Try Smitty's. He's just a half mile or so from here on Orchard Boulevard."

As he joined her, he saw the problem close up. "That damn tire almost came off. How'd that happen?"

"This isn't an accident. Somebody removed the other lug nuts while we were inside. Glad I wasn't heading back to the Rez and turning right instead of left. Otherwise I might have yanked the tire off and crashed," she said, looking more closely at the wheel. "I'm hoping there's no real damage to the wheel or bolts and all I'll need is a jack and five new lug nuts."

Ella stepped back onto the sidewalk, standing beside Dan and watching people gawk as they drove past them.

"This has all the markings of a prank—a dangerous

one," Ella said, remembering the attempt made to burn up her SUV earlier in the day.

Dan nodded. "If the intent was to make you wreck, the perps would have done more than just loosen the lug nuts."

Ella's gaze drifted back to the Horny Toad's parking lot. "What do you say we go ask the working girls on the street corners a few questions?"

"Yeah, good idea," he said. "It's possible one of them saw something useful. They probably watch vehicles leaving the bar, hoping to catch somebody's attention."

"This wasn't an isolated incident, and no way it's just a coincidence. It's the second time today the vehicle I've been riding in has been attacked," Ella said.

"Huh?"

As they walked up the sidewalk, she told him about the firebomb.

NINE
—— ✖ ✖ ✖ ——

Earlier, Ella had noticed two
women standing on opposite street corners a little farther
up—prostitutes, judging by the way they waved at passing
drivers. Their profession often made them excellent sources
of information—but only if they chose to cooperate.

Ella took the one closest to her while Dan crossed the
street to speak to the other. As she approached the young
woman, Ella realized that she couldn't have been more than
a few years out of high school—if that.

Instead of flashing her badge, Ella reached for her wallet
and pulled out a twenty-dollar bill. "I need some help."

The Anglo girl gave Ella a tentative smile, then pushed
her jet black hair away from her face. "My name's Candy.
What did you have in mind? A threesome is going to run
you eighty dollars, but if you want—"

Ella held up her hand. "I just need some information."

The young woman's eyes widened. "You a cop?"

Ella didn't answer directly. "Someone was tampering

with my pickup. Did you happen to notice anyone sneaking around the parked cars over there, say within the last hour?" she said, and pointed to the parking area.

"You're the one with the wobbling truck, aren't you?" she said. "I saw that. You got lucky."

"Yeah. Turns out someone removed the lug nuts off my front wheel and my insurance company is going to want details of what happened. Did you see anyone?"

She jammed the twenty-dollar bill Ella had just given her into the pocket of her painted-on jeans. "No, but I've only been here about fifteen minutes. Do you want me to ask the other girls and give you a call if I get anything?"

"Sounds good." Ella took a card from her wallet and handed it to her.

Candy glanced at the card. "So you are a cop."

"Yeah, but I'm off duty, so this repair bill's on me. I'd appreciate any help you can give me."

"Sure."

As Candy walked away, Ella saw a tow truck drive past, then pull into the lane just ahead of her pickup. As it started to back into position for a hookup, Ella whistled to Dan, then turned and jogged back to her truck.

Ella gave the tow truck driver her keys and waited while he hauled her pickup off the street and into the parking lot of the real estate office.

Five minutes later, Leroy, judging from the embroidered name on his work shirt, took a closer look at her tire. "No obvious damage. I can fix this right here, if you want, Officer."

"Go for it," she said.

He worked efficiently, using battery-powered tools and

a bright lantern, then lowered the vehicle to the ground and disconnected the winch cable.

"Your truck's ready to go," he said, putting his tools back into a metal storage bin. "You got lucky, ma'am. None of the bolts were bent or stripped too much to use, so all it really took were new nuts. The wheel's on securely now, your tire is scuffed but intact, and you're ready to roll. You might want to drive slow at first, just to make sure. And better have the alignment checked, sooner rather than later."

Ella gave him a credit card as Dan joined her. While Leroy went back to his truck to make out her bill, she hung back with Dan. "Did the woman you spoke to see anything?"

"Nah. She was too busy 'making friends.' She said she's come and gone twice within the past hour."

"It was easy for our suspect to stay under the radar out here. I'll have to be more careful from now on, even off the Rez."

Dan waited by the cab of her pickup while she finished finalizing the bill. When she came back, he opened the door for her.

"You look so serious, Dan. What's on your mind?" Ella said, climbing in back behind the driver's seat.

Resting one arm on the frame, he leaned in slightly through the open window, obviously wanting to keep the conversation private. "Have you considered the possibility that Navajo witches are sending you a message by tampering with your ride?"

She thought back to the jawbone she'd found in the bed of her truck, something Dan didn't know about, and realized he was probably right. Before she could say anything, he continued.

"You mentioned that cooking oil fire, now this. With that in mind, think of Coyote, the trickster in our creation stories. What's been happening to you is right in line with that kind of thinking," Dan said. "The suspect probably figured you'd catch the problem with your tire in time—and if not, that was just too bad."

She nodded slowly. "It fits, in a sick way."

He glanced at his watch. "I better take a pass on the Bucking Bronco. I've got an early court date tomorrow and I need to go over my notes and get at least a few hours' sleep."

"Okay. Thanks for all the help."

"No problem," he said, then after a beat added, "I don't believe in the supernatural, Ella, but I've dealt with crazies and saw plenty of weird stuff when I lived down by Winslow. Watch your back."

"Yeah, I know," she said. "I've had run-ins with skin-walkers before. Let's just say they leave a lasting impression."

"I know your father died at their hands," he said, his voice gentle. "They'll use those memories against you. It's the way they work. They're crazy, but they're also cunning."

Dan was right. They'd zeroed in on her vulnerabilities with uncanny precision. Even after all these years, she still missed her dad. His death had created a void in her life, one that would never be filled. Ella checked out the wheel repair again, needing a second or two to compose herself before answering.

"I have powerful allies, Dan—my mom and brother," she said at last. "And my backup is top notch, you included."

"You know I'll help you any way I can," Dan said.

"I appreciate that. The problem is I don't even have a

suspect yet. That's why I'd like to ask you a big favor," Ella said slowly. It wouldn't be a fair request, but she had to try anyway. "Can you compile a list of officers who have direct access to county inventory? I'm looking for someone who's fairly competent with a rifle and has a good working knowledge of Navajo culture, or has access to contacts who do."

He stared at the ground for a moment, then looked back at her. "I don't like the idea of putting people from my department under the microscope just so you can rule them in, or out, as potential suspects. However, I trust what you're doing, so I'll see what I can find out. But no promises."

"Fair enough," she said. "And, Dan, thanks."

"Just watch your back," he said. "You're becoming a magnet for trouble."

"Hey, at least I'm not a boring date."

He laughed. "Boring? That's not an adjective I'd ever use to describe you."

"How would you describe me?"

He looked at her and shook his head. "Ask me when I'm not on duty."

As he walked away, Ella studied his long-legged stride and tight buns. Work always managed to get in the way. She sighed. Unfortunately, that also summed up her entire history with men, even with Eugene, her late husband. He'd been a soldier, deployed for half their brief time together.

Dan stopped by his truck, then glanced back and smiled. "Window shopping?"

Ella laughed. Maybe this time things would turn out differently. "You can't blame a girl for admiring the scenery."

Ella drove back toward Shiprock and the Navajo Nation

feeling wide awake and a little wired after everything that had happened. No way she'd be able to fall asleep anytime soon.

Not ready to go home, she considered paying Teeny a visit. He was a night owl and very seldom went to bed before midnight. She dialed his cell, knowing that if he'd already sacked out, she'd get his voice mail.

Teeny answered after the second ring. "Hey, Ella."

"If you're not turning in early, how about letting me come over? I need to chat with someone."

"Sure. Night's still young."

"See you in twenty."

When Ella drove into Teeny's fenced-in compound, she spotted Jayne Goodluck's truck and cringed. Justine's sister and she had never managed to get along, but things grew decidedly worse after Jayne started dating Teeny.

Ella's friendship with Teeny went all the way back to high school. They were close, but there'd never been any romantic involvement between them. Despite that, Jayne had always been jealous of that relationship. No amount of reasoning, or reality, could dissuade her.

Teeny met Ella at the door. As she stepped inside, Jayne came out of the back bedroom wearing one of Teeny's T-shirts, which draped over her like a tent.

"Ella," she said, "kinda late for you to be roaming around, isn't it?" Not waiting for an answer, she ducked back out of sight into the bedroom.

"You should have mentioned you had company," Ella said, biting off the words.

"Jayne came looking for a fight tonight and I'm not in the mood for battles. Step into the kitchen with me and ignore her," he said. With a wave of his hand he invited Ella to take a seat, then offered her a Mexican Coke, the kind that used sugar, not syrup. "Are you any closer to catching the killer?"

"No, which is why I wanted to talk to you."

"I've told you all that I can, Ella. I'm still waiting to hear from my client."

"Okay," Ella said. "So how about this? Can you tell me which county offices have reported missing items?" Seeing him hesitate, she added, "Help me. I really need a lead."

"Okay, I'll give you that much, but that'll be it," he said. "The county commissioner's office and the sheriff's department."

"So I assume your client is pretty high on the food chain?"

"Don't push it, Ella, and stop trying to narrow down the list. I've given you all I can," he said.

"You're being stubborn," she said, taking a sip of Coke.

"I'm respecting my client's right to privacy. Like it is in police work, there are lines in the private sector that no one should cross."

"Okay, okay. I'll drop it for now."

He grinned. "You're a real pain in the ass, but my company could really use someone like you—skilled, smart, and stubborn. Just name your terms."

"I'm still thinking about that," she said. "I'm tempted, too. I just don't like what's happening at the PD. If it all falls apart and I get transferred to Window Rock, I might just quit."

"My door's always open."

Jayne came up the hallway, fully dressed now, her boots

clicking on the tile floor. "I'm leaving. You're obviously going to be busy," she said, then shot Ella a dirty look.

"No, listen, I'm just—," Ella started, but Teeny uncharacteristically interrupted her.

"Nothing's stopping you, Jayne. Go," he said.

From the way Jayne slammed the door on her way out, it wasn't hard to tell that she was furious.

"I really didn't have to stick around," Ella said.

"I wanted her gone—seriously. I'm not happy with the way things are working out. What's worse, I don't see them getting any better."

"I understand." Ella gave him a sympathetic smile. "Your track record with relationships is a lot like mine. Nothing works for long."

"Tell me about it," he said. "I'm set in my ways, but your problem is that your heart and loyalty are already given to your family and the tribe."

"Yeah, maybe so," she said.

"That's one of the reasons you should come work for me. You'll determine your own schedule, and in the majority of cases, you would still be working in behalf of the *Diné*, just from the private sector."

"I'm really considering it, Teeny. Police work doesn't give me the same satisfaction it did once, and I'm not cut out to be a paper pusher, if it comes to that."

"I'm willing to bet that you're really going to like the freedom of working for a private company, Ella, and if there's a problem, we'll work it out. You and I think alike in a lot of ways."

"We're both reasonable people," she said, nodding. "You'd think we'd have better luck with relationships."

"It's hard to find someone who understands that we choose to give the work we do everything we've got, and that there'll be times everything else will have to take second place." Teeny leaned back, making himself more comfortable. "Take Jayne. She loves meeting people for dinner, but I work most evenings. My company handles a lot of cases and that's the way I like it, but she wants me to change my life to suit her. So the fights start, and that gets old in a hurry. When I cash it in for the day, I don't want to argue. I just want to relax."

"Yeah, guy—me, too," she said, moving toward the door. "And with that thought in mind . . ."

"You gotta get home," he said.

She nodded. "Some Friday night, huh?"

"Par for the course."

Ella was passing through Shiprock when her cell phone rang. Considering the time, she picked it up quickly, and glanced at the caller ID. It was a blocked call.

Thinking it was one of her team, she answered immediately.

"Listen carefully," came a fast whisper. "There's a body out by Rattlesnake, near where you found the last one. The skinwalkers are playing with you."

Before she could ask the caller for a name, the man hung up.

Ella picked up the radio and requested that any officer in the area of Rattlesnake provide backup. Big Ed was the first to respond, but he used her cell phone to contact her instead of going through dispatch.

"What's the deal, Shorty?" he asked.

She was surprised that he was still at his desk, but then again, even the chief had reason to be looking over his shoulder these days.

Ella reached the intersection of 491 and 64, turned west on 64, then gave him a quick situation report as she raced past Shiprock High.

"With the weekend here, most of our officers are answering calls or working the DWI checkpoints north and south of town. I'll try to free up a patrolman, but if I can't, I'll back you up myself."

Ella returned her cell phone to her pocket. She knew why Big Ed had chosen to use the phone instead of the radio. Even the word "skinwalker" was enough to start a media circus. News stations and some former officers often monitored police radio calls. Since their department was already under the microscope, using the phone had become part of the CYA approach to law enforcement, another unfortunate sign of the times.

Ella switched on her siren. Though traffic wasn't particularly heavy, there was always the risk of encountering a drunk walking down the center line or livestock that had found a gap in the fence.

It wasn't a long drive, a little under twenty minutes, which by Rez standards qualified as just down the street. As she topped the hill where they'd found Harry's body, the badger fetish she wore around her neck began to feel warm against her skin. Although she'd never been able to figure out if it was simply the result of her own rising body temperature during moments of stress, the inescapable fact was that it always signaled trouble.

Ella remained inside her pickup, but with the windows down, it didn't take long for the scent to reach her. Death—there was no mistaking that odor. Using her headlights to cut into the darkness and hoping her backup would come soon, she proceeded slowly.

Ella drove along the fence line, then slammed on the brakes as her headlights revealed a skinwalker's calling card. A human body had been strung up like a scarecrow on the fence. She took shallow breaths, hating the stench and the fact that she'd have to go in even closer.

Ella reported her position to dispatch, then used the phone to call Big Ed.

"I'm not far behind you now, Shorty. I'll be there in less than three minutes."

Grabbing her flashlight, she got out of her truck and approached the corpse slowly, making sure that she didn't obliterate any tracks as she walked. Bitsy Willie, Dawn's friend, lived just down the road and this was a sight she didn't want her daughter's friend, or anyone outside of law enforcement, to see.

The corpse was wearing a suit, and on closer inspection, she could see it wasn't a fresh kill. It had to have been dug up from a cemetery somewhere. From the sallow skin that still clung to the facial bones, she had a strong suspicion that the body didn't belong to a Navajo. The bone structure indicated Anglo or Hispanic. The body had been mutilated, however, with missing fingertips, as with Harry. But there was more. . . .

Hearing another vehicle approaching, she rested her hand on the butt of her pistol, but seeing the emergency lights on the SUV, she relaxed. It was Big Ed. Not wanting to draw attention to the incident, he'd turned off his siren after leaving the highway.

Big Ed aimed his spotlight at the figure on the fence, then got out of his SUV. "Do you know who that is?"

"No, do you?"

"Yeah, there's enough of him left. He's one of the Anglos who'd opposed the casinos. He spent the last few years working against the tribe, trying to cut any federal funding we received. He claimed that we were doing the Devil's work, and until that stopped, he wanted to make sure the good people's tax money wasn't used to help the tribe in any way. He died several weeks ago," Big Ed said, stepping a little closer and illuminating the body with his own flashlight.

He whistled low. "Somebody really did a number on his body. At least he was dead at the time."

"How'd he die, anyway?" Ella asked.

"If I recall, he had a heart attack. He made a lot of noise when he was alive, and now in death he's still going to make headlines—if this gets out." Big Ed stepped over a low spot on the fence and moved closer to the dead man.

"Then our people will be blamed, and that'll generate even more ill will," Ella said. "It won't stop there, either. Inside the Rez, this kind of news will create a panic. This is a skinwalker's MO. Skin whorls are prize catches, and so are the bones at the back of the head."

"Which explains why the back of his skull is missing," Big Ed said, examining the body from a different angle. "At least they didn't do that to Harry," he added, stepping back and checking the ground for footprints.

"We'll need the ME to tell us what else is missing from

the body," Ella said. "Skinwalkers particularly like dried skin, so we need to know how much was stripped off the body."

"You're thinking for use as corpse poison?" he asked, retracing his steps and coming back across the fence.

"Yeah, that's part of their bag of tricks. That, along with powdered bone fragments, are used to make special ammo," she said. "But there's other stuff that doesn't fit in. Why bother telling me ahead of time that it's here? If one of the area residents had found this, fear would have spread faster than the flu, and played right into their hands."

Ella called the ME and heard the electronic pause before Carolyn answered.

"We have a body," Ella said, filling Carolyn in, then added, "I heard the pause, so I know you've got your phone forwarded. How soon can you get here?"

"Half hour to forty-five minutes. I'll need to stop by the hospital and pick up the van."

Irritated, Ella shoved the phone back in her shirt pocket. Kevin's home was about twenty minutes from the hospital, and the ride from there would take another twenty minutes or so. It didn't take a genius to know where Carolyn had been.

For some reason she really didn't understand, the thought of Carolyn and Kevin dating each other bugged her. Logically, it made no sense. She wasn't particularly close to Kevin and hadn't been for years, but they did see each other more or less regularly when he came by to pick up Dawn for the weekend, or just to visit his daughter.

Carolyn, on the other hand, was one of her closest friends, and if anyone deserved a good life, it was her. She'd sacrificed everything for the tribe, and there just weren't many Navajo men who could accept the work she did. Yet it still felt like a betrayal—but of whom and by whom?

Unwilling to think about it anymore, she called Justine and the rest of her team. As she did, Big Ed walked up the road, checking the area with his flashlight and staying on hard ground, not wanting to obliterate any tracks.

Once finished, Ella joined Big Ed, who was now standing beside his vehicle. "They'll be here in about thirty minutes," she said.

"While we're waiting, why don't we begin the search by working outward from the body in a spiral pattern? No sense in wasting time."

Flashlights aimed at the ground, they were busy working when they both heard a hair-raising, mournful howl in the distance, somewhere off to the west.

"That wasn't an animal," Big Ed whispered. "Stay sharp."

A second howl rose from among the waist-high brush and stunted junipers about two hundred yards away. Ella peered into the shadows, focusing on any sign of movement. The person was coming closer. Feeling a burning sensation at her neck, she reached up with her free hand and touched the badger fetish. It was scalding hot. Danger had found them.

TEN

—— ✖ ✖ ✖ ——

We're being stalked," Ella said in a harsh whisper. She moved the flashlight away from her body to keep from becoming a target, and reached for her pistol with the other hand.

Big Ed, his weapon out, crouched down and stabbed the night with his flashlight, looking for the howler. Seconds went by and they could hear movement but couldn't pinpoint its location.

Without warning, an explosion of light and sound erupted from behind a waist-high boulder less than twenty yards away. The spotlight on Big Ed's vehicle shattered, instantly throwing the area around them into darkness.

They dived to the ground. Ella dropped her flashlight, and as she reached for it, the ground beneath it exploded, shattering the light into shards of metal and plastic. Something stung her hand, and she knew she'd been hit by flying debris.

As she rolled to one side, she heard running footsteps moving from right to left. Ella fired two low shots, then crawled farther to her left. Big Ed fired once, then moved off somewhere to her right. His flashlight was off now.

They both remained still, listening for movement. All she could hear, beyond the faint ringing in her ears, was the sound of Big Ed's car engine.

"Where'd he go?" he whispered.

"To my left. Cover me while I head up the side road." Ella inched along the ground, pistol extended, trying to advance and keep from being flanked at the same time.

After crawling for several feet, she stopped to listen.

Nothing. The guy was patient, but she was a better sniper. She'd wait him out.

Several minutes went by; then she heard a faint footstep to her right. Her night vision was back now, and spotting movement against the dark mountain background, she squeezed off a shot, then rolled to her left.

Within seconds, two shotgun blasts came at her in response, buckshot whistling overhead.

Big Ed fired three quick rounds at the muzzle flashes; then everything became silent again.

Another minute went by. "You hit?" Big Ed called out to her.

"Yeah, Bob . . . my leg." By using the wrong name, she was letting Big Ed know she was fine, and at the same time hopefully drawing the shooter in.

She inched back several feet, then waited, scarcely breathing, searching for her target.

Seeing a flash of light to her right and hearing the sound of vehicles approaching, Ella knew backup had arrived. Unfortunately, that was also bound to drive the gunman away.

"Cover me," she whispered, then ran forward, darting

left and right. After fifty feet she stopped, crouched low, and listened.

Moonlight made an object on the ground glimmer and it caught her attention. It was the brass base of a shotgun shell, but the shooter was long gone.

Somewhere behind her she could hear Big Ed issuing instructions, positioning their backup.

Holding her ground, she waited.

One of the vehicles soon raced past them, then headed up the side road to her left. Far to the right, she could see a spotlight probing the slopes of the hillside beyond.

"Cover me," Big Ed called out.

She watched and listened, looking for any sign of movement ahead.

Big Ed moved quietly for a big man, and a minute later he crouched down beside her. He aimed his flashlight at the area where the shotgun shell lay, and as he swept the beam of light from side to side, found another.

"His second position," Big Ed said.

She nodded. "And now we have tracks."

Staying apart to avoid giving the shooter two targets with one shot, they tracked the size 10 footprints about three hundred yards to a wide arroyo. Ten feet down, on hard-packed sediment and bedrock, were vehicle tracks. The footprints led right up to it, then disappeared.

"He took off east, toward the highway, with his lights off," Ella said. "Do we have any units in that direction?"

Big Ed shook his head. "If he makes it to the highway, he'll have clear sailing all the way to Arizona." He brought out his cell phone and called the tribal officer covering the Teece Nos Pos area near the state line.

After a moment he put the phone away. "It'll take a good half hour for her to get into position," he said at last. "Let's see what we can find here."

Distracted by the pain, Ella glanced down at her hand. Big Ed, following her gaze, aimed his flashlight lower.

"You're bleeding," he said. "What's that black thing stuck in your palm, a piece of your flashlight?"

She nodded. "Yeah, debris flew everywhere. At least it wasn't buckshot. I'll dig it out when Dr. Roanhorse arrives. She's got tweezers and disinfectant."

"Glad it was just your hand, Shorty," Big Ed said in a gruff tone. "Back to work now."

She smiled, knowing he cared more than he ever allowed himself to show.

It wasn't long before Carolyn came up in the van. The locals had given it a name—the body bus—and spoke of it in whispers, if at all.

Ella went to meet her. "Mind if I dig into your supplies for some disinfectant?" She held out her hand.

"I've got my first-aid kit back here somewhere." Carolyn lifted a big metal box out from behind the seat. "What happened?"

While the ME looked through her supplies, Ella gave her the highlights of what they'd found and the subsequent confrontation.

Carolyn shook her head slowly. "It could have been worse. Bone ammunition can be especially nasty. Steel shot, even worse."

Ella nodded, but didn't comment.

"This has got to be difficult for you," Carolyn said in a

whisper. "I remember when you returned to the Rez to investigate your father's murder."

"What's hard is knowing that evil is never really defeated. The best we can do is beat it back for a while. After I retire, it'll still be there for the next generation of cops."

"The more things change, the more they stay the same?" Carolyn said, dabbing disinfectant on the back of Ella's hand. "Stop squirming."

"It stings," Ella said.

"Suck it up."

"Your bedside manner needs some work," Ella said.

"My patients never complain."

Seeing that Carolyn was wearing fancy shoes, leather pumps that were a beautiful crimson color, Ella smiled. "So how was your date with Kevin?"

"I had a feeling you knew." Carolyn looked at her. "I like him, Ella. More to the point, I really like the way he makes me feel when I'm with him. To Kevin, I'm not just the ME. He treats me with respect and . . ."

"Go on," Ella said.

"Tenderness," she said in a barely audible tone. "Most people look at me and see a hard-ass, tough, coldhearted bitch. Yet Kevin sees me as a desirable woman, one who's doing her best to serve the tribe," she said. "I can't remember the last time I leaned against a man's chest, hearing his strong heartbeat, and felt so . . . protected."

Ella looked at Carolyn in amazement. Kevin had made her feel a gazillion things, but she would never have described any of her emotions the way Carolyn just had.

"Surprised? You don't think I should need that?"

"Not at all. If anything, I'm a bit jealous," she said truthfully. "I never felt that way with him. In fact, I've never felt that way with anyone."

"It's nice, particularly for women in our professions. Most men exclude us from things like that, or maybe we exclude ourselves, I don't know. What I do know is that when I retire, I don't want to spend the rest of my life alone."

She finished taping a small bandage on Ella's hand, then reached inside the van to bring out a second, larger medical bag. "Leave that on for a few days and you'll be fine. Time for me to get to work."

Ella walked over with Carolyn and then, after putting on latex gloves, helped her free the corpse and lay out the body on a plastic ground cloth Big Ed had placed close by.

"This man was embalmed, check the tiny stitches by the right carotid artery. That's where the embalming fluid went in. The blood and body fluids were drained from the right jugular vein."

"According to the chief, this man was buried a few weeks ago," Ella said. "We'll need to know what was taken from the body—in addition to his fingertips and part of his skull."

"Skinwalker trademarks," Carolyn said with a nod. "Okay, then. I'll need to bag him and get him in the van."

Big Ed stepped up, also wearing latex gloves. "I'll help you."

Long after Carolyn had driven away, they continued processing the scene—searching for anything and everything.

"We've got shotgun shells for a twelve-gauge shotgun, athletic shoes size ten or thereabouts, and vehicle tracks, a pickup's most likely, about a quarter of a mile up the road," Big Ed said.

He stopped speaking, but Ella could tell that he hadn't finished, so she remained quiet.

"The shotgun shell that took out my spotlight held more than gunpowder, Shorty. That leaves a black residue, but this was lighter, gray colored. Justine is going to take it to the lab and verify what else was in that load besides gunpowder and a few steel balls."

"You think he added corpse poison?" Ella asked in a hushed voice.

"It's their MO. That might also explain why he didn't even come close to hitting either one of us. Long shotgun range, coupled with reduced power and velocity, equals lousy marksmanship," Big Ed said. "Talk to your brother and see if he's heard of anyone who might be a possible suspect."

"I've already done that, but I'll check with him again first thing tomorrow morning," she said.

Though exhausted by the time she got home and crawled into bed, Ella found it hard to sleep. After tossing and turning, she finally drifted off. Hideous images haunted her dreams until, drenched in sweat, she woke up abruptly, her heart racing. Ella looked at the clock on her nightstand. The red numbers glowed back at her. It was three forty-five.

She lay back and stared at the ceiling for what seemed like an eternity. Carolyn was right. Nothing ever stayed status quo, and there would come a time, sooner or later, when she'd be retiring, too. The future was calling to her, and maybe now was the time. Teeny's job offer was almost too good to be true, and she'd be a fool to pass it up. Although giving up her badge would be like leaving a piece of herself behind, there was something freeing about moving on, too.

The thought comforted her somewhat, and this time when she closed her eyes, she slept.

The sounds of people moving about in the kitchen nudged her awake. Saturday morning. That meant Dawn would hurry outside and spend most of her day with the horses. All things considered, Ella was happy her kid was more involved with horses than with boys, but Dawn's interest in barrel racing worried her. It was a dangerous sport.

With a sigh, Ella tossed the covers aside and got up. She had another long day ahead.

Even before meeting her family for breakfast, Ella called Justine. "Have you had a chance to process anything from last night?"

"No, not yet. I came in early to play catch-up on lab work, but I've got a huge backlog that needs my immediate attention. I'm hoping to have something for you later on this morning."

"Good. Call me as soon as you do and make sure you check Harry's belt buckle for prints other than his own. I have a feeling about that."

"You've got it, boss."

Ella showered quickly, put a little salve and a bandage on the cut on her hand, then went down the hall and met her family for breakfast. Pouring herself a strong cup of coffee and taking a large chunk of leftover fry bread smeared with honey, she listened to her daughter talk about her plans for the day. Dawn tackled everything with such enthusiasm, it was impossible not to feel energized just listening to her.

Soon Dawn headed out the back door. Herman filled his faded Washington Redskins coffee mug, then excused himself to go work out in the garage.

Rose, with a newly poured cup of herbal tea in hand, sat across the table from Ella.

"Something's worrying you, daughter. Is it work?" She watched Ella's expression, then shook her head. "No, it's more than that, isn't it? Are you upset because your doctor friend is dating your child's father?"

Ella looked up at her, surprised. "I just found out the other day. How long have you known?"

"Some detective you are," she said. "It's been going on for at least a month."

"No one told me," Ella said, then shrugged in dismay. "I had no idea."

"I've asked your daughter's father to wear a medicine pouch whenever he's around my granddaughter. He doesn't believe in such things, but he'll do it for me."

Ella smiled. Few ever had the courage to say no to Rose. "Does having someone so connected to family at the moment—a woman with Caroline's profession—still bother you, Mom?"

"Yes, but things are what they are. Your daughter has also promised me that she'll continue to wear her medicine pouch." Rose smiled, then added, "She's glued some sequins on the outside of the bag in the outline of a horse—to make it prettier, she said. It's a new day, I suppose."

"Progress," Ella said softly. "Change comes, whether we want it or not."

"Maybe that's part of what's bothering you, daughter. For years you've had three loves—your daughter, your family, and your work. Now, your daughter's growing up, my husband and I have our own lives, and at work you're being asked to give up what you love most about your job."

"Mom, I don't know what to do. Bureaucrats have taken control of the tribal police. Cost cutting is bleeding the department dry. They demand more and more from each officer, but aren't willing to give anything in return. Their priority isn't effective law enforcement, it's smaller government. To me, that's not what the job's all about, and I don't know if I can work around that mind-set. The worst part of it, I have the feeling that they'd take me out of the field and try to turn me into a paper pusher."

"So what are you going to do?"

"This isn't a battle I can win," she said. "I've got the years I need to retire with full benefits, but I don't want to just sit around doing nothing. Teeny's offered me a great job, and I'm seriously considering working for him. My only holdback is that I've worn the badge for so long, giving it up is going to be really hard. It's part of me, you know?"

"Retirement wouldn't be so bad. You'd then be able to look around in peace and think about what your next step should be. You'd also have more time to date that county detective."

Ella looked at Rose and laughed. "You never give up, do you, Mom?"

"I want my daughter to find the other half of herself. Maybe this man is right for you."

"If he is, you'll be the first to know."

Rose stood and smiled. "Just give him—and yourself—a chance."

After Rose left, Ella finished her fry bread, then stood. It was time for her to get moving. She wanted to stop by her brother's place and talk to him before she headed to the station this morning.

Ella hurried outside and got into her truck. Many years back, her brother had described her job as restoring the balance between good and evil. At first, she'd thought it was just a fancy way of saying that law enforcement was about keeping the peace. These days she understood the Navajo Way better, and Clifford's statement echoed her own sentiments. Just as evil needed good to define it, good was needed to keep evil in check.

With or without the badge, that need to restore the balance would be a part of her forever.

ELEVEN
✖ ✖ ✖

Clifford was stepping out of his medicine hogan as Ella drove up. She parked, and in case he had a patient, waited in the truck to be invited to approach. Seconds later, Clifford waved at her to join him.

"I had a feeling you'd be coming by," he said as she walked up. He looked down at the medicine pouch on her belt. "I'm glad you're wearing that. I've heard some stories. . . ."

Ella glanced around, wanting to make sure they couldn't be overheard. "Is your family around?"

He shook his head. "My wife and son are still up at the sheep camp. I've encouraged them to stay longer. I don't want them home right now, it's too dangerous. A deformed calf was stillborn northeast of Rattlesnake and people are saying that it's the work of the evil ones."

"I hadn't heard about that," she said, realizing once again how well connected Clifford was to their community.

"What brings you here this morning? Has there been another incident?"

She nodded and gave him the highlights regarding the body they'd found on the fence. "I have some photos I'd like you to look at."

He watched her slide several close-ups across her smart-phone display. "It seems to be the work of the evil ones, but there's something I don't understand. *Who*—or *what*—is their target?"

The question made her stop and think. "That's a very good question and I don't have an answer. The activity started a while back, even before my friend was killed. Do you think this could be a turf war directed at everyone in this particular area?"

"Land disputes are common and people often come up with real crazy ways to settle things. When I first began my practice many years ago, an elderly Navajo over on the Arizona side of the Rez wanted to farm land that belonged to his neighbor. The men couldn't work things out, so one of them decided to pretend he was one of the evil ones, hoping to scare the other into doing things his way."

"Did it work?" she asked, curious.

"He succeeded in scaring his neighbor," Clifford said, "but things didn't work out the way he'd planned. The people who lived in that area got real scared, so one night they all got together and killed him." He paused. "Officially, the man just disappeared. The truth never came out."

"I never heard of the case," she said.

"It was before you returned to the Rez. There was no of-ficial report—nobody would talk to the police. It just hap-pened."

She nodded thoughtfully. Strange things happened

deep on the reservation, incidents that never reached the files of law enforcement agencies.

"What made you think of that now? Do you think someone's just pretending to be a witch?"

"Anything's possible. The person wants to scare others, but what remains unclear to me is who his target is and why he's doing this. My advice is be very careful who you trust."

"Thanks."

Ella was on her way to the station when her cell phone rang. After glancing at the caller ID, she put Justine on speaker. "What's up, partner?"

"Good news, bad news. I found a print on Harry's belt buckle. The bad news is that there's no match in the system," Justine said. "If the woman with him had ever been arrested for prostitution, we'd have gotten a hit."

"It's something. Take it as a win. Once we find Harry's date, we'll have a way to confirm her ID," Ella said. "Will you be spending most of today in the lab, or are you almost done?"

"I have a lot of pressing work to complete, so I was planning to stay here, but there's that nonlethal-weapon seminar this morning. If I don't go, I'm off payroll."

"What? That's crazy. We're in the middle of a homicide investigation. That takes priority over a training workshop."

"Not these days. Big Ed said that I have to go. Nelson Natani will conduct it and he's at the station now."

"Good thing I'm not coming in for a while," Ella said, instantly changing her plans.

"Lucky you. Where will you be?"

"I'm meeting Dan. He's on the county pistol team and

practices at the shooting range every Saturday morning. I need to talk to him about the case."

"Ella, I know it's the last thing you want, but you really should consider attending this session. It's nonlethal-weapons training. There's nothing new about it, according to Benny, who already took the class, but you might want to have it in your personnel file. Natani's got you in his cross-hairs now."

"It's to be expected. Selina Ute said she'd be putting on the pressure, and Natani's her cousin. But thanks for the heads-up."

"I'll tell him you're following up an urgent lead—if he asks about you."

"You won't be lying. Not completely, anyway."

Ella called Dan next and arranged to meet him. Getting some firearms practice was just what she needed right now. Spending a little time with Dan wouldn't hurt, either.

An hour later, Ella arrived at the county's shooting range northwest of the city of Aztec, which was also the county seat. Dan was a top-rated marksman who'd won plenty of interdepartmental shooting competitions, including back in his days as an officer in Arizona.

The shooting range had an indoor and an outdoor section, including a tactical course, and was equipped with paper silhouettes at the twenty-five, fifty-, and one-hundred-yard ranges. After grabbing a set of ear protectors from the backseat, she went inside the main building and found Dan there, waiting.

"What's the tribal PD doing here?" another deputy called out in greeting.

Ella glanced around and saw a familiar face. "Hey, Jack. How've you been?"

Sergeant Jack Koehler was in charge of the range, maintained the facilities, served as gunsmith, and also reloaded most of the practice ammunition for the SJCSO. He came up to them and gave Dan a sixteen-ounce tin can filled with bullets. "This is your quota of competition loads."

A second later, he smiled at Ella and gave her a gallon can half full of .40-caliber reloads. "Here you go. A little interdepartmental courtesy. Go show the boys of the San Juan County Sheriff's Office how it's done."

As Jack walked off, Dan glowered at him. Ella laughed, knowing that Jack and Dan didn't get along. She suspected that there was something about the two alpha males that made them completely incompatible.

"He's messing with you," she said, then put the can down. "We use the same ammo, and I'll share."

They walked outside to the handgun firing line, backed by earthen berms tall enough to trap all but the most errant shots. Ella took a position to Dan's left. No other deputies were present, so they set up their targets at the twenty-five-yard distance, then both fired off several rounds.

Ella, despite the nuisance of a small bandage on her hand, placed most of her rounds in the heart area of the paper silhouette, but Dan chose head shots and grouped the rounds in a cluster about the size of a golf ball.

"Nice shooting," Ella said. Yet even as she spoke, she could feel her competitive edge spark to life. She had a tight grouping, too, but it was more the size of her fist. It was time to up her game. "So what do you say we try for head shots at fifty yards?"

"Sure," Dan said, smiling. "If you think you're up to it."

"Watch and learn," she said.

Another county officer arrived, then walked over and stood behind them to watch as Ella took aim. At this distance, her shots were all grouped within a six-inch cluster centered on the bridge of the nose.

Dan placed his first shot on the nose area of his target, then proceeded to place shots above and in a curve to the right, forming a crude letter *D*.

"Not enough ammo to write your entire name?" Ella smirked. "Show-off."

He laughed. "You're an excellent shot, but I have an edge. My hand's bigger and can handle the recoil a lot better. In competition, you'd be better off with lower-velocity rounds and lighter bullets."

"Yeah, but this is the weapon I use out in the field," she said. "When my life is on the line, I want to know exactly what I can or can't do with my pistol."

While they were talking, the deputy sergeant who'd been watching them had time to set up his target. Ella watched him empty a magazine downrange. His shots went wide of the silhouette twice, but he managed to get the rest in the black.

"Good thing I'm not in the field anymore," the older officer said.

The sergeant—his name tag said ROBERT KIRK—shot another full magazine at the target, improving slightly, then turned to them. "I'm done, thanks for not laughing," he said. "Let me get my target, then I'm back to my desk."

Five minutes later, the sergeant left, wishing them good shooting as he walked toward the parking lot.

"Kirk could retire anytime he wants," Dan said, watching the officer load his gear into a department vehicle. "If I were in his shoes, I would have been long gone instead of working Hit and Run at headquarters."

Ella, who'd been refilling the two magazines she'd expended, inserted a clip and moved the slide, placing a round into the chamber. She'd run a patch through the barrel later. As she returned the handgun to the holster on her hip, she looked over at Dan.

"Retirement—we look forward to it all the years we're in, but when you actually get close to it, the picture changes," she said as they headed toward the parking area.

"Are you worried that you won't have enough to do?" Dan said.

"It's not that, not exactly, anyway," she said. "For the past twenty years, I've gotten up each morning knowing pretty much what I'd be doing that day. I find the thought of getting up without that sense of purpose off-putting somehow."

"You're barely over forty, in great shape, and with pretty much half your life ahead of you. There's no end to what you can do."

She smiled. It was the optimistic response most people who weren't considering retirement always had. Dan was younger than she was, still in his mid-thirties, so to him retirement had all the reality of a movie on the science fiction channel.

She smiled politely.

He laughed hard. "You think I don't know what the hell I'm talking about."

It wasn't a question, so she didn't answer.

"To tell you the truth, I can't see you staying at home and learning how to weave, but there's always the possibility of you going into business for yourself."

"Doing what?" she asked, more curious than anything else.

"Setting up a firm that offers personal security for the high-ranking women of the tribe."

She looked at him in surprise. "You know, that's not a half-bad idea."

"I've taken off-duty gigs protecting celebrities and politicians of both sexes, and I can tell you that many of the women would prefer their security being handled by someone of their own sex."

"Less testosterone can come in handy, particularly when you want to go to the ladies' room," she said.

"Plus you can stay in the same room and she doesn't have to worry about someone sneaking past outside security and coming after her in the middle of the night."

"You know that's really a great idea. I'm not sure I'd start my own firm, but I can certainly hire out my services to someone who already has a company."

"Like Bruce Little?" Seeing her nod, he added, "That's also a good idea. You'd be a great asset to him. You're practically a law enforcement legend around here. People trust you."

"Do you?" she asked, taking the opportunity to get back to business.

"Yeah, I know where you're heading with this. You've found out more about the thefts?"

She nodded. "The stolen inventory came from the

county commissioner's office and sheriff's department, and both are housed in the same building."

"I'll ask around off the cuff and see what I can get, Ella, but that's as far as I'm going with this. I've been with the department less than two years and I'm not really sure who I can trust. It's possible I'll end up making a bad enemy—one that'll cost me my job."

"There's no reason why it has to come to that," she said. "Just tell me who actually has physical access to the inventory."

"Sheriff Taylor, for sure, but I'm not sure who else. Probably some of the office staff, heads of the divisions, and the physical plant supervisors, like maintenance."

"Sheriff Taylor . . . ," Ella said in a thoughtful low voice.

"You don't think he's your man, do you?" he asked, surprised. "The thief?"

She shook her head. "No, no way. I've known him for a long time, and he's as straight as an arrow." She paused. "I was just wondering if he's Teeny's client. He's certainly high up the county's food chain, and Teeny would protect him, knowing the sheriff's one of the good guys."

"But what you're saying doesn't make sense. Taylor's got an entire department under him. Why would he hire an outsider, a glorified rent-a-cop?"

Ella smiled. "Bruce Little is a skilled professional, don't ever let him hear you call him that."

Dan grimaced. "Yeah, I've heard what happens when someone disrespects him. One time an off-duty Farmington cop called Bruce a hired gun and got himself tossed into the bed of his own pickup."

Ella laughed. "Yeah, I was there. Sergeant Tsosie shot off

his mouth, like he always does. But he apologized afterwards, so all was cool again."

"So, as I was saying, why would Sheriff Taylor go to an
outsider? He could have handpicked an IA detective to do
the job and instructed him to keep it under wraps."

"In Taylor's shoes, I might have also gone to Teeny, if for
no other reason than to keep rivalries and office politics out
of it. Teeny is completely loyal to his clients and to his
friends."

"You obviously know Sheriff Taylor and have worked
with him before. Why don't you speak to him yourself?" he
asked.

"I thought about it, and Big Ed's been in contact with him
about this case, but if Taylor's Teeny's client, I'll be putting
him on the spot and undermining his efforts to keep the
theft investigation under the radar," she said. "If he's not
Teeny's client, I can give him a call, but I'd rather put it off
until I run out of other options. Of course, if I find out that
there's no connection between the thefts and the murder,
there'll be no reason for me to get involved any further with
Taylor's county operations."

"Yeah, good point." Dan met Ella's gaze and held it. "So
I work with you under the radar on this and you owe me
one?"

"Yeah, and you can call it in anytime," she said.

"Good. It'll keep the balance between us."

She smiled. "Navajo Traditionalist thinking?"

"It comes naturally when dealing with the oldest crimi-
nals on our land—skinwalkers."

"Did you hear about the latest body?"

"Yeah. The dead dude was taken from a graveyard in

county jurisdiction," he said. "Nobody saw a thing, apparently. Taylor sent me a copy of the report. Have you spoken to your brother about it yet?"

"Yeah, and he pointed out that to get a better handle on what's happening, we need to figure out who or what is the skinwalker's target. Usually that's pretty straightforward," Ella said.

"You may not be their primary target, but you've already been given a warning, so watch your back," Dan said.

"They tried to scare me, but all they've done is piss me off, Dan. I'll stay on my guard, but I'm going after them."

After saying good-bye, Ella got under way. She was driving west through Aztec when her cell phone rang. A look at the caller ID told her it was Justine. She answered.

"I made it to class and it was a lame rehash of stuff right out of the academy training manual," Justine said. "A total waste of time."

"It doesn't surprise me," Ella answered.

"After it was over, I was able to pick up the warrant we needed to access Harry's calls and get his mail. My uncle, Judge Goodluck, always keeps the red tape to a minimum," she said. "I also have preliminary findings on the rounds used against you and Big Ed. Some were ordinary buckshot, but the ones that smashed the headlight and sent shrapnel into your hand had something else."

"Corpse poison?" she asked in a muted voice.

"There were bone fragments mixed in with the buckshot. I've sent samples to the lab in Albuquerque to see if they can match the DNA to the corpse that was dug up. Otherwise, we may have another body we've yet to find. Assuming the bones are human, of course."

"This just keeps getting better and better."

"Are you coming into the station?"

"Yeah. Now that we have a warrant, we can get the post office to turn Harry's mail over to us. Whatever arrived after his death has been sitting in one of those boxes on a shelf," Ella said. "Did you ever find out what cell phone carrier he was using? Once we get that, we can also look through his calls for a lead."

"I haven't made any progress on that front. I even called his ex-wife, but Selina was no help. Maybe we'll find a bill in his mail," Justine said.

Ella walked through the side doors of the station ten minutes later, said hello to the duty officer, then chose the hall to her left. As she approached Justine's lab, Benny stepped out the door.

"Morning," he said, then hurried off.

Ella smiled. It was good to see Justine with someone. Maybe she and Benny would take that final step in their relationship before too long.

As Ella went into the lab, she found Justine seated behind her computer terminal, a yellow rose in the vase next to her.

Ella fingered the soft petals gently. "Gift from Benny?"

Justine nodded. "Ever since he found out that I love yellow roses, he makes sure to bring one by every other day or so," she said. "That's what I like most about him. He isn't big on special dates. What he does is take the little moments and finds a way to make them memorable. Last weekend he rented an old romantic comedy he knows I like and brought it over to my place along with a box of microwave popcorn and a six-pack of Mexican Cokes. It was a great evening."

Justine logged off her terminal and stood, reaching into a drawer for her firearm and extra magazines. "You ready to go?"

"Whenever you are," Ella said, heading for the door.

"Oh, good news for a change. Our Suburban has been checked out. Nothing but cosmetic damage. The department doesn't have the funds for a new paint job on an SUV with two hundred thousand miles on it, but we're back in the saddle again."

"Small victories, cuz—take 'em when you've got 'em," Ella said.

They were soon back on the highway, Justine at the wheel as usual. Though Justine hadn't spoken, Ella could see that she had something important on her mind. Rather than rush her, she waited.

After a few minutes, Ella began to worry. Reluctance to speak her mind was not something she'd ever associated with her partner.

"I'm not sure how to bring this up," Justine said after a while longer. "My uncle mentioned it in passing, assuming I already knew. I tried to get more details from him, but when he realized that was the first I'd heard of it, he refused to say anything more."

"Just come straight out with it."

"Selina Ute and Nelson Natani got one of the tribal attorneys to agree that your involvement in the murder case could jeopardize its outcome in court. They took that legal opinion to Gerald Bidtah and filed a formal protest," she said. "Bidtah came to our station to talk to Big Ed about that, apparently, but the chief refused to budge, insisting you were the best person for the job."

"Are you telling me that Selina went all the way to tribal government with that nonsense about my having ruined her marriage?" Ella shifted in her seat to face Justine.

"I don't know about that, but my uncle said that the way things stand, if you fail to close the case, Bidtah's going to use that against Big Ed. He's already trying to dig up everything he can to force Big Ed into retirement."

Ella cursed. "I hate petty, political games that cross over into our arena. Bidtah has no idea how to run a police department, much less a murder investigation."

"Bidtah's argument that our department needs new blood has swayed some powerful people, Ella, including the tribal president and some in the tribal council. He's actually using one of our creation stories to get the People's attention and persuade them to side with him."

"Huh?" Ella said, totally confused. "What story are you talking about?"

"I forget the details, but it's the one that explains death and the need for renewal."

"I remember the story, and I can tell you that the guy is really reaching," Ella said.

"How's it go?"

After a brief pause, Ella began. "It was during the time of the beginning," she said, her voice as soft and entrancing as Rose's had been when she shared the sacred knowledge. "The Hero Twins, sons of Sun and Turquoise Woman, were sent out to defeat all the monsters that preyed upon the earth. The Twins were invincible in battle and eventually only four dangerous enemies remained—Cold, Hunger,

Poverty, and Death. The Twins wanted to kill Cold the second they saw her, but she warned them that if they killed her, there would be no snow or water in summer."

"Oh, I know this story! It's a good one. So they let her live," Justine said.

Ella nodded. "Hunger then introduced himself. He told the heroes that if they killed him, no one would ever take pleasure in eating again and that's why he was allowed to continue."

"Everything has two sides," Justine said with a nod.

"Poverty was an old man dressed in dirty rags," Ella said, continuing. "He begged them to kill him and put him out of his misery, but he also warned that if he died, old clothes would never wear out, and people wouldn't make new ones. The incentive to better yourself would vanish, so everyone would be as dirty and ragged as he was."

"Now I remember. Poverty was allowed to live as well," Justine said.

"Finally they turned to Death," Ella said. "She was old and frightening to look at. The Hero Twins wanted to kill her as quickly as possible, but Death warned them to reconsider. If she ceased to be, old people wouldn't die and the young wouldn't be able to take their places. They needed her so young men could marry, have children, and life could continue its endless cycle of renewal. She assured them that she was their friend, though they didn't realize it."

"So Bidtah's saying that Big Ed should step aside and allow the renewal cycle to continue," Justine said.

"Yes, and they'll probably want me out, too. They're using a little more finesse to do it, but I have a feeling they're going to keep pushing me till I quit."

"I think the real reason Bidtah is targeting you is because you're too big a name—too well known. People look to you and your family for answers more often than not, and Gerald would rather be the one the People depend on. It's a matter of ego—and positioning."

"The whole thing's just crazy," Ella said, and shrugged. "There was a time when I would have fought this nonsense a lot harder, but experience tells me this isn't a battle I can win. So let's concentrate on what's really important here, finding Harry's killer."

TWELVE
— ✖ ✖ ✖ —

They arrived at the Bloom-
field post office a little before noon, just beating the Saturday hours. The one postal worker still behind the counter
was about to close up when Ella produced the warrant.

In a rush to leave for the weekend, he asked Ella to sign
a receipt and quickly gave her the rubber-banded stack of
mail that had accumulated.

Once back inside the tribal SUV, Ella had Justine roll
down the windows as she sorted through the stack. "There's
only one credit card bill, so I think Harry may have used
that card exclusively."

"The charges may tell us what he's been doing and
where he's been," Justine said.

Ella opened the envelope and studied the lengthy multi-
page bill. "Here's something. It's a monthly fee paid to an
Internet data-storage service. It looks like he backed up all
his laptop files online, automatically. We need to take a look
at those."

"We'll need another court order," Justine said.

"It would be faster to get permission from Harry's family," Ella said slowly.

"Not really. Harry's daughter is most likely the primary heir, and Selina's her guardian. After all the noise Selina's already made—"

"I know, but I wasn't planning on being the one doing the asking, not directly, anyway. I have another idea. Stop by the Totah."

They pulled up in front of Teeny's place twenty minutes later.

"Have you ever noticed that Teeny looks mean even when he smiles? It comes out looking more like a snarl. Yet when the guy wants something, he can charm the heck out of people," Ella said.

"Let me guess. You want *him* to ask Selina?"

"Yeah. I don't think she'll turn him down. She knows that Harry was working for Teeny and any job-related files are also company files. It makes logical sense for the request to come from him."

"So all you need to do now is convince Teeny to ask her, and then give you a look at the files."

Ella glanced down at the four covered Styrofoam plates. "Two for Teeny and one apiece for us. Stuffed sopaipillas with fresh green chile are his all-time favorites—particularly when Mrs. Curley makes them."

"We lucked out there."

Teeny was waiting for them at the front door. "Good to see you both." He sniffed the air. "A bribe! Did you happen to stop by the Totah?"

"You bet. Mrs. Curley works there on Saturday."

His face broke out in a wide grin that to the uninitiated might have looked positively frightening. "Stuffed sopaipillas with green chile. The favor you want must be a doozy," he said, leading the way into the kitchen.

Ella told him what she needed as they began to eat.

"Selina hates your guts. You know that, right?" Teeny said.

"Yeah, which is why I'm asking you to do the asking," Ella said.

"All right. I'll do it after lunch, but you might want to watch yourself, Ella. She intends to do everything in her power to hurt you."

"Yeah, I know. She doesn't realize that I was just a footnote in H's past."

"You were more than that," Teeny said. "A lot more."

"Not you, too!" Ella shook her head. "There was nothing there after our breakup."

Teeny stared at her for a long time. "You really *don't* know, do you?"

She opened her arms, palms up. "What?"

"His ex-wife is right—he never really got over you. Every time your name came up, his voice changed and he couldn't look at me. I think he wished he'd stuck around and fought to change your mind."

"You think he still had feelings for me? You're wrong," Ella said.

"I'm not saying he was still in love with you, but he never forgot the time you two were together." He took another huge bite as he thought things out and then tried to explain. "It's kind of like a guy's first car. Sooner or later, it's gotta go, but that feeling he had for it never goes away."

"I wasn't his first . . . anything," she said.

"You were the first woman he actually wanted to marry."

"No way. H had loads of girlfriends—before and after me."

"Sure, he dated a lot, but what he felt for you was on a whole different level. You were the love of his life."

Ella stared at him for a moment, then took a bite, mostly to have another few seconds to think. "No, I don't think so."

"Think what you want, but I'm still right," he said, finishing his meal. "Thanks for the sopaipillas, Ella. I don't know what Mrs. Curley does to her fry bread, but she's the best cook around."

"Coming from you, that's a huge compliment," Ella said, knowing that Teeny was a master chef. She'd tasted some of his creations, and they were second to none.

"I'll go make that call now. Give me a few minutes," he said, rising from the table.

Teeny walked into the next room, closed the door behind him, and Ella and Justine ate in silence.

He came back ten minutes later and gave her a thumbs-up. "Selina said okay. I also spoke to my client. Since his name is not on H's files, he has no objection to you having the information. I've downloaded what H stored with that online backup service onto a flash drive for you. For future reference, his password is '19Hosteen70,' all lowercase except for the *H*," he said. He handed her the flash drive and a folder containing several sheets of printouts.

"I also printed out something I think you'll find particularly interesting," he said, continuing. "He made a list of missing county inventory, including some serial numbers. In addition to that, you'll find the names of county employees who have direct access, or supervise those who had access to the inventory. The list includes warehouse employees, the sheriff, county commissioner, unit leaders, and their various office staffs. In that same file I also found the name of those civilians known to have purchased stolen items. Most were returned to the county once the buyer discovered they were hot."

"Thanks, I really appreciate this."

"Pay particular attention to the name at the top. You might have noticed in the past that H arranged lists in order of significance, not alphabetically. Billy O'Donnell is out of your jurisdiction, so you may need county cooperation, but he's worth checking out closely. He runs a huge retail store—almost a warehouse, located between Farmington and Bloomfield. The Emporium offers almost anything and everything you can think of—new or used. The county cops have been keeping a close eye on that place for months now because they suspect it's an outlet for stolen property. No one's been able to prove anything, though."

"Did H have any evidence against O'Donnell?"

"If he did, it went to the grave with him," Teeny said.

"Which may explain why he was killed," Ella said.

"Thieves aren't necessarily murderers," Teeny said.

Ella nodded slowly. "True, but skinwalkers are both."

"I can't shake the feeling that H was killed because he saw someone or something he shouldn't have," Teeny said.

"At first I thought that, too, but now I'm thinking he may have been set up," Ella said.

"Like you and Big Ed were when you came under fire?"

Ella looked up at him quickly. "How—?"

He held up one hand. "Come on, of course I heard. People know and trust me."

She shouldn't have been surprised. Teeny had sources all over the reservation. "Are there any rumors about who may have been responsible for that shooting incident?"

"No, not a peep, and I've been pushing," he said. "Go check out O'Donnell. Greed's always a motive, and good ole Billy knows a lot of Navajos." He walked with them to the door. "One last thing. I have it on good authority, via a woman deputy, that he finds ladies who carry a badge a real turn-on."

Ella rolled her eyes. "Good to know. Thanks."

As they went back outside, Justine glanced at Ella. "I've met a few guys who are really into women cops, but I've never understood the attraction. Is it the idea that they could dominate an authority figure?"

"I'm not sure, but to be fair, plenty of women find the idea of a male police officer a turn-on, too. Maybe it's the opposite of what you just said—wanting to be dominated by what they consider an alpha personality."

"I'm no shrink, but what's the big deal? If that's your thing, you can buy a real-enough-looking badge on eBay, pin it on any guy or woman you want, and play around."

"Role-playing versus the real thing?" Ella laughed. "Our problem is that we deal with the reality of the job on a daily basis. It's hard to even want to envision a fantasy around something you know so well."

As they pulled out of Teeny's compound, Justine at the wheel, Ella glanced over. "Head for Blalock's office next. I'll call him on the way."

While Justine drove, Ella texted Dan, telling him that she had the names she needed. Right after that, she called Blalock.

Special Agent Blalock answered his phone after the third or fourth ring, then growled his name.

"Is it that bad a day?" Ella asked.

"Computer problems, Clah," he snapped. "The thing keeps locking up on me. I've rebooted three times today already. It's making me crazy."

"Let me guess. You still haven't hired a new office assistant?"

"Not yet. I'm thinking of leaving that to the next resident agent. You know I'll be fifty-seven soon, which means mandatory retirement in the FBI. I could apply for a couple of years' extension, sure, but why postpone the inevitable?"

"So, have you figured out what you'll do next? Join a security firm? Set up a business?"

"Hell no. I'm ready for a little Dwayne time. I'm going to remodel half of the garage into a train room and build a replica of the Georgetown Loop. That's an old mining line west of Denver. My grandfather worked as an engineer there. Dad and I would drive up from time to time to see the depot, and Grandpa would tell me stories about the place."

"I never realized you were into all that."

"I love everything to do with the rails, and now I'll finally have the opportunity to indulge myself. Ruthann is going to help with the construction and scenery."

"Sounds like a good plan," Ella said, knowing how close Dwayne and his wife were, now that they'd found each other again and remarried.

"But that's not why you called. How soon will you be here?"

"Twenty minutes."

After Ella hung up, she stared out the passenger window for a while, noting how different the landscape was from when she was a kid. Everything was changing. Almost everyone she knew was moving in a new direction.

"What's up?" Justine asked, looking over.

She told Justine what Blalock had said. "I've never had a hobby like that, something I want to do but just never had the time. My life's always been centered around my family and police work."

"You love horseback riding."

"Yeah, I enjoy that, but a few hours a week is enough for me."

"Maybe your problem is that you don't have a grand passion outside your family."

"Yeah, I do," Ella said. "It's investigative work. I like digging for answers, interviewing witnesses, and trying to get into someone else's head so I can solve the puzzle. It gives me an incredible sense of accomplishment and it's one helluva rush."

"You were born to be a cop, Ella," Justine said .

"No, you're wrong," she said after a beat. "What I love most about our work isn't necessarily tied to my badge."

"In that case, I hope O'Donnell doesn't fantasize too much about you."

Ella burst out laughing. "Drive, partner, and keep your mind on the road."

They soon arrived at Blalock's office, located in Shiprock on the northern mesa among various tribal agency buildings. He was standing behind the computer terminal, checking connections as they entered the cool, air-conditioned office.

"Can I help?" Justine asked as Blalock looked up.

"If you get this thing to stay up and running, I'll adopt you, Officer Goodluck."

Justine laughed. "Let me take a look."

"While she's doing that, I need to talk to you," Ella said, then sat atop an adjacent empty desk. Though it had been originally intended for a second resident agent, none of the ones who came had ever stayed for more than a few years. This wasn't the kind of field assignment most young agents wanted, particularly those intent on climbing that proverbial career ladder.

Ella told Blalock about her conversation with Teeny. "I want to interview Billy O'Donnell regarding possible crimes on the Rez and in county, and you're the only one here with joint jurisdiction. I need you to be there, Dwayne."

"No problem."

"You can try to boot up your network again," Justine said. "Your ethernet cable has been damaged and has probably been cutting out. I think it got pinched between the wall and the desktop and the insulation wore off. I straightened out the kink, but you need to replace it or your Internet will be coming and going."

"Thanks," Blalock said, then started searching through desk drawers. After a few minutes, he brought out a yellow cable in a plastic bag. "Will this work?"

"That's the one. Let me switch out the cables for you," Justine offered, taking the bag.

A few minutes later, Blalock nodded and sat back in his chair. "Finally. I'll print out the file I need, then we'll go."

They left in two separate vehicles and, forty-five minutes later, pulled into the large asphalt parking lot in front of the Emporium. The front had been designed like an Old West general store, with a false second story. Facing a major intrastate highway, this was clearly an attempt to appeal to the tourist trade, not just county residents.

Once they were inside, Ella looked around, circling the inside perimeter of the main display area while Blalock introduced himself to the clerk and asked to see the owner. Seeing an open doorway on one side of the hall, Ella positioned herself at an angle so she could see inside the small room. On a table with a photo-studio-type curtain backdrop rested a Native American clay pot decorated in grays and black. A camera on a tripod, flanked by two lights on stands, was aimed at the object.

Ella stepped into the hallway and took a closer look, trying to recall if there had been any reports at department briefings of museum thefts or pieces stolen from private collectors. The pot on the table looked really old and genuine, at least to her untrained eye.

As she crossed the hall, a man coming out of the next room saw her. He turned around in a flash and headed toward a door at the opposite end of the hall.

"Stop!" she said. "Police."

The man doubled his pace.

"Runner! Cover the rear," Ella called out to Justine.

As the man ran outside, Ella raced down the hall. Help was already on its way. She could hear Blalock's heavy footsteps right behind her.

By the time she reached the loading dock, the man had jumped onto ground level and was running toward the far corner of the building.

THIRTEEN

—— ✖ ✖ ✖ ——

Justine was waiting in ambush. She appeared from around the corner and tripped the man as he cut the corner, knocking him to the ground.

When Ella and Blalock caught up, the suspect was already lying facedown on the ground. Justine handcuffed him and began reading him his rights.

"No tribal cops have jurisdiction here!" he yelled. "This is San Juan County, not a reservation."

"I'm Special Agent Dwayne Blalock of the FBI, and you're under arrest for fleeing an officer and possibly theft," he said. "What's your name?" he asked as Ella helped Justine haul the thirty-something Anglo to his feet.

"I'm Billy O'Donnell." He was wearing a Western-cut short-sleeved dress shirt, blue jeans, and a wide leather belt with a big silver and turquoise buckle. His boots looked expensive, either snake or alligator. "I'm not a thief, I'm the owner of the Emporium."

"Then why did you run?" Blalock asked. "The lady identified herself as a police officer. We all heard."

"At the time, I didn't believe her. I saw three people come into my business carrying guns," O'Donnell said smoothly. "I thought I'd better take off and call the cops."

"The phone inside doesn't work?"

"I had to get away before I could call, didn't I?"

"So you fled because you wanted to protect your customers and employees," Ella said. "That's your story?"

"You understand me perfectly," O'Donnell said.

Blalock laughed derisively. "Better than you realize, buddy. Let's go inside. We need to talk."

"You have no right to keep me cuffed," O'Donnell said. "Not unless you're charging me with something."

"Evading an officer is at the top of my current list, but we'll uncuff you," Blalock said, and gave Justine a nod. "If you try to run, your next stop will be the county jail. You get me?"

"Sure," he said as the cuffs came off. "My office?"

O'Donnell led the way to a large room at the far end of the building. A beautifully crafted mahogany desk had been carefully positioned opposite a window with a view of the river valley and mesas rising to the south. Closer to the center of the room was a comfortable-looking brown leather couch and several matching leather easy chairs.

"Nice setup," Ella said.

"I never settle for second best. You only live once, pretty lady," he said, giving her a wink.

Ella suppressed the urge to punch him. "Then why risk spending some of that precious time in jail for dealing in stolen merchandise?"

His eyes narrowed and his jaw clenched. "I thought I'd settled all that nonsense last month. I admitted using poor judgment buying those laptops at the flea market. I had no idea they were stolen."

"Forget the laptops. I'm talking about that pottery in the back room, the jug you're set up to photograph," Ella said. "Do thieves issue four-color catalogs to their buyers now?"

"That's a *private* room. You have a search warrant?" he clipped.

"The door was open, Einstein, and what I saw was from the customer area. If you wanted it to remain private, you should have closed the door. I now have all the probable cause I need," Ella said. "I'm very familiar with the laws dealing with antiquities. Are you? Give yourself a break and tell us about that artifact."

"In the spirit of cooperation, I'd be happy to," O'Donnell said. "I picked up some nice Native American pieces from a roadside vendor near the Rez. Just to be sure, I had a friend in the sheriff's department check the hot sheets, and they weren't stolen. I went back as soon as I could, hoping to buy more items, but by then the vendor wasn't around anymore."

"Can you give us a name, a description, anything?"

He shook his head. "Didn't get a name, and it was strictly a cash transaction. The man was elderly, maybe in his eighties, and said they were pieces he was given when he got married, decades ago."

"Was he Navajo?" Ella asked.

"Yeah. Well, Indian. I guess he could have been Ute or Apache. I didn't ask."

"You really expect us to believe that story?" Blalock said.

"It's true," O'Donnell said.

"Unauthorized digs are illegal. You know that, right?" Ella said.

"So who's digging?"

"We can charge you with illegal possession of Native American antiquities," Ella said. "To comply with the law, you'll have to prove ownership and document the purchase."

"I didn't dig them up or steal them," he said flatly. "You can't prove I did, either."

"We don't have to prove anything other than the fact that you have them. We can arrest you for possession alone," Ella said.

"You need permits to have those items in your possession unless you can prove you've got Native American blood, or that they weren't obtained illegally," Blalock said.

Ella saw O'Donnell squirm and decided to press him harder. "Where were you on Tuesday between, say, twelve and five?"

"Here, mostly, though I did take off for lunch at one."

"Was it anyplace where people would remember you?" Ella asked.

"No. I usually have lunch at home and come back at around two. It's my routine. You can ask Cassie, she's at the front register. She takes lunch from twelve to one."

"I'm going to take a closer look at those pottery pieces," Justine said.

"Go right ahead," he said, though it hadn't been a question.

"We'll need you to come to the sheriff's department and make a statement," Blalock said.

"I want my lawyer there with me."

"Make the call. I'll wait."

Leaving Blalock with O'Donnell, Justine and Ella walked back into the room where she'd seen the pottery. "What do you make of this, partner?" Ella asked.

Justine took close-up photos of the clay pot at the center of the table, then walked over to look at other Native American artifacts on a shelf at the far end of the room.

"These stone corn grinders and ceremonial objects look genuine, Ella. I remember seeing similar pieces at the tribal museum in Window Rock. Look how these have been worn down and weathered. I'm betting they're older than the ones on display at the museum." Justine studied the corn grinder. "I'm no expert, but I'd say most of these are Pueblo or Anasazi in origin. If O'Donnell can't show proper documentation, or prove that he dug them up on private land *prior* to 1979, when the Archeological Resources Protection Act kicked in, we can arrest him. Dealers aren't immune from prosecution."

"We need to authenticate them first and also verify they're not on a hot sheet," Ella said. "As for O'Donnell, he was about two years old in 1979. So unless he found these artifacts in his sandbox—"

"Or inherited them—which he didn't even suggest— we'll treat them as stolen goods," Justine said. "Let me call in Victoria Bitsillie from our robbery and burglary division. She's got a degree in cultural anthropology and may be able to authenticate these."

"I've only met her in the halls, coming and going, but from what I heard, she's got Gerald Bidtah's backing," Ella said. "He calls her the best of a new generation of tribal officers. Maybe she is, maybe she's not. I don't trust Bidtah's judgment all that much."

"In this case, Bidtah's on target. She's very good at what she does," Justine said. "Big Ed speaks highly of her, too. She gets results and doesn't let her ego get in the way. According to her, it's all about restoring the balance."

"That's a plus. She sounds like a Traditionalist."

"New Traditionalist," Justine said, referring to those who still held to many of the old ways, but not at the exclusion of the new.

"Give her a call, and let me know what she says after she sees the pottery."

After speaking with Ella, Blalock turned O'Donnell over to the county sheriff's deputy who'd responded to his call. "You have no documentation for those artifacts, Billy, so I'm placing you under arrest for possession and trafficking in Native American antiquities."

"I'll be released before you get to the station."

"I wouldn't count on that," Blalock said. "I've got a feeling that there's more to find around here."

"Good luck with that," O'Donnell said, shaking his head.

Blalock went to speak to the woman behind the cash register, and Ella followed.

The sturdy young Hispanic woman wearing a turquoise polo shirt with a CASSIE name tag and the Emporium logo appeared to be barely out of her twenties. As she stared at the gold badge in Blalock's hand, she turned a shade paler.

"What do you know about the artifacts in there?" Blalock said, pointing to the room where they'd been kept.

"Not much. I just work the cash register and keep things

in order out here, dusting, straightening, like that. Every once in a while, Mr. O'Donnell brings in a Native American item, takes photos, and shelves it in the back room. Eventually, he packs and ships them off. I guess he finds the buyers himself, because he never puts them on display out here."

"Are there other pieces around the store in addition to what we found in that room?" Ella said.

"There's another pottery jar in the stockroom over there," she said, and pointed to the north wall. "I think he was planning to take photos of it next. I don't know for sure, but I figure that's part of the inventory he sells online."

While Blalock remained with Cassie, Justine and Ella went to check it out. This room wasn't much larger than a walk-in closet, and the artifact was inside a clear acrylic case.

"It looks like the real thing, Ella. I mean, just look at the corrugated pattern on that jar. That's hard to fake."

They went back to talk to Cassie. "Does Mr. O'Donnell do a lot of online selling?" Ella asked.

"I think so. I've heard him talking about it from time to time."

"Do you know which sites he uses?" Ella asked.

Cassie shook her head. "Sorry, no. I give him plenty of space when he's working at the computer. He doesn't like anyone looking over his shoulder."

Justine, who'd moved away to answer a call, came back. "I just heard from Victoria. She's on her way and should be here within a half hour."

"Good. Let me know when she arrives," Ella said.

Blalock took Ella aside. "We know O'Donnell's fencing stuff, but we're after a killer, not just a high-end thief. The real question here is whether can we tie O'Donnell to Ute's murder. Are those artifacts really pricey enough to kill for? How does Ute play into that?"

"I have no idea, but maybe the answers will come to us once we narrow our focus. Let's concentrate on finding evidence that'll link O'Donnell to the case Harry was investigating—the theft of county property."

"Agreed," Blalock said.

Using her smartphone, Ella pulled up the list Harry had prepared of missing county property and sent a copy of it to Blalock's BlackBerry. "Let's see if any of these things are here."

As they searched the Emporium's merchandise, they managed to find several computers with altered serial numbers as well as other office equipment, including copiers and high-speed backup systems. Once the original serial numbers were restored, they'd be able to see if they matched any on Harry's list of missing inventory.

Victoria Bitsillie arrived a short time later. Ella spotted the stately Navajo sergeant through the store window as she drove up in a tribal SUV.

Ella pointed her out to Blalock, and together, they went to greet her. "We understand that you can authenticate the items for us," Ella said as they walked back into the store.

"My uncle is a curator at the UNM Museum of Anthropology in Albuquerque, and he taught me ways of sorting the real from the fake," Victoria said.

Ella led her to the storage room and stood back, watching Victoria work. The sergeant was tall for a Navajo woman, only a few inches shorter than Ella's five foot ten. Victoria had broad, high cheekbones and intelligent brown eyes. In her mid-twenties, she wore her hair in a tight bun, but judging by its diameter, Ella had a feeling it fell down to her waist when loose. Overall, Victoria was a striking woman.

Victoria silently studied the pieces on the table. After a while, she removed a pair of latex gloves from her purse, put them on, and very carefully examined the surface on each of the pots.

"Visually, these appear to be genuine and in incredibly good condition for their age. From traces left in the cracks, I think they've probably been buried in dry, sandy soil for centuries. If I had to guess, I'd say these came from an illegal dig, since they appear to be Anasazi in origin. The markings and wear are consistent with artifacts dating back two to three hundred years, but to be absolutely certain, I'd have to run some tests."

"I'll see if we can get permission to take custody of the pieces," Ella said.

Blalock nodded. "Go ahead. I'll do the paperwork for you."

A petite auburn-haired woman in jeans and a sleeveless blouse knocked on the open door. Seeing Blalock's gold badge, she smiled.

"Agent Blalock, you called for a forensic computer analyst? I'm Mandy Stillwell and I work for the SJCSD out of the Kirtland station." She handed Blalock a file folder. "And here's the warrant you need."

Blalock shook her hand. "Thanks for getting here so quickly."

"No prob. My job's to recover and analyze computer data on behalf of the sheriff's department. When it deals with encryptions, deleted files, and backtracking intrusions, I'm your man."

Ella nearly laughed out loud. Although the tech was much too cocky and looked no older that a high school senior, Ella liked her at first glance.

Blalock stepped out into the hall with Mandy, then waved her toward O'Donnell's office. "We have reason to believe that the suspect is selling stolen merchandise online. We want a full list of anything he's uploaded and sold on the Internet. His computer's on the desk."

"I'll get on it," Mandy said.

As his phone rang, Blalock answered it and moved away. Ella glanced at Justine. "Call Teeny as a courtesy. Tell him where we are and what's going on."

"Sure, boss."

Blalock returned and joined Ella. "I'm assuming you'll want to be in the room when we question O'Donnell?"

"You bet."

"We know Ute was working a case involving stolen county property and some of the items we've found here with altered serial numbers match the descriptions and may match the serial numbers, too," Blalock said. "We also know that O'Donnell was on Ute's radar. Of course, that doesn't prove O'Donnell was involved in his murder, but since O'Donnell's alibi's shaky, I want to continue to push him. Let's see what we get after we squeeze him a bit."

Before Ella could reply, Mandy came out to find them. "I've got something. It looks like O'Donnell has been dealing everything from computers to cell phones on RogersList."

"You broke his password already?" Blalock said, surprised.

"Didn't have to, he'd taped it beneath a drawer. It's the first place I look."

"Good job," Blalock said.

"I'll go back and search for anything specific to Indian artifacts," she said, then returned to O'Donnell's office.

Ella walked across the customer area to Cassie, the clerk, who sat on a tall stool behind the register. Though they'd just closed the store and locked up for the day, she remained there, matching cash, checks, and credit receipts with the computer data.

"Cassie, it appears that your boss was involved in some shady business," Ella said.

"I know. I've been listening to you all talking," she said, "but I had nothing to do with any of that. I've only been working here for about three months, and all I do is handle the cash register, do light bookkeeping, and maintain the displays. Sometimes I work late and lock up."

"Where does your boss spend most of his time—out here on the floor or in the back?"

"Definitely the back—the storeroom, in particular. Personally, I hate going in there. That place is just plain spooky."

"What do you mean?" Ella asked.

Cassie gave her a wry smile. "He carries boxes and boxes of stuff into that place, but it never fills up. I kid him, saying that it's not a storage closet, it's a transporter, like in *Star Trek*."

"Maybe we should take a closer look," Blalock, who'd been listening, said.

Ella nodded. "Sounds good."

The storeroom was paneled with cheap, laminated wallboard and crammed full of office and janitorial supplies.

"Claustrophobic place," Ella said.

"If you wanted to hide something in here, where would you put it?" Blalock asked, looking around.

"I'd pick a place I could access easily but one that's not highly visible . . . like maybe behind those file cabinets against the far wall. Let's see how easy those are to move."

Blalock went over and began opening drawers. They all contained file folders and paper office supplies. When he pulled on one of the cabinets, it started to tip, but it didn't slide. He pushed it back. "Not this one." Blalock went down the line, but had no better luck with the rest.

Lost in thought, Ella stared at an enormous watercolor painting of Shiprock that was propped against the wall. "How about behind that? What's the painting doing in here in the first place? Shouldn't it be out in the display area, mounted on the wall?"

"Is there a space for it out there? Or maybe it's been sold," Blalock suggested. "Either way, let's take a look behind it."

They tipped the heavy painting forward, but there was nothing behind it except the wallboard panel and a few grandaddy longlegs spiders.

Ella continued to look around, mentally dividing the room into quadrants and carefully studying each, searching for anything that didn't fit in with the rest.

"That metal shelf unit," Ella said.

Blalock shook his head. "With all the crap on those shelves, one man would have the devil of a time pulling it away from the wall."

"No, look closer. I think it has casters. It's not flush with the floor." Ella walked up to it, placed her hand on one end, and pulled carefully, not wanting it to topple over on her if she was wrong.

The five-foot-tall, four-foot-wide unit moved out easily. Seeing that nothing on the shelves wobbled even slightly, she reached over to pick up a bottle of bleach. It wouldn't budge.

"It's glued down," she said. Reaching for another item, a box of paper towels, she found it was stuck as well. She lifted the box, using pressure, and it broke free. "There's some kind of goo here, like clay."

Blalock stepped over. "That's museum putty. Put it at the base of a fragile figurine, and it won't tip over even in an earthquake."

"And you know this because . . ."

"Used it on my childhood train layouts. It kept the hobo by the train track from tipping over every time the train raced by."

"Good to know," she said. "Hey, Dwayne, look over here. See this? The corner panels aren't quite flush. Something's behind there," she said.

Blalock went out of the room, trying to figure out what butted up against it, and returned in thirty seconds. "The break room's on the other side, but things don't line up right. There's a section of unaccounted space there."

They tapped the wall, listening for a hollow sound, but found none. "Something's back here, inside this wall, but where the heck is it?" Blalock muttered.

"And how does he access it?" Ella ran her hand along the end of the wall panel where it met the corner. "Nothing here, but look at that scuff mark on the left by the baseboard," Ella said, tapping it with the tip of her boot.

"Don't just tap it. Give it a push," Blalock said.

As she did, they heard a click, and the wall popped out a half inch. Blalock pushed it to the left, and the panel rolled aside easily, revealing shelves holding bullet-resistant vests printed with the letters SJCSD. There were also handguns and shoulder weapons of several different types—revolvers, pistols, shotguns—even rifles with scopes.

"Look at this hardware! How did he get his hands on all this without anyone noticing?" Ella asked.

"I've got an idea," Blalock said, then stepped out into the hall. "Mandy," he called out.

She came out of O'Donnell's office. "Here."

"Can you get me a list of evidence that was confiscated by county and scheduled for disposal by the department? Firearms, ammunition, explosives, tactical gear, things like that. Serial numbers in particular would be helpful."

"Sure, Agent Blalock," Mandy said, quickly glancing inside the room and seeing what they'd found. She pulled out an iPad, then after another second showed him what was on the screen. "Read off the serial numbers on the gear one at a time. I'll type it in and see if I get a match."

Seeing Blalock give her a nod, Ella went to a shelf containing several revolvers. Choosing the closest one, she read the serial number off a Smith & Wesson.

"Got it." Mandy typed a few keystrokes, then looked up. "According to records, that gun was one in a batch of weapons destroyed by the bomb squad four months ago. It was part of the old inventory, before the department switched to Glocks."

"Looks like Mr. O'Donnell's going down," Blalock said. "Let's go have a talk and see what else he's trying to hide."

FOURTEEN

——— ✖ ✖ ✖ ———

Ella was on her way out the door, Justine beside her, when her cell phone rang. As she glanced down, Ella saw that the call was from Sergeant Neskahi. She answered quickly.

"What's up, Joe?"

"I'm on patrol duty today, and right now I'm answering a call at Truman John's place. Mr. John claims that Norman Yazzie took a shot at him."

"Did he actually see Yazzie do that?"

"No, but a few hours before the incident, Mr. John got into an argument with Norman's grandmother and threatened to kill her sheep if she didn't keep them off his land."

"Did the grandmother file a report?"

"No. Truman said he apologized later for losing his temper, but Norman's out for blood now. John's words, not mine."

"We need to question Yazzie—the grandson. I'll meet you over there as soon as possible."

Ella glanced at Blalock. "Can you hold off questioning O'Donnell for a couple of hours? I need to deal with another issue relating to the case," she said, filling him in.

"Go. I can hold O'Donnell for forty-eight hours. While you're on the Rez, I'll have the deputies process O'Donnell's stash and the compartment itself and see if they can get prints."

"I'll be back as soon as possible." Ella glanced at her partner. "Head over to Norman Yazzie's. I'll update you on the way."

Later, as they reached the hill where Harry had been shot, Ella felt her chest tighten.

"It's hard coming back here," Justine said softly, echoing her thoughts.

"What makes it even harder is knowing that we still haven't found any answers," Ella said. "We don't even know why he was killed."

"We will, and we'll also find his killer. None of us will give up till we have the shooter behind bars," Justine said.

Silence settled between them until they passed that spot in the road.

"Something else has been bothering you lately, Ella," Justine said. "What's up?"

Ella sighed. "I'm wondering just how good a detective I really am. Maybe I am losing my edge," she said. "Things have been changing all around me, partner, and I never even noticed."

"This have something to do with Carolyn dating Kevin?"

"That's only part of it. The lives of the people I love most have been changing—a lot. Look at you and Benny. You're ready to take things to the next step, but until you brought it up, I had no clue. I should have been more aware."

"You can't know everything that's going on around you, Ella. Your family's your priority."

"Things are different at home, too. You should have seen my family's reaction to that skinwalker's attempt to scare them. Mom was as cool as could be and so was Herman, though I'm sure he's keeping his hunting rifle loaded and ready," Ella said. "My daughter kept her head, too. She went to look up skinwalkers on the Internet. I expected them to panic, but that never even entered the picture."

Justine nodded slowly. "I get it. Up to now, you've been the one who kept things running smoothly, but now they aren't so dependent on you. They've found their own strengths."

She nodded. "Mom has Herman, and Dawn's growing up. Their lives are leading them in new directions, away from me, and I feel . . . left behind."

"You've moved on, too, Ella. You're pursuing a brand-new relationship, and good things are just beginning. Dan's nuts about you."

"True, and I care about him. But don't assume this is going to result in anything like marriage. There's still a lot more we need to know about each other."

"So go with it and see where it takes you."

"Sage advice from my single cousin?"

"Ella, I know you better than most. You're gun-shy about relationships because of your past."

"Which is why we're taking it slow," Ella said, then

grew quiet for a while. As they turned off the main road and went down what amounted to a residential lane, Ella's focus shifted back to business. "Keep your eyes open, especially along the fence line."

"You think we'll find more skinwalker surprises?"

"I'm not sure." The badger fetish around her neck felt cool, but training and instinct told her not to let her guard down.

Justine soon pulled up in front of a double-wide trailer. Joe's cruiser was parked about ten yards away behind a big Ford pickup.

Within seconds, Joe stepped out of the home and waved at them, signaling it was okay to approach.

"Investigator Clah, Officer Goodluck, this is Norman Yazzie," Joe said.

"I'm glad you're here, Investigator Clah," the short, stocky man said, ignoring Justine. "This officer's taking a skinwalker's word over mine."

Ella looked at Joe, who shook his head.

"I'll join you inside in just a moment, Mr. Yazzie. I'd like to speak to the officer first."

Norman glared at her, then strode back inside.

Ella motioned for Joe to join them by the SUV.

"Bring us up to date," she said.

"Yazzie was really agitated when I first arrived. He said that the skinwalker, meaning John, needs to be dealt with. Norman and his friend—the woman inside named Alice— both maintain that there's no way Norman could have taken a shot at John today. They'd been in Farmington, walking around town and window shopping, and only returned home a few minutes before I got here."

"Do you believe them?"

Joe paused. "I checked and noticed that Yazzie's pickup engine was hot. That tells me he went somewhere recently, but I have no idea where. I also went to the spot where John said the incident occurred, it's not far from here, and looked around. I figured that the shooter must have chosen high ground because of the rolling terrain, so I climbed up and looked around. I didn't see any spent cartridges. In fact, I found nothing—no tracks, and no evidence at all that anyone had been there," Joe said. "When I asked John about the shot, he'd said it whistled overhead and missed his truck."

"Did you question the woman with Norman?" Ella asked.

"I did, but she's almost hysterical. She thinks we should arrest Truman John right away because he's a danger to Mrs. Yazzie."

"Wait a sec, guys. Are we talking 'girlfriend,' here? I thought Norman was married," Justine said.

"Yeah, you're right," Ella said, remembering her conversation with the elder Mrs. Yazzie, Norman's grandmother.

"Norman told me that he and Alice are just friends, but they're too familiar with each other for that to be true. The way he's constantly reaching for her tells me something more's going on." Joe paused.

"Something else bothering you, Joe?" Ella said.

"Yeah. I think Alice's afraid of him. It's nothing overt, but she always looks to him before she answers a question."

"Okay, I'll handle it from here on. Thanks. You can take off now."

"I'll be in the area if you need backup."

"Thanks, Joe," Ella said.

"One more thing. I saw the sketch of the woman that was supposedly with Harry that night. I wouldn't rule out Alice as a match."

"Interesting, thanks," Ella said.

As the sergeant walked to his patrol car, Justine spoke up. "Do you want me to go inside with you right now or stay out here and do some quick digging into Norman Yazzie's background first?"

"Run him through the system and see what you get. That'll give me time to assess the situation. I may want to split the two subjects up. If Alice is afraid of her boyfriend, I'll probably need to talk to her privately." Ella turned in a complete circle, studying the area. There were no moving vehicles anywhere on the horizon.

"Worried about another drive-by? Last time we were talking to the locals, our unit got toasted," Justine said.

"Yeah, exactly, so stay sharp," Ella said. "Do your thing, then come join us."

As Ella entered the trailer, Norman waved her to the living area. The woman, Alice, was sitting on the bench seat next to the built-in table.

Norman spoke first. "That husky cop—he's got it all wrong. I'm no killer. I wouldn't shoot that crazy skinwalker even if he does deserve it," he said. "Truman's nuts, and dangerous, too, but he plays it smart, hiding it from people. Instead of giving a good Navajo a hard time, why aren't you arresting him?"

"On what charge?"

"Haven't you been paying attention? He's a skinwalker! What more do you need?"

"Oh, I don't know. How about actual evidence that he's broken the law?" Ella said.

"So you believe *him* when he says I took a shot at him, but you don't believe me when I say I didn't? Find any bullet holes?" He glared at her; then suddenly his angry expression changed and he smiled. "Wait a sec. I get it now. You think he's a skinwalker, too, and you're afraid you might get witched or something."

"I'm armed, and not just with the strong medicine that's in this pouch. Until skinwalkers become bulletproof, I have no reason to fear them," Ella said. "So tell me. Why would your neighbor assume you took a shot at him?"

"He's crazy, I'm telling you. We'd just come home from Farmington when the officer arrived."

"Is there anyone who can verify you were there, or on the road about an hour or so ago?" Ella pressed.

He considered it, then shook his head. "Probably not. We looked in store windows downtown, then stopped at the McDonald's on the west side. But I doubt they'll remember us. We used the drive-up window."

"Do you have the receipt?"

"Nah, we decided to eat at one of the outside tables and threw it out with our trash."

Ella looked at the young woman who'd remained on the sofa, sitting quietly. "I'm Investigator Clah. What's your name?"

"Alice Cisco," the Navajo woman said, eyeing Justine suspiciously as she came in.

Ella remained focused on the young woman's face. Although the similarities to the sketch were there, including an appropriate figure, the shape of her nose was off and her eyes were rounder and bigger. Of course, that didn't elimi-nate her; sketches based on eyewitness testimony were never exact.

One thing caught Ella's attention and held it. It was the way Alice kept glancing at Norman, then back at her. Joe had been right.

"While my partner talks to Norman privately, I'd like you to step outside with me," Ella said, instantly aware of the sus-picious look on Norman's face and the hard look he gave Alice.

"Anything you want to say to her has to be in front of me, understand?" Norman said.

"You don't get to vote on this." Ella gave him a cold glare, looked back at Alice, and saw the woman cringe. "Let's go for a walk, Alice," Ella said, and smiled, hoping to set her at ease.

As they stepped outside, Ella allowed Alice to lead the way. The woman went to the east side of a metal shed and stood in the shade there.

"Do you think that Truman John is what Norman claims he is?" Ella asked.

"I can't be sure, no, but someone around here is a witch, that's for sure. Look at all that's happened."

"It wouldn't necessarily have to be someone who lives in this area, would it?" Ella said.

Alice looked at Ella in surprise. "Why would an out-sider want to come here and take over the place? We don't have a spring or good grazing land, or oil, or natural gas. A few people have water wells, sure, but that's the biggest prize I can see."

Ella said nothing. and silence stretched out between them.

"There's evil close by," Alice said at last. "If you close your eyes, you can feel it. A man was killed in his pickup on the road over there." She gestured in the direction of the hill.

Ella nodded. "Do you think the skinwalker did that?"

"Who else? Witches get their power by killing, and then they steal parts of their victim's body to make bad medicine. That's what I've always heard."

Ella once again allowed the silence to stretch. Alice kept tugging at her long skirt, bunching the fabric in her fist, then releasing it in a continuous cycle.

"What's bothering you, Alice? We can talk about it." Ella saw her look at the trailer, then back at the ground. "Norman can't hear us out here," she added, hoping to set her at ease.

"He's a good man," Alice whispered, "even if he doesn't act like it sometimes. His temper just gets away from him."

"These days, we're all going through tough times," Ella said, trying to keep the woman talking.

"He works hard. He owns the Little Bear Café in Beclabito, but sometimes he doesn't know how to stop being the boss. I get ordered around all the time, even off the job."

"That can make any relationship difficult. How did you meet?"

"I applied for a job at the café," she said. "I was a waitress, but then he gave me a promotion. He taught me to handle all his bookkeeping. Now I have a skill I could use anywhere. I owe him."

"Is that what he said?"

She shrugged. "Without him, I'd still be busing tables."

"So how does he collect?" Ella asked her bluntly.

Alice cringed. "It's not like that. I'm just here for him when his wife's not around."

"Is that what *you* want?"

She hesitated, then nodded. "He's there for me when I need help, too, and I've never had anyone do that for me. Take last year, when I had to pawn my squash blossom necklace, something my mother had given me. When he found out, he went to the pawnshop and bought it back. I didn't know until I came back here with him one afternoon and saw it on the table. He told me to take it home and not lose it again."

"How did he know you pawned it, and what happened that forced you to pawn something that special?"

"I stop at the casinos when I go to Albuquerque. Last time I was there, I was on a winning streak, so I kept playing, but then my luck changed," she said, and shrugged. "After that, I was broke. It was the middle of winter, and they were going to turn off my gas 'cause I kept missing my payments. I pawned the necklace so I could catch up."

"How did Norman find out? Was he with you at the casinos or did you tell him?"

"Sometimes I guess he follows me." She stared at the ground. "He always knows where I've been."

"And that doesn't bother you?"

"He only does it to protect me."

"So why are you afraid of him?"

Her eyes grew wide. "I never said I was."

"No, but I can see how careful you are around him. Does he hit you?"

She shook her head. "No. He yells a lot and gets upset, but he's never hurt me."

"Emotional threats can be scary. Is that what frightens you?" Ella asked.

She shook her head once more. "He can have anyone he wants, but he chose me. I'm lucky to have him. I want him to be happy with me, so I try not to get him upset. I've got a good thing going here."

Alice started walking back toward the mobile home. Halfway, she stopped and turned to face Ella. "For what it's worth, I think he's right about his neighbor. Something's really wrong with Truman. I work with Eileen at the café, and I've seen what he's done to her when he gets angry."

"He hits her?"

She nodded. "She didn't say so, but one day when she came in to pick up her check, she had a black eye and a split lip. It's what a man's fist does, I know. My dad used to do that to my mom. That's why I'd never stay with Norman if he ever hit me. Bruises hurt, but what a man breaks inside a woman—that never heals."

Ella watched her walk away. What amazed her was that Alice didn't see that she'd allowed herself to become just as trapped and controlled as her mother, and Eileen.

As they went back into the house, Norman immediately met them by the door and placed his arm around Alice's shoulders. "Are you okay?"

"Yeah, I'm fine." She looked back at Ella. "You should hear the calls at night—the howling. It makes your hair stand up on end. You can tell it's not an animal."

Norman nodded. "She's right. I went out last night, trying to figure out where it was coming from, but the howling stopped once I started getting serious about tracking it down."

Ella gave him her card. "If you hear it again, stay inside and call me."

"The cops have been out here plenty of times, trying to find the howler. Ask your patrol officers," Norman said. "The really bad stuff just started happening, but those calls have been going on for over a month."

"I'll look into it myself, so if you hear it again, call me."

Ella nodded to Justine. "Let's go, partner."

Neither of them spoke on the way back to the SUV. Once Justine switched on the ignition, she glanced at Ella. "Where to, boss?"

"Go straight to the sheriff's office in Kirtland. I want to be there with Blalock when he questions O'Donnell."

Ella called Blalock on the way and updated him.

"It's interesting that even before Harry was killed, someone was busy trying to scare the residents," Blalock said in a thoughtful voice. "We need to figure out if Harry's murder was part of someone's strategy to frighten the residents, an escalation of events already taking place, or a completely separate incident."

"I still have no idea why a skinwalker would target that area. As Alice said, there's nothing much there."

"Don't let the skinwalker angle sidetrack you, Clah. Right now we need to focus on Billy. The deputies didn't get any usable prints. We've got a date for the revolver but no idea when the other gear was taken. Get over here and let's see what we can get from Billy. He knows a lot more than he's told us."

Ella ended the call and turned to Justine. "While I'm

helping Blalock question O'Donnell, I want you to look deeper into Truman John's past. He's almost flippant about the presence of Navajo witches, and I don't trust someone with that attitude. Also, have Benny and Joe pull a photo of Alice and show it to the bar patrons and Alan Scott, Harry's neighbor. See if anyone can ID her as the woman who was with Harry that Monday night."

"You think maybe Alice moonlights as a hooker?"

"It's possible. A sexy outfit, wig, and some makeup would bring her up to speed. She has a gambling problem, too, and people like that are usually short of cash. It's worth a try."

FIFTEEN
✕ ✕ ✕

By the time they arrived at the sheriff's station, Ella was eager to start questioning Billy. There were too many intangibles in this case, and frustration was eating at her. What she and Harry shared back in the day hadn't been perfect, but his name was indelibly written on the pages of her past. No matter what it took, she'd find his killer.

As she walked into the building, Justine remained behind to follow up with the state lab in Santa Fe, where she'd sent some of the evidence for further testing. As she entered the station, Ella noticed Blalock talking to Sheriff Taylor. His office was in Aztec at SJCSO headquarters, but he spent a lot of time in the field, and often dropped by the Kirtland station.

She was at the front desk clipping her visitor's pass onto her shirt pocket when Blalock, alone now, came up to her.

"Let's go. I caught up to Taylor while he was in the

neighborhood briefing his deputy sheriff. Once we're done with O'Donnell, we'll turn copies of everything we've got over to county."

As she entered the small interrogation room just behind Blalock, Ella noticed that Billy was already reacting to the uncomfortably warm temperature.

"It's really hot in here. How about turning on the air conditioner?" he said.

"I'm comfortable," Ella said, though she knew it was near eighty.

Everything in the room was designed to make the suspect uncomfortable and anxious to leave. There was one small table in the center, with one chair for the suspect, and two chairs on the opposite side for the officers. A second detective would take the seat across the table while the primary investigator would sit in front of the suspect, literally backing him up against the wall. If the suspect had an attorney, a fourth chair would be brought into the room.

"Talk to me, Billy. Right now we've got enough to put you away for fencing stolen merchandise—multiple charges, of course, and each one kicking in a few more years of jail time. Your only option is to cooperate. If you do, we may be able to cut you a deal of some kind," Blalock said, having seated himself right across from the suspect.

"Cooperate how? What do you want to know?"

"Start by telling us where you got the antique pottery we found at your store," Blalock said.

"I pick up stuff on the Internet, at yard sales, out of the back of a pickup, flea markets, you name it," O'Donnell said. "Items like pottery don't show up that often, so I don't have any special inventory codes in my system for it. To me, it's just miscellaneous merchandise. I bargain hard, buy cheap, and sell at the best price possible. It's business."

"Tell us about the merchandise in that hidden storage area?" Ella said, trying to rattle his composure. "I'm talking about inventory behind the big metal shelf. That tactical gear and the weapons in there didn't come from a yard sale or off the back of a truck."

For a moment, O'Donnell just stared at them, a blank look on his face. "I have no idea what you're talking about."

"You're a lousy liar," Blalock said. "It was right behind the storage shelf. Press the trim, and the door pops open. Don't add giving false statements to the FBI to the list of charges you're already facing."

"Honestly, I have no idea what you're talking about," he said. "And because I'm at a loss here, it looks like you'll have to wait until my attorney arrives."

"Look, Billy, I'm not really interested in stolen county property. That's for the sheriff's department," Ella said. "I'm a tribal police officer and I'm working a different case." She pulled a photo of Harry from her shirt pocket and placed it in front of him. "Do you know this man?"

O'Donnell glanced at it, then after a half a beat, spoke. "Never met him. Sorry."

Ella noted the pause. "We have reason to believe he was investigating you. Take another look."

O'Donnell didn't look down. "Friend of yours?"

Ella continued to look at him but didn't answer.

"I suppose it's possible he may have made a purchase at the Emporium, but I don't remember him. You might ask some of my employees," he said, leaning back. "Cassie works the register most of the day, show it to her."

"Count on it," Ella said.

Just then, a tall redheaded "suit" carrying a briefcase came in. "Don't say another word, Billy." He looked at Blalock and Ella. "I'm George Franco, Mr. O'Donnell's attorney. Why don't you tell me what this is all about? Is my client being charged?"

Blalock gave him a description of what had transpired at the Emporium, including his client's possession of unregistered Native American antiquities and stolen county law enforcement tactical gear and confiscated weapons.

"Those are very serious charges. I'll need time to confer with my client in private," Franco said.

"I've already told them that this is the first I've heard about a hidden storeroom, and have nothing to do with those weapons and tactical gear. I took over the place after my dad passed away three months ago. He never said anything to me about this, and there's no way you can hold me responsible for what he may or may not have done."

"That's a valid argument, Billy, but for now, don't say anything else," Franco said, then looked at Blalock and Ella. "We'll need some privacy. And get me a chair."

"Take mine," Ella responded, not about to fetch for the man.

As Blalock started for the door, Franco gestured to the window. "And turn off the mike."

Blalock led the way back out; then they went to the break room. "I didn't know that about O'Donnell's father. If that's true, O'Donnell could be released within the hour. Though the circumstantial evidence is abundant, we can't physically connect him to anything in that closet."

Ella nodded. "Along with the county property, we have the pots and other antiquities, but the Emporium has been there for at least thirty years. It's almost a landmark. I'm guessing you're right. He's going to make bail unless we can get more on him—in a hurry."

"Along with all the stolen inventory, the county judge included O'Donnell's cell phone in the warrant. Let's see what calls he's got logged in there. If he spoke to Harry, that would give us a link between the men," Blalock said.

"And prove that Billy lied to us," Ella said.

Blalock stepped inside the first open office door to his right. "Where can we find your computer specialist, Mandy Stillwell?"

"Try the lab," the office assistant said. "All the way down this hall, then turn right past the restrooms. It's the first door to your left."

"Thanks," Blalock said.

They quickly arrived at a small work area resembling a storeroom. Metal shelves were piled high with monitors, CPUs, and layers of keyboards and other components. A wooden counter, probably a shop table at one time, contained two oversized monitors, a laptop, and a CPU underneath. At the end of the counter closest to the door was a large laser printer. Beside it was a box of printer paper, and on the wall above it a large sign with an arrow pointed down, labeled PRINTER.

"Hi, guys," Mandy greeted, turning in a swivel chair from the counter where she was working.

"We need to ask you about O'Donnell's cell phone," Blalock said.

She nodded. "I'm already on it. I figured you'd need to know who he'd been talking to or texting—particularly if it was someone from the department."

"And what did you find out?" Blalock said.

She looked down at her iPad. "The cell phone he's using is a cheap throwaway, a burn phone. No numbers are stored in memory, and he's only made five outgoing calls—one to his barber, two to his bank, one to a take-out place, and one to a commercial landscape service."

"That's all?" Ella asked, surprised. "How long has he had the phone?"

"Three weeks," Mandy said.

"He's got to have another one somewhere," Blalock said.

"I also checked calls made to and from the landline at the store, but there are hundreds of those for this past month alone. It'll take a while for me to check them all out, but so far I've got nothing that shows a pattern."

"All right. If you find anything, let me know," Blalock said, handing her his card.

"No problem, Special Agent Blalock," she said, putting the card beside her keyboard.

As they walked back to the lobby, Justine met them and Ella updated her on what she'd learned.

"Why a disposable phone? People usually have those for a specific reason," Justine said. "Sometimes it's just economics, but all too often it's because the user is trying to avoid being tracked."

"We're thinking there's another cell phone, one he wasn't carrying on him when we met up," Ella said, looking to Blalock, who nodded.

"After we go another round with Billy, let's head back to his store. We don't have a warrant for his residence yet, but I've made the request and maybe by the time we're done, we will," Blalock said.

They returned to the interrogation room, and Franco stood as they came in. "I've had an officer lower the thermostat in here. My client has a heart condition and keeping it that hot was a willful disregard for his safety."

Ella forced herself not to roll her eyes. "He didn't mention any heart problems to us, Counselor."

"You're a tribal officer and you have no jurisdiction here. Why are you talking to my client at all?" Franco said.

"She's with me, Counselor," Blalock said, holding up his Bureau badge. He motioned for Ella to sit, and she positioned herself facing the attorney.

Blalock stayed on his feet, across from the suspect, and began to question Billy again, but Franco answered each time "on behalf of his client," refusing to allow Billy to say a word.

After ten frustrating minutes, Blalock stepped back, throwing up his hands. "I'm done here."

"Will you, or the sheriff's deputies, be booking my client?" Franco said.

Blalock shook his head. "I'm not taking any further action at this time. Sheriff Taylor's investigators will interview him next. I don't know what their plans are for the suspect or what charges he'll be facing."

Blalock and Ella met Justine out in the hall. "We're getting nowhere," Blalock growled.

"Let's go back to the Emporium. I've got that clerk, Cassie's number, and she has a set of keys to let us in. My gut tells me Billy recognized Harry's photo but chose to play dumb. He hesitated before responding, then wouldn't look directly at me for a while afterwards. Like you said, he's a lousy liar," Ella said.

"Billy was at the top of Ute's list for a reason, and I trust your instincts about him, so let's go," Blalock said.

By the time they arrived at the Emporium, the sun was on the horizon. "It's been a long day, boss," Justine said.

"Yeah. After we finish here, why don't you come home with me and have dinner with the family?"

Justine shook her head. "I can't tonight. Benny's cooking."

"He cooks? You've got a good deal going there, cuz," Ella said as they stepped onto the porch.

"Yeah, I think so, too."

Blalock met them at the entrance. Cassie had already arrived, and was standing there, waiting with the keys. After being shown a copy of the latest search warrant, Cassie opened the door and went inside with them. She remained at the front register while they continued on to Billy's office.

Ella glanced around the room. "Okay, let's try to find that second cell phone."

Twenty minutes later, Blalock stopped and shook his head. "It's not in here."

Justine appeared in the doorway. "I decided to search the cell phone display by the electronics. None are activated."

"Did you talk to Cassie?" Ella asked her.

"Yeah, but I didn't tell her what I was looking for, if that's what you meant."

"I don't think she's involved in what O'Donnell has been doing, and she certainly won't want to be implicated in any of this," Ella said. "Let's enlist her help."

Ella walked out to the main room and approached the young woman, who was killing time straightening items on a candy display beside the register. "Cassie, I need to ask you something important," Ella said. "What do you know about Billy's cell phone?"

"It's cheap and old school, all he did with it was talk and text. I tried to get him to upgrade, but he said he wasn't into all that techno stuff."

"So he only used the cheap model he carried?" Ella asked.

"No. He'd also use the cell phone we have here at the cash register. It's stuck with Velcro to the bottom of the counter. It's supposedly only for emergencies, like if a customer is causing trouble, but Billy used it a lot. He said he wanted to make sure it was always charged and problem free."

Ella smiled. "Can I see it?"

"Sure."

Cassie brought it up and handed the phone to Ella. "It's top of the line, or was last week. You know how competitive the mobile device market is these days."

Ella moved away from the register and searched for a contact list. There were no saved numbers, but she was able to retrieve a list of sent calls. "These date back several months, but there's one local number that shows up frequently."

"Call it," Blalock said, looking over her shoulder.

Ella shook her head. "I'd rather get a reverse directory and find out who it belongs to first," she said.

Blalock nodded. "Okay, let's get Mandy."

Moments later, Mandy returned Blalock's call. Stepping outside with Ella, Blalock told Mandy what he needed and put her on speaker.

After several moments, Mandy got back on the phone. "I have what you need, Agent Blalock. That cell number is registered to SJCSO Sergeant Robert Kirk. He's currently assigned to the Hit and Run desk at headquarters in Aztec. Sergeant Kirk's home address is in Fruitland."

Ella was surprised to hear his name in connection to their case. She remembered him from the county shooting range. To her, he'd come across as someone coasting toward retirement.

"What's his work history with the department?" Blalock asked.

"He's served with the sheriff's department for twenty years and six months. He worked homicide, then robbery and burglary, but he got shot in 2008 while on duty and was assigned to the evidence room. Currently he's been working Hit and Run."

"Sounds like he's paid his dues. Thanks, Mandy."

"I've got something else for you, Agent Blalock. I continued digging into Mr. O'Donnell's computer files. Some were doubly encrypted, so it took me a little longer to crack them. Mr. O'Donnell has active listings on Rogerslist for a ten-millimeter Glock Model 20 and three bullet-resistant vests."

"Good job, Mandy," Blalock said, and ended the call. "Let's see if I can speed up that warrant. After we lock up here, I want to search O'Donnell's house while he's still in custody. Since the request has already been put through, it's just a matter of giving things a little nudge. Should be a piece of cake."

"I sure wish you hadn't said that," Ella said. "That practically guarantees that something's going to go south."

SIXTEEN
——— ✖ ✖ ✖ ———

After discovering that the warrant would take more time than expected, they decided to grab dinner. They went to the closest grill, a place that specialized in Mexican food. Justine hadn't been too happy about canceling her dinner date with Benny, but personal plans were subject to change whenever they were working a case.

Ella and Justine chose stuffed sopaipillas, big, golden fried pastries stuffed with the works, including fresh green chile. Blalock ordered the jumbo burger loaded with red chile and fries with the skins on.

They ate leisurely while waiting for the warrant call, and though the food was a little greasier than Ella would have preferred, she had to admit everything tasted wonderful.

"I'm going to miss meals like this after I retire," Blalock said, savoring each bite as if it were his last. "Ruthann is always worried about her weight, or too much salt or too much cholesterol. That means I eat way too much salad. She doesn't understand that sometimes a guy just needs guy food."

Ella laughed. "Hey, healthy eating is a good thing. She cares about you."

"Yeah, I know. Things *are* good between us," Blalock said, smiling. "What about you, Ella? You've got a kid entering high school this fall. Are you ever going to settle down?"

"Maybe. I have someone new in my life, so we'll see how things work out."

Blalock was about to say more when his phone rang. "Finally. Hopefully this is about the warrant."

Blalock identified himself, listened, then spoke. "Wait a minute, Sheriff Taylor. Could you repeat that?"

As he hung up, Blalock cursed. "That slippery SOB O'Donnell is already out on bail. Despite being in possession of undocumented Native American artifacts, his buddy on the county commission fast-tracked the process by suggesting that Billy could wear an ankle bracelet. We got the warrant to search his place, but now that the suspect's been released, we'll need to play things a little differently."

"How so?" Ella asked.

Blalock motioned toward the exit. "Billy's already home, Sheriff Taylor tracked him there, so we better get there ASAP. County's sending a detective over to Billy's place to serve the warrant and await our arrival. That should at least keep O'Donnell from trying to move any evidence off the premises."

"So we'll play it by the book but stay on target," Ella said. "Search for evidence that'll show a link between Billy and Harry."

"If it exists," Blalock said. "I hate to say this, but there's a chance all we'll end up finding is more evidence of a stolen-property operation."

Twenty minutes later, they stood on the front porch of O'Donnell's Bloomfield residence, a sprawling ranch house surrounded by a well-maintained lawn beneath the shade of a half dozen pine trees. County Detective Velasquez, a dark-skinned Hispanic with huge biceps, was waiting for them, warrant in hand.

"I've rung the bell, pounded on the door, even circled the house and tried the back, but I can't get a response," he said. "I checked with our tech people back at the station, and according to them, O'Donnell's inside."

"His ankle bracelet is, but maybe he cut it off and left it there," Blalock said, banging on the door. "We have a warrant to search the property, O'Donnell," he called out after identifying himself. "Open up or we'll break the door down."

There was no answer, so Velasquez stepped up. "I've got this." He kicked hard, aiming his boot heel at a spot just below the doorknob. The wood splintered and the door swung open.

"That's some kick," Ella said, her pistol out now and at her side.

"Tae kwon do—black belt," he said, flashing a wicked grin.

Blalock pushed his way in, pistol ready as he checked the front room. "Come on, O'Donnell. Don't make me shoot you."

"No chance of that," Ella said, pointing to the ankle bracelet that lay on the floor beneath a glass-topped coffee table. "He's in the wind."

After issuing an ATL, attempt to locate, they began a thorough search of the house. An hour passed, but their efforts failed to turn up any new evidence.

As they worked, Blalock stepped away to answer a phone call. He returned moments later. "We've got a lead. O'Donnell's phone at the Emporium showed that he made several dozen calls to a burn phone, not the one that county's holding. Mandy hasn't been able to get anything on the phone's owner, but each time, the call went through a cell tower in Fruitland."

"West of Kirtland . . . Isn't that where Robert Kirk lives?" Ella said.

"Yep. The calls reveal a pattern, too, and give us probable cause, so I'm going to ask Judge Harris for a warrant to search Kirk's home next. If we find something, we'll place him under arrest," Blalock said. "Damn, I hate dirty cops."

As Ella went into the bedroom, where Justine was continuing to search, something shiny on the floor by the edge of the bed caught her eye. "This money clip . . . I gave Harry one that looked just like it," she said, bending down to retrieve it.

Justine came over to take a closer look. "I noticed it before. It's sterling silver, but besides that, there's nothing distinctive about it. Can you say for sure that it's the same one?"

Having overheard their conversation, Blalock hurried over. "If you could prove this was Harry's, then we'd have the link we've been looking for."

Ella shook her head. "No, I can't swear it's the same one. I bought the clip at the Outpost, a trading post outside the Rez, but it wasn't a one-of-a-kind."

"According to the conversation I just had with Sheriff

Taylor, Sergeant Kirk's off duty and should be at home now," Blalock said. "You want to go pay him a visit? He won't know we're waiting for a warrant and we might be able to convince him to talk to us."

"Keep him busy till it comes in?" Ella nodded. "Good idea. With Billy O'Donnell on the run, something tells me that we need to get there quickly or we'll be looking for two missing suspects, not just one."

Ella knew that because it was possible O'Donnell had already contacted Kirk, they had to go in prepared. If the sergeant was involved in the crimes, he could decide to make a run for it, or resist being taken into custody. Although from what she'd seen that day at the range, that Kirk wasn't that good a shot, facing a well-armed opponent was always dangerous.

It was eight thirty, close to dark and well past sunset, when Ella and Blalock pulled into the driveway of Kirk's modest tract home. There was a light on somewhere inside, but the room facing the front was dark.

They parked beside a brown Jeep Wrangler loaded up with duffel bags and several suitcases. "Looks like someone is about to go on vacation," Blalock said, gesturing to the Jeep as he stepped out of his unmarked unit.

"Must be a road trip, I don't see any camping gear," Ella said, maintaining the "business as usual" tactic they'd decided upon before arriving.

Ella walked with Blalock up the sidewalk. Though they were both wearing vests beneath their jackets, she still regretted not having argued with Dwayne when he'd decided to ignore tactical training and approach the front door together. He wanted to make it all seem more casual and avoid putting Kirk on the defensive. Yet by grouping like this, they were also easier targets.

Although they were obviously hoping to avoid a firefight, they'd also taken steps to protect the residents. Deputies had evacuated Kirk's neighbors, and a SWAT team was positioned behind the corner of the now-empty house to her left. A sniper was also set up across the street, behind some low junipers.

"Once we're done here, wanna grab a late dinner?" Blalock said, making conversation. His casual tone was in direct contrast to the intensity of his searching gaze—and the fact that his hand was inches away from his handgun.

When they stepped up onto the front porch, Ella noticed movement behind the curtained window. "Looks like somebody's home," she announced pleasantly, not moving her head but showing Blalock the direction with her eyes.

The badger fetish around her throat suddenly felt very warm. Heeding the warning, she stepped back from the door and reached down to her waist, removing her Glock.

Blalock nodded, then rang the doorbell and also stepped back. Drawing his own weapon, he kept it at his side, down low. "Sergeant Kirk—Robert. Got a minute?"

"Back!" Ella yelled, instantly pushing Blalock with the heel of her left hand.

The sleeve of Ella's jacket fluttered, and she felt a slight tug just as the left center of the door splintered from two rapid bullet blasts.

"Down!" Blalock yelled.

Ella sank to one knee, held her weapon out at an angle with her left hand, and fired two shots blindly into the door.

The heavily armed and armored SWAT team came down the side of the house at a practiced jog. The lead officer was holding up a metal shield to protect himself and the three men behind him. All the officers had on gas masks and radio headsets.

"You okay?" the fourth officer in line asked as they passed Blalock. Dwayne was prone now, his pistol aimed at the window.

"Fine. Clah?" Blalock asked, not taking his eyes off the window.

"I'm okay," Ella said, staying low but inching out from the wall, hoping to provide cover for the upcoming assault.

Two SWAT members carrying MP-5 submachine guns with attached flashlights provided cover for a third officer, who carried a battering ram.

The officer looked at the lead officer to his right and, getting a nod, swung the ram, breaking the lock away from the jamb.

The SWAT leader, pistol in one hand and the shield in the other, gave the door a mighty kick, and it swung open with a crunch.

A shot went off inside, and the officer with the shield flinched as a bullet clanged against the metal shield, ricocheting off into the wall.

Both men beside him returned fire, then advanced into the room. "Drop your weapon!" one of the SWAT team members yelled.

There was another shot, then the sound of a door slamming.

Ella reached the shattered entrance, Blalock behind her, and in the soft glow of a hall light saw the silhouettes of the

SWAT team. All four were crouched low in the living room, their weapons trained on a door down a short hall. The SWAT leader called for the next move via his radio link. "Tear gas, front bedroom."

Ten seconds passed before there was a muffled bang; then tear gas began to seep from beneath the door. Ella quickly detected the fumes, and her lungs started to react. Moving fast, she and Blalock backed out of the house and into the yard.

Less than a minute later, they heard the sound of loud coughing, followed by several men yelling "Clear!" in succession.

Robert Kirk, coughing and cursing, was led out of the house by two members of the SWAT team. His hands were handcuffed behind his back.

One of the officers still inside turned on the porch and house lights, and suddenly everything became brighter.

Kirk was ordered to lie facedown on the grass by the SWAT team leader, but seeing he was still in distress, Blalock jogged over to a garden hose coiled by a faucet. "He needs to be hosed down," he said.

The SWAT leader nodded his okay, and Blalock turned on the water. "Sit up and close your eyes," Blalock told Kirk, coming closer, then spraying his face and hands with a fine mist from the sprinkler head.

After the SWAT team's medic wiped the prisoner's face and arms with a cloth soaked in some kind of neutralizer, Kirk was ready to be questioned.

Ella and Blalock were soon joined by a young sheriff's deputy, who began reading Kirk his rights.

"Save it for someone who cares, kid," Kirk said, shaking

his head. His eyes were red, floating in tears from the after-effects.

"You might want to save yourself some prison time by helping us out, Kirk. Where's your partner?" Blalock asked.

"If you're looking for Billy, you're wasting your time. He's long gone."

"Where is he?" Blalock said.

"How should I know?"

"How long have you been selling O'Donnell county property?" Blalock demanded.

Kirk sighed, a sad, resigned expression on his face. "A year and half, maybe two. In the beginning, it was a real sweet deal—no one got hurt, not even the department. I only removed inventory that was scheduled to be destroyed, either because it was confiscated weaponry, obsolete, or sur-plus. All that crap was just taking up space. I had a set of keys that gave me access, and it seemed a shame not to get rid of the stuff and make a buck. Billy's old man didn't have a clue what was going on. . . . " His voice trailed off at the end, and he shook his head slowly, clearly defeated.

Ella looked at him curiously. Though it wasn't fancy, Sergeant Kirk had a nice home, a decent vehicle, and, being employed and single, was probably not hurting for money. "You draw a good salary from county. Why did you risk it all like this?"

"I gave twenty years to the department, but I never made it past sergeant. My time was almost up, so this was my last chance to score before I was put out to pasture. I wanted money to travel anywhere I chose—first class. The way I saw it, I had nothing to lose," he said, and shrugged.

"But why get greedy now?" Ella pressed. "You could

have retired with a decent pension and taken it easy for the rest of your life. Or you could have chosen a new career. Now you'll be going to prison."

"Six months—max."

"Not with Harry Ute's death on your hands," Ella said, pushing just to see how he would react.

"You mean the Navajo PI on Billy's trail?" Seeing her nod, he perked up and continued. "Hell, Billy and I had nothing to do with his death. Okay, we'll cop to firebombing your unit with that cooking oil. I was the guy behind the wheel. But that was just a sideshow to misdirect the investigation of the stolen inventory. Trust me, neither of us were involved in any shooting."

"If that's true, and you give us something we can use, we might be able to cut you a deal," Blalock said. "You don't want to go into the general population with the other inmates."

"Billy's not a killer. A thief, yes, a con man, absolutely, but a killer? No way. He doesn't have the stones."

"Do you?" Ella asked, continuing to push.

"If you think I blew that PI away, you're way off the mark. Okay, so I took stuff the county was going to end up chopping into scrap metal or recycling, but murder?" He shook his head. "No way. In twenty years, I've never even fired my weapon on duty. I know what it's like to have your days cut short."

"I don't follow you," Ella said.

"I'm dying. I've got pancreatic cancer. I look perfectly normal, don't I?" He shrugged. "They found a mass, and what lies ahead for me ain't pretty."

"Then why on earth did you risk the time you had left?" Ella said.

"Don't *you* want to die on your own terms? I was hoping to take the dirt nap while lying on a beach in Costa Rica. I wanted to know how the one percent lives for a month or two. You read me?"

"Yeah. But now you'll die in jail, or prison," Ella said.

"Hey, all I needed was a few more months and I'd be outta here. It was a calculated risk," he said.

"You should have taken longer to calculate," Blalock said. "Where were you last Tuesday between noon and four?"

"At the hospital, getting more tests. I spent the whole day there. You'll have plenty of corroboration," Kirk said.

As the county officers led him over to a squad car, Ella and Blalock talked to the county crime team now working the scene. A big exhaust fan had been set up and was venting the gas from the interior of the house.

Justine, who'd been with the officers covering the back, joined them inside once it was safe to enter without a mask.

"Deputies have already found items stolen from county in two closets, including computers with altered serial numbers, four handguns, and two vests with ceramic body armor inserts," Justine reported. "But there's nothing here that connects him to Harry's murder."

"Then there's a third player out there, one we haven't identified yet—maybe the shooter." Ella examined the vests found in a box in the study. "Kirk didn't bother wearing either of these. I think once he realized that he wasn't getting away, his plan shifted to suicide by cop. That would have solved his biggest problem."

"Pancreatic cancer is particularly nasty, Ella. I had a cousin who passed away from that. Believe me, it's a real hard way to go," Blalock said, his voice somber. "I think that once Kirk found out what he was up against, he laid it all on the line, figuring he'd either get rich or eat a bullet. I don't think he factored in the possibility that he'd end up in jail."

"All things considered, does it really matter?" Justine said. "If you're going to die and there's no hope, what difference does it make where you are at the time? If it was me, all I'd really want is enough morphine to be in la-la land when the reaper showed up."

"I'd fight every step of the way," Ella said.

Blalock shrugged. "There are battles you can't win. Face it, we're here, then we're gone. No one checks out alive."

SEVENTEEN
—— ✖ ✖ ✖ ——

Once the house was searched, Justine was given permission to access Kirk's laptop computer. Typing with gloved hands, she got down to work quickly.

"His files aren't encrypted," she told Ella, "and there's one in particular you're going to find interesting. It has the list of items he's taken from county, apparently for years, and it includes a lot more than what we saw on Harry's list. Kirk even snagged an old trencher used for heavy-duty digging, a radial arm saw, and a drill press taken from a burglary raid. The rightful owners were never found, so they stayed locked up in storage."

"Why on earth would he *keep* a list like that?" Blalock asked. "That's as good as a signed confession."

"Thieves rarely believe they'll get caught," Ella said. "Or in this case, maybe Kirk wanted people to know what he'd done *after* he died—a last in-your-face type of thing."

"Maybe," Blalock said, "but none of this ties him directly

to Harry Ute. Is it possible for us to get a look at Ute's actual case file? Even in the private sector, he must have had some written record of what he'd done up to the time he died."

"Teeny said he gave Harry plenty of space. We accessed the backups of his laptop files but there were no specifics other than what I've already told you about," Ella said. "It's possible Teeny's got more information he hasn't shared with me in addition to his client's name, but legally I can't force his hand. All I can do is go talk to him again."

"You'll have better luck without me there," Blalock said. "I'll follow the deputies to the station and give them a statement. While I'm there, I'll check to see if their people lifted any prints off that money clip—other than O'Donnell's, that is."

About fifteen minutes later, Ella and Justine were on their way back to the Rez. It was already nearly nine thirty, but their workday wasn't over yet. As they crossed the border into tribal land, Justine's phone rang and she spoke to Benny briefly.

After she hung up, Ella looked at her partner. "I didn't hear his side, but from what you said, it sounded like Benny was upset."

"No, that's not it. He knows we work long hours. He's a police officer, too. It's just that . . ."

Ella didn't interrupt. Long pauses were common among Navajos. She'd learned to wait.

"He has a double standard. He can't always call me ahead of time when he's working a case, and I don't sweat it, because I figure it goes with the badge. Yet when the reverse happens, like me not calling, he acts as if I've let him down, that I should have found a way to let him know. It's been hours since I called and canceled dinner. He was worried, not hearing from me."

"If you want to keep Benny around, find a way to work it out. Ignoring the problem means it'll stay beneath the surface and blow up when you least expect it."

"Is that why you're so careful around Dan? You're afraid your relationship will blow up in your face?" Justine said.

"You bet," Ella said. "He's fun, Justine, and sexy, too, but there are a lot of things I still don't know about him. He's not the type to talk about his feelings over tea."

"What cop is? Try single malt scotch," Justine said.

Ella laughed. "Okay, partner, drive. I've got some things to think through, and I'm hoping to get home before midnight."

Forty minutes later, they were inside Teeny's main room. Though surrounded by computers, the leather couch and chairs in the center were soft and comfortable. As she settled into the cushions, Ella suddenly realized how tired she was. Looking at the watch, she saw it was close to ten.

"You ladies want a cup of coffee? You look beat," Teeny said. "It's a strong Italian blend. It should give you some energy, or at least prop those eyes open a few more hours."

They both took a cup of the steaming liquid, then accepted his offer of fresh cream.

After a few minutes, Teeny spoke again. "I'm glad you two dropped by. I finally have permission to tell you who my client is, but please keep this as private as possible." Seeing them both nod, he continued. "It's Sheriff Taylor. He hired my firm because he wasn't sure who he could trust inside the department."

"I had a feeling about that," Ella said.

"Taylor's determined to avoid a scandal. This happened

on his watch, and if it doesn't get resolved quickly, it could cost him his job. He's doing his best to keep it out of the press—that is, until he has the perp in handcuffs."

Ella nodded, lost in thought. "H had lots of friends in county, people who knew and trusted him."

"That's why I assigned him the case," Teeny said, then continued. "I've got some other news, too. I did a comprehensive background check on the residents in the vicinity of where H's body was found. Truman John, it turns out, has an interesting past."

"I didn't see anything out of the ordinary," Justine said, "and the background check that was run for his teaching job showed he was clean."

"You didn't go back far enough. To find the interesting stuff, you would have had to check his family, too. Herman John, Truman's grandfather, lived just outside of Greasewood, Arizona. His neighbors thought *he* was a skinwalker, too. Then one day Herman just disappeared. Word has it that his neighbors got together, killed the old man, and buried him out in the desert."

"It's been known to happen," Ella said, remembering the story Clifford had told her. "By any chance, did that all start with a land dispute?"

Teeny nodded. "That's what I heard."

"How did you get the information? Is it reliable?" Ella asked.

He nodded. "I made time to go talk to some of our old ones, like Ely Benally, who lives over by Little Shiprock Wash."

"So, if the rumor's true, Truman may have learned about skinwalkers from his grandfather," Ella said.

"Or maybe they're both victims of gossip," Justine said.

"Yeah, and your guesses are as good as mine," he said. "The key to solving this is finding out what H was doing parked all the way out there southwest of Rattlesnake. Once you do that, I think the answers will come to you."

"This case keeps getting tougher with each passing hour. Every time it looks like something's about to break, we hit another roadblock." Ella rubbed the back of her neck with one hand. "Did you ever find any additional notes on the case, something H might have handwritten and left behind on his desk?"

He shook his head. "He kept most of the details in his head and in that little spiral notebook he carried in his shirt pocket."

"The killer took that along with everything else H had on him," Ella said. "We still haven't found any of it."

"You will," Teeny said, and poured them each a second cup of coffee. "I picked up a bit of interesting gossip. I heard that Bidtah wants you to transfer to Window Rock, so he's going to sweeten the deal by offering you a driver and transportation."

"I hadn't heard that," Ella said. "Not even a job offer."

"You still haven't. My source is a little iffy, and I haven't had the chance to verify it yet."

"Boss, transportation *and* a driver? That's big time," Justine said. "My partner is now a celebrity."

"Oh—and housing, too," Teeny said, "but I think we're talking a double-wide close to Gallup, maybe over by the Twin Arrows casino."

"Wow. Sounds like he really does want you to stay with the department, Ella," Justine said. "He's finally realizing what you're worth to the tribe."

Ella ran a hand through her hair. "I had no idea he was actually that serious. I thought he was planning to force me out and make it look like it was my decision."

"No, that's not it at all," Teeny said. "But tell me, why would you be set against moving to Window Rock?"

"Dawn," Ella said. "My kid got herself into truckloads of trouble last year, but now she's finally back on the right track. She's currently in an advanced placement program for eighth-graders, courtesy of a U.S. Department of Education grant, but the program is only offered here in Shiprock. If she works hard, once she graduates from high school, she's almost guaranteed a full college scholarship at a top school. We can't afford to pass up a chance like that."

"You could let her stay here with Rose and Herman," Teeny said.

Ella shook her head. "For four years of high school? No way. My kid—my responsibility. The best place for her is Shiprock, so that's where we'll be, job or no job."

Ella's phone rang. After glancing at the caller ID, she answered it quickly, identifying herself.

"This is O'Donnell," came the hurried reply. "I want to make a deal. I'll give you Harry Ute's killer and the people involved in the thefts over at county if you grant me immunity."

"I'd have to check that out with a prosecutor, Billy, but you might as well turn yourself in. Half the county's out looking for you now. You're not going anywhere."

"I have something you want," he insisted. "Let's trade."

"You're wasting my time. We searched your home and found Harry Ute's money clip. I'm thinking you killed him. No way you're getting off the hook that easy."

"If you found something in my home that belonged to Ute, it was planted there by the person who really killed him. I know who he is, and I can give him to you, along with all the proof you need."

"Make me believe you."

"Ute's killer is one of my regular suppliers, and he likes money clips. I'm not saying anything else unless we have a deal."

"If what you've got results in an arrest, we'll work something out—assuming *you're* not guilty of murder."

"There's no way you can pin that on me. How soon can we meet?"

"You're in a rush, I take it?"

"I'm next on the killer's list. He knows I want to cut a deal," O'Donnell said. "I can give you everything you'll need to nail him. I've kept records that'll give you the proof you're looking for, and then some. Are you ready to trade?"

"Tell me who's after you," Ella said.

"If I talk now, I'll have no leverage. Meet me with a written offer signed by the county DA, saying the charges against me will be dropped. Then I'll turn over everything you'll need to collar this guy. I'll call back in an hour."

Ella hung up and looked at Teeny, then Justine. "O'Donnell's ready to turn himself in, but he wants a deal—all the charges against him dropped. I know it's late, but we need the DA or her deputy. Any suggestions?"

"My grandfather, Judge Goodluck, has the DA's private cell phone number. I'll get things rolling," Justine said.

"Good. I want to put a face to our friend's killer," Ella said. "Then we'll bring him down."

EIGHTEEN

✖ ✖ ✖

Teeny was at his laptop when Ella's cell phone rang. "Keep him on the line and I'll try to zero in on his location," he said.

Ella picked up her phone and identified herself.

"Do you have it?" O'Donnell said.

"The DA says you'll get immunity *if* your testimony results in a conviction. That's the best I can do. Now, where do we meet?"

"Drive over to Space-4-U. It's east of the Salmon Ruins, outside Bloomfield on the north side of Highway 64. I rented a storage unit, number seven, under the name of Don Williams. Meet me there, and I'll turn over what you need."

"Just so we're clear. I'm not interested in stolen merchandise. I'm looking for a killer."

"I know, but don't worry. I have the evidence you need. Be here."

O'Donnell broke the connection, and Ella looked up at Teeny. He shook his head. "Sorry, I've got zip, not even a cell tower."

"That's okay." Ella told him where she'd be meeting Billy.

"That's outside of tribal jurisdiction. I'm backing you up," he said.

"Good. And since it's in county, I'll also call Dan in on this," Ella said, looking over at Justine. "While I'm doing that, get Blalock and tell him what's going down. He lives in Bloomfield and is a lot closer to the storage units."

It was after midnight when they set out, flashers and siren on. Their destination was forty miles across the county, but at this time of night, traffic was way down. Justine kept her eyes glued on the road. With two eastbound lanes here, they were making good time and could skirt most of Farmington by using the southern truck bypass.

"There's a possibility you need to consider," Justine said. "What if O'Donnell's the one who killed Harry, and he's planning on taking us out tonight? He could hide in the dark with a rifle and pick us off. You saw all the weapons he had in that stash. He could have easily kept a high-powered rifle with a nightscope."

"No, that's not going to happen. That man's scared spitless. He's got a killer after him," Ella said. "Right now, Billy's the only person who can ID the shooter, and that makes him a loose end."

"You couldn't get him to name the guy gunning for him?"

Ella shook her head. "He's desperate, but he's smart. He's not about to give up his only leverage. I'll have to show him the paperwork first."

"Something's coming through now," Justine said as the printer light came on.

Ella took it in hand as the device fed out the paperwork. "This is just what we need. Thank your grandfather for us."

Justine nodded. "He saved us a lot of time, but as I always say, family sticks together. That includes us. No matter how this goes down, I've got your back, cuz."

"And I've got yours," Ella said. The badger fetish at her neck was cool to the touch. So far, so good.

They arrived less than fifteen minutes later, without emergency lights or siren. Seeing Blalock's car parked off the highway on a side road a hundred yards from the storage facility, Justine pulled in behind it. Dan was there, too, in an unmarked car, parked across the highway from the Space-4-U.

As soon as Blalock climbed out of his car to join Ella and Justine, Dan crossed the highway. The two arrived together.

"How do you want to handle this?" Blalock asked Ella, standing about fifty yards from the facility, watching for activity.

"Let me go in alone," Ella said. "O'Donnell wants to surrender to me, and I don't want to spook him. The guy's already on edge, terrified of one of his suppliers, the man he says killed Harry Ute."

"Cover the parking lot," Blalock told Dan, who nodded.

Just then, a big pickup pulled up alongside them. It was Teeny. Blalock walked over to the passenger-side window and shook his head. "Bruce, I'm sorry, but this is strictly a police matter."

"I disagree. I bear some responsibility for the death of my employee, so consider me backup."

Blalock thought things over for a moment, then rather than argue, nodded. "Okay, come along, but stick with me."

Blalock and Teeny waited near the closed gate, Justine, several yards back while Ella presented her badge to the guard at the small office. With the sudden appearance of law enforcement, the armed security man seemed to have become energized despite the late hour. He opened the gate, but at Ella's insistence, remained at his post.

Ella walked into the facility and passed a pole with a surveillance camera that monitored the interior grounds. Lights on other poles directed downward helped illuminate the area and made it possible to work outside at night.

The fenced-in compound comprised two rows of flat-roofed, cinder block storage units, each sharing common walls. The garage-type overhead doors on each compartment opened into an interior area wide enough accommodate two vehicles side by side.

A pickup with a Texas license plate was parked at the far end of the enclosure near the closed back gate, and despite the fact it was nearly one in the morning, a young couple was busy unloading cardboard boxes and plastic containers into one of the units.

Ella looked at the numbers painted on each of the doors. The odd numbers were on the left. From what she could see, the door to number seven, about twenty-five yards away, was half open.

She was walking toward it when two loud blasts echoed out from its interior. A few seconds later, a third shot was fired.

Ella flattened against the closest wall, her pistol out. Hearing running footsteps behind her, she turned her head and saw Justine and Blalock, weapons in hand, holding their badges up at the camera, racing in. Teeny, also armed, followed close behind.

When no more gunfire erupted, Ella moved forward, her shoulder close to the units. She stopped beside compartment three and called out to the confused young couple who'd been caught in the open at the far end of the compound.

"We're police officers. Lie flat on the ground."

"Which unit did the shots come from?" Justine asked Ella, coming up behind her.

"Unit seven," Ella said, gesturing ahead. Just then a man sprinted out of the partially open unit, racing toward the far end.

"Stop! FBI!" Blalock yelled, his pistol up.

The figure—a man, judging from his gait—ran toward the pickup and the couple on the ground. For a second, Ella thought she'd have to risk a shot to protect them. At that distance and in the dim light, she couldn't tell if the suspect was armed or not.

Ignoring the frightened couple, the fleeing man jumped onto the bed of the pickup, then leaped up onto the twelve-foot-high chain-link fence, grabbing hold of the mesh.

"Crap!" Ella increased her speed. "He's gonna get away. Justine, call Dan to circle around and cut him off!"

The subject swung a leg over the fence, dropped to the ground, and disappeared into the darkness.

Leaving him to Dan, who was covering the outside, Ella went back to unit seven and looked inside. There was enough light coming in for her to see cardboard and wooden boxes stacked ceiling high in the small space. In the corner of the room, wedged between two rows of boxes, was

O'Donnell's body. An ever-widening pool of blood surrounded him like an unholy halo.

"I'm here," Teeny called out from behind her.

"O'Donnell's down." Ella brought out her pocket flashlight and hurried over to check for signs of life.

"All that blood—he's gone," Teeny said even before she checked the pulse point at his neck.

As Ella crouched down, she knew instinctively that Teeny was right. Although the round to O'Donnell's leg hadn't been fatal, the bullet to his forehead had been. Finding no pulse, Ella stood.

"Protect the scene," she told Teeny. "I need to have Dan call county homicide and get them out here."

Ella went outside, searching for the others, and saw Dan walking up.

"The runner got away," he said. "He had a truck parked on a dirt road on the other side of the fence. I saw the outline as he took off, but he didn't turn on the lights, so I couldn't get a read on the make or model."

Blalock came around the opposite side of the enclosure. "You checked inside the unit?" he asked, then studying her expression, added, "O'Donnell's dead, right?"

"Yeah. We need a county crime scene team here," Ella said.

"Any chance he gave you a name?" Blalock asked.

"No, he was dead when I found him," she said. "But the evidence Billy mentioned may still be here. No way he would have turned it over to his killer. I'd like to search Billy's pockets and the boxes closest to him, but I'll wait for permission from county." A little courtesy went a long ways.

"This is clearly FBI and county sheriff business now,"

Teeny said, "so I'm heading home. They'll know where to find me if they need a statement."

"Thanks for the help," Ella said. "And not just the backup."

"Anytime."

As Teeny left, Ella put on two pairs of gloves and went inside to look around. "There were two quick shots, then a third a few seconds later," Ella said, thinking out loud. "One struck the vic's leg, another the head. So where'd the third bullet go?"

"I'm thinking the killer wanted to keep Billy from escaping and went for the leg with his first shot, but missed," Blalock said. "So let's look for a thigh-high impact point. The bullet has to be here somewhere."

Ella glanced at Justine and saw the look of relief on her face as she turned away from the body and focused on the room. When it came to corpses, Justine, like her, had been raised with the rule of three—don't touch them, don't look at them, get away from them. Although as police officers they'd had to learn to overcome that urge, doing the opposite still required strength of will.

"The boxes behind the vic have been disturbed," Ella said, taking in the immediate area around the body. "Maybe he was moving those around when he was interrupted."

"If you're right, the bullet may have struck one of those boxes or the wall on the far side. Let's check it out," Blalock said.

"Any sign of shell casings?" Justine asked.

"No," Ella and Blalock replied at the same time.

They looked around carefully. Following the most likely trajectory based on the location of the body, Ella soon found a bullet embedded in the hollow concrete block wall.

"It traveled between the stacks," Ella said.

"Looks like a .38, or maybe nine-millimeter," Justine said, coming up for a closer look. "It's hard for me to tell for sure in this condition, but I'll confirm it in the lab. If it's a nine-millimeter, I'll check to see if it might have come from Harry's gun. It's still missing, so you never know."

"You're saying that Harry's killer kept the weapon and used it to kill O'Donnell?" Blalock asked, looking at Justine, then Ella.

"It's only stupid if you get caught with it," Justine said.

"With no shell casings around, though, I'm guessing this murder weapon was a .38," Ella said.

"You're probably right," Blalock said. "Okay, then, moving on—what's next? Top-to-bottom search?"

"Yeah. Once the crime scene team arrives, we need to go through all these boxes," Ella said. "I think the evidence O'Donnell was offering to trade is still here someplace."

When the sheriff's deputies arrived on the scene, along with the OMI investigator, Ella, Justine, and Blalock stood back while the newcomers unpacked their gear and set up a crime scene perimeter.

Blalock spoke to Sheriff Taylor on the phone, then joined Ella. "I'm working this crime in conjunction with county, so we have the go-ahead to search each box before it's taken away. Plan on being here the rest of the night."

Ella turned around, visually examining the storage unit. There were two small clusters of what looked like white gravel in front of the garage-type overhead door. She looked up.

"The killer came over the fence, onto the roof, then dropped down here right in front of the open door," she said, pointing to the ground. "This is gravel from the fiber-glass roofing."

"It makes sense," Justine said. "If he'd have come in via the front gate, the guard would have seen him, and had he chosen to enter by jumping over the back fence, he would have been seen by the couple working by their storage unit."

"Exactly. He took O'Donnell by surprise, and when the vic tried to run, the killer shot him to keep him from getting away. His first shot missed, but the other brought O'Donnell down. When O'Donnell refused to hand over the evidence, the killer shot him at point-blank range," Ella said. "By then, we were here, so he had to make a run for it."

"Makes sense to me," Blalock said.

"From what O'Donnell told me, the killer was someone he'd done business with, someone he said was crazy. Once the man showed up here, O'Donnell must have known that his options were limited. Protecting the evidence meant moving away from it." Ella studied the immediate area. "Look at those boxes. They've been moved recently. See how the dust and sand beneath them has been disturbed?"

Justine opened the top box. "This one has ballistic vests, all with SJCSO labels." Setting it aside, she looked inside the second box. "Office supplies in this one, everything from ink cartridges to external drives." Justine tried to push the box at the bottom out of the way to make the most use of the limited light. "It's heavy," she said, then opened it where it was. "Handcuffs and belts."

"A full box of them? Those would have been hard to steal without anyone noticing." Ella joined her and shone her flashlight inside. "Wait a sec. There's something taped to the side of the box." Ella reached in carefully and pulled

out a small flash drive. "I think this may be what we're looking for."

"If that's the backup, where's the original?" Justine said,
thinking out loud. "Let me take a closer look at the other
boxes."

Justine first emptied the box with the office supplies.
"There's an ultra-thin laptop at the very bottom, beneath a
layer of ink cartridges." Justine pulled it out, then glanced at
Ella. "No way this is surplus, it's pretty new and top of the
line. I'm guessing it was probably O'Donnell's. I could turn
it on and take a look at the files, but if they're encrypted—"

"Do what you can, but don't risk losing the data," Ella
said. "We don't know for sure that the flash drive *is* a
backup."

No one rushed Justine, and she booted up the laptop
immediately. As she worked, they searched the other containers. One was a wooden crate that had been carefully
sealed.

"There's something in here," Blalock said, calling out to
Ella. "It's nailed shut, so we're going to need something to
pry it open."

One of the crime scene people, a young Hispanic woman
in her twenties, came over. "More than a big screwdriver?"

"Oh, yeah," Blalock said.

The detective returned a moment later, holding a pry
bar. Working carefully, they were able to pull away the lid.
Inside were several Anasazi pots surrounded by a heavy
layer of packing materials. Most of the protection came from
foam peanuts and wadded-up newspaper, though there was
also some straw present.

"Can we narrow down the location of the dig site by

identifying the plant matter inside and around those pots?" Ella asked Justine.

Justine left the laptop and came over. "Not all the plants around the Rez are cataloged. We'll need an expert."

"Like Mom," Ella said. "She's spent years cataloging plants for the Plant Watchers and identifying where various species are generally found. I'll talk to her as soon as possible."

"I have access to the research she did for the tribe. It's up in a digital database, including identification keys. If I can take some of these samples to the lab, I can start working on that right away," Justine said.

"Let me get an okay from county. They're handling the evidence." Blalock moved away to speak to the ranking detective, then returned. "Take a few samples, but make sure you sign off on it, and make sure you don't lose anything."

"Did you get anywhere with the laptop?" Ella asked as Justine collected what she'd need.

"I need more time. Any chance I can take it to my lab and finish up?"

"I doubt it, but I'll ask." Blalock left to talk to the lead detective. He came back and shook his head. "No, they'll handle that at the forensic lab in Aztec."

"If they let me have a few hours with it, I could return it tomorrow morning, early."

"No, sorry," Blalock said.

Ella looked at Justine, puzzled by her insistence, but there was no time to ask her about it.

"Clah, I need your help with another crate," Blalock said.

They continued working for two more hours, but found nothing else that tied in to Harry's murder.

After checking with county and making sure she'd still be able to access the scene if necessary, Ella joined Blalock over by the crime scene van.

"I'm beat, Dwayne. Let's call it a night. With luck, we may be able to get a few hours of sleep before we have to get going again," Ella said, and waved to Justine, who was talking to one of the techs.

Blalock looked at his watch. "Yeah, I'm getting too old for this all-night crap."

Ella smiled. "That's attitude, not age."

Blalock chuckled. "Maybe so, Clah, maybe so."

Ten minutes later, Ella and Justine were on their way west toward Shiprock. "When are you planning to tell me what's going on with that laptop?" Ella said, interrupting the long silence that had settled between them.

Justine gave her a sideways look. "How did you—?"

"You have too many 'tells,' like rubbing your forehead with your index finger, or tugging at a strand of your hair. I know them all," Ella said. "What's going on?"

Justine took a long deep breath, her eyes on the road. "I've got to tell you, Ella, I've never been so tempted to delete a file in all my life."

Ella stared at Justine in surprise. "What on earth did you find?"

"A list of customers who bought Billy's stolen merchandise and the dates each sale was made. Some of it, like the construction equipment, went to legitimate buyers who are now going to take a loss and maybe face some bad publicity."

"How can people not know this stuff is illegal when the serial numbers are altered?"

Justine almost winced.

"You recognized a name among the buyers, didn't you?" Ella said, taking what she was sure was an accurate guess. She was starting to get a real bad feeling about this.

"Yeah, I did," Justine said. "E. Atcitty Construction in Shiprock."

Ella's eyes widened. *"Elroy* Atcitty?"

"I don't know of another one."

Ella stared out the window. The endless expanse of darkness matched her mood. Elroy Atcitty was Big Ed's brother.

"Gerald Bidtah has been gunning for Big Ed ever since he took over the tribal agency. If news of this gets out, the scandal and allegations could finish off the chief's career," Ella said. "If Elroy somehow manages to avoid jail time or a crippling fine, accusations will be made that Big Ed got him off. Even if Elroy goes to jail, the taint will remain, and pressure will build for Big Ed to resign."

"I thought of deleting it, I really did. But if I did that, I don't think I could have lived with myself."

"We don't withhold or hide evidence, cuz. That's not our job," Ella said.

"So what do we do next? Should we tell anyone, or just step back and let county figure things out on their own?" Justine asked.

"I'll talk to Big Ed first thing tomorrow," Ella said. "Right now it's county's business, so it's out of our hands. Don't speak about this to anyone."

"Including Blalock?" Justine asked.

Ella nodded. "For now."

NINETEEN

—— ✖ ✖ ✖ ——

Ella didn't have much to say at the breakfast table the following morning. She was still processing last night, but her daughter was talking and she realized she had to focus.

"Mom, I've been thinking of what college I'd like to go to, and there are so many choices. If I stay in the advanced placement classes, I can get a scholarship to practically anywhere," Dawn said, "not just state colleges."

"You'll know what to do when the time comes," Ella said, wondering why her daughter was in such a rush to decide. She was only fourteen, and there was lots of time.

"I wish I could be more like Bitsy. She knows *exactly* what she wants—which college and everything. She thinks we should both apply to Stanford."

"California is so far from home," Rose said.

Dawn nodded. "Sarah says that big-name colleges open more doors once you graduate, and that if I want to get into the FBI Academy, I've got to have top credentials."

Ella choked on her coffee. "You want to do *what*?"

Rose silently slipped away from the table, making herself scarce.

"Mom, I want to join the FBI just like you did. I thought of going to Cal State, since they offer a Bachelor of Science degree in criminal justice. It's supposed to be the best anywhere, but Bitsy says that a degree from a place like Stanford carries a lot more weight."

"That's true, but the impact a big-name college creates also depends on what career you choose," Ella said, still trying wrap her head around Dawn's new career plans.

"Yeah, maybe you're right. At Stanford I'm going to need a lot more financial help, too."

A car honked outside.

"Gotta go. That's Bitsy's mom. She's taking us to Durango for the day, shopping and stuff. I'll tell you all about it tonight." Dawn kissed her good-bye and rushed out.

Ella stared at the empty chair where Dawn had been sitting, then glanced at Rose as she walked back into the kitchen. "Law enforcement? Did you know about that, Mom?"

"She admires you, daughter. She wants to do what you've done—only better," Rose said, and smiled.

Ella laughed. "Yeah, that sounds like her."

Rose brought Ella a piece of fry bread and a jar of honey.

"Eat something, daughter, and tell me what's really bothering you."

Ella smiled. Her mother's favorite comfort had always been fry bread with honey. Considering that Rose's recipe for fry bread was to die for, she heartily approved.

"Now, tell me what's on your mind," Rose pressed gently.

Ella lathered honey all over the bread and ate in silence for a while. "The department's headed for some serious shake-ups, Mom," she said at last.

"I've heard that some of the tribal leaders in Window Rock want you to work down there." She gave Ella a long look. "But that's not what's worrying you, is it?"

"I can't give you any details, it's police business, but there might be some serious trouble ahead for some people at our station."

"Including you?" Rose asked.

"No, I have my own problems, but it's nothing like what's facing some others. I'm talking about having reputations ruined and careers destroyed."

"Is there anything you can do?"

Ella shook her head. "Not really."

"Then let things work out on their own. Eventually harmony will be restored."

Ella leaned back in her chair, idly glancing down at her hand. At least the cut was healed over now. "You're right," she finally said. "My focus has to remain on the case, and that brings me to a favor I'd like to ask you." She told Rose about the unidentified Anasazi pottery.

"That's somebody else's history—their property. I don't like to handle those things," Rose said.

"You won't have to, Mom, but no one knows the Plant People like you do. I need you to help my second cousin. Come down to the station and see if you can recognize the seeds and the bits of plant debris we found on the pots. That may help us figure out where those pots might have been dug up."

Rose considered it in silence, then finally nodded. "Will it be okay if I come in later this morning?"

"That'll be perfect."

Ella headed to the station. The first thing she'd have to do this morning was speak to Big Ed. Although this was a meeting she would have preferred to avoid altogether, he had to know what was going on.

She reached the station's parking lot just as Big Ed pulled into his assigned space near the front doors. She parked two rows behind him and went inside.

Seeing Big Ed striding down the hall, Ella jogged to catch up. "We need to talk, Chief."

"My office," he said with a nod.

Moments later, Ella sat across from Big Ed's desk, searching her mind for the best way to give him the news.

"What happened?" Big Ed asked. He'd stopped rocking back and forth in his chair and was leaning forward. He'd obviously picked up on her mood. "What's going on?"

Ella gave him the details. "County has the laptop in evidence, so it's only a matter of time before they find the file."

"Are you sure it was my brother's firm?" He held up a hand before she could answer. "Of course it is."

"Maybe you should ask your brother to come in and explain. It may be easier for both of you that way."

He shook his head. "No special treatment. It's up to county to follow up on this. If Elroy ends up facing charges, I'll make sure he gets a good attorney. That'll be the extent of my involvement."

Ella went to her office, got on the phone, and called in

her team. A half hour later, with everyone there, she started their briefing. By the time she finished, she could almost feel the somber cloud that had descended over all of them.

"Benny, Joe, check out E. Atcitty Construction," Ella said, "but your sole objective will be finding any possible connection to Harry's murder. The actual purchases of stolen goods aren't part of our case unless they lead to uncovering the killer. What we want is to learn the identity of the man Elroy Atcitty dealt with, if not O'Donnell. Keep in mind that if it wasn't Billy, this contact could be the same guy who killed O'Donnell—and our friend."

"Before we even leave that construction company's site, word will get out that we were questioning the chief's brother," Benny said. "Speculation will go wild, and Big Ed's critics and the local press will eat him alive."

Ella rolled her eyes. "We have no other choice. We're working a homicide investigation."

After Joe and Benny left her office, Ella looked at Justine. "You got here early, I saw your car when I pulled in. Anything new from the lab?"

"The bullet we recovered was from a .38, so that rules out Harry's weapon," Justine said.

"Okay. What about those plants?"

"I haven't been able to narrow things down much. Plants just aren't my field. I'm cross-referencing against some of the data I've got, but it's slow going. The only thing I've identified is fresh straw—kind of obvious—and that could have come from anywhere."

"You're gonna get some help soon. Mom will be coming in this morning."

"That's great news!" Justine said, brightening up almost

instantly. "I'll leave word out front and ask the desk sergeant to bring her straight to my lab."

"Take me there yourself," a familiar voice said from behind Justine.

"Hi, Aunt!" Justine said, and smiled at Rose, who had her hair down and was wearing her baggy khaki garden slacks, a long-sleeved cotton blouse, and her favorite old chambray jacket with worn cuffs and a half dozen pockets. In Rose's hand was a tablet computer Herman had bought for her on her last birthday.

"I see you brought your references," Justine said, eyeing the computer. "Let me show you the way, and we can sort things out there."

Ella watched them walk away and smiled. Justine adored Rose, and the feeling was mutual. Both would enjoy working together, and had spent several days earlier in the year scanning all her reference maps and charts into digital form, then onto the tablet so Rose could carry them out into the field.

Ella was glad that her mother had decided to help. Rose's expertise when it came to the Plant People was second to none. For years she'd worked tirelessly for the tribe, locating and identifying native plants and cataloging the ones with special medicinal uses. She'd charted the location of hundreds of plant populations, and her research had also predicted other sites where particular species might be found.

The project had been mostly a labor of love. She certainly hadn't been paid enough for the time she'd spent on the work, but Rose had performed an invaluable service for the tribe, and now that information, in digital form, could be preserved forever.

When Ella went to answer her ringing phone, she was surprised to hear Gerald Bidtah on the other end.

"Investigator Clah, I'm planning to be in Shiprock and I'd like to meet with you this morning. Will you be available?" Bidtah asked.

"No, sir. We're at a critical point in a double homicide investigation and we've just uncovered an important lead."

"Your people can't follow it up for you?" he snapped.

"As lead investigator, I handle certain aspects myself. It's even more so in a complicated case like this one."

"Harry Ute's murder?"

"Yes, sir. And another victim just last night."

"Stay on the trail, then. You've done excellent work coordinating federal, county, and tribal law enforcement, Clah," Bidtah said. "I know that you've undoubtedly heard about the restructuring within the department, but rest assured your future is secure. Your experience is invaluable to us."

"Thank you, sir."

"Make good choices, Investigator Clah, and the sky's the limit."

"Yes, sir," Ella said, her voice strained. What she really wanted to do was hang up on the sanctimonious prick.

"Call me as soon as you can free up an hour in your schedule. We need to talk about your future with the department."

"Yes, sir." Ella placed the receiver down and swallowed back her distaste.

Maybe once Harry's murder was solved, she'd have a

better feel for what her next step should be. Until then, she had work to do. Ella hurried to her partner's office and found Justine and Rose seated beside the large central counter. Her mom was wearing gloves, probably a double set.

"Seeds plus this tiny fragment tell me all I need to know. In Navajo, that plant is called *Ch'il lizhini*. It means 'black plant,' but most just call it blackbrush. Look at the stem. It's a distinctive dark gray. The leaves were a dull green once, and those long spurs eventually become thorns," Rose said. "It's one of the few plants without any recorded medicinal or ceremonial use. It grows around sand dunes, and helps stabilize them."

"Mom, do you know if it's a species that's prevalent in any areas right around here?" Ella asked, joining them.

Rose took a deep breath. "The closest one I know of is around Little Wash, west of Rattlesnake," she said. "I'm sure there are some other sites in that general area, too. Wind distributes the seeds."

"We really appreciate your help," Justine said. "Can you give us a list of other places around the Four Corners where it can be found?"

"I'll have to look that up for you once I get home and have a chance to check my notes," Rose said. "But remember that the Plant People like to move around, and they settle where they will. No one can tell them where they should go."

Rose picked up her purse and Ella walked her mom back to her pickup.

"I'll get you that information as soon as I can," Rose said.

"Thanks, Mom."

After Rose drove off, Ella hurried back inside, where Justine was waiting. "Where's the rest of our team?"

"Joe and Benny are at E. Atcitty Construction," Justine said. "Ralph broke a tooth eating piñon nuts on break, so he's off at the dentist's."

"So it's just you and me," Ella said. "Little Wash isn't far from where we found Harry's body. Let's go over there. We have to take a closer look around and check for disturbed earth, tool marks, or tracks. If an illegal dig is taking place in the area, maybe that's at least part of the reason Harry was killed."

"An illegal dig, skinwalkers, murder . . . It doesn't get any worse than that."

"I sure wish you hadn't said that," Ella muttered.

By the time they arrived at the edge of Little Wash, Ella could see how tense Justine had grown. "What's up, partner?"

"It's the feel of this place. There's evil out here, partner. We've seen the evidence of skinwalkers for ourselves."

"Fear is one of their most valuable weapons, cuz. If you refuse to be afraid of them, they lose their power over you. Stay strong."

Justine turned off the path and parked. There, on ground zero, they began a careful search for the plant Rose had identified. Little Wash was a long, meandering arroyo that ran for several miles. Their plan was to search the sandy areas along the perimeter of the arroyo first.

After ten minutes of searching fruitlessly, Justine glanced at Ella. "I'm going up that rise to get a better view of the entire area. From there, I'll look for clusters of blackbrush."

"I'll stick to lower ground and check out places where runoff collects," Ella answered, continuing to work.

Ella worked north to south, and reaching a section between two low hills, saw Mrs. Yazzie's sheep grazing nearby. Mrs. Yazzie, Norman's grandmother, stood in the shade beneath a tall juniper with her dog and waved. "If you're going to be working here, I'll take them back to their pen," she called out.

Ella jogged over to talk to her. "Do you come out this way often?"

Mrs. Yazzie nodded. "I like eating lunch on that hollowed-out rock over there. It's cool and I can keep watch over my sheep," she said, pointing. "You're not looking for more bodies, are you?" Her eyes were widening with fear.

"No, just a species of native plant," Ella answered quickly. "The locals call it blackbrush or black plant. Do you know it?"

She shrugged. "Not really. I don't pay attention to all of the Plant People, just the kinds that can harm my sheep, like broom snakeweed. It's one of our Life Medicines—good for people, but bad for livestock. At least my flock has always had the good sense to avoid it." She looked up at the sky. "It's time for me to move them on. That way they won't overgraze."

Mrs. Yazzie said good-bye, then, with the assistance of her nondescript-looking but well-trained dog, began herding her sheep in the general direction of her home, visible in the distance.

Ella quickly turned her attention back to work. Glancing around, she saw the hollowed-out rock Mrs. Yazzie had mentioned. As she walked over to check it out, something on the ground caught her eye.

On a flat layer of sandstone beneath a low overhang was a small ash painting. She had a feeling it had been placed there for the express purpose of scaring Mrs. Yazzie. It was a good thing she hadn't come here today.

"Justine," she called out.

Her partner jogged over, followed Ella's line of sight, and stopped about six feet away. "What's that doing *here*? Are skinwalkers after Mrs. Yazzie now?"

"That's the way it looks to me," Ella said. "I'm going to call my brother. I want him to see this firsthand."

Ella pulled out her cell phone, but unable to reach Clifford, was forced to leave a message instead. "He knows it's urgent," she told Justine, "so hopefully he'll call me back soon."

"There's something that looks like a little medicine bag over there, on top of that flat rock," Justine said, pointing with her chin.

Ella circled toward that high spot, searching the ground for footprints along the way but finding none. "That's not a regular leather pouch. From the looks of it, I think it's made from the skin of a horned toad. It's one of their calling cards."

"There are other things here," Justine said, going over and studying what was on the ground. "It's a bunch of human hair, like the tangle you'd pull from a hairbrush, weighed down with a rock. And there are nail clippings, too."

"Try to get a DNA match on those," Ella said. "Skinwalkers steal personal things like those and use them to cast spells to make their victims suffer and die."

Justine shuddered.

"It's just somebody's hair and nails," Ella said. "Stay focused, cuz." As her phone rang, Ella glanced at the caller ID and saw that it was Clifford.

Ella described the scene to him, then waited for her brother to comment, but there was only silence at the other end. "Did you get all that?" she asked. "I can send photos to your cell."

"I'd rather see the display in person, and frankly, I don't want this kind of evil showing up in my cell phone gallery. These things, if they are real, have power of their own, and my family uses this phone sometimes. Humor me on this, okay?"

"Okay. But so far, what's your take on this, brother?"

"From your description, I've got to say it sounds like the real deal, but I've never seen those signs and displays all in one place," he said at last. "I'll come over and take a look, but in the meantime, don't touch anything with your bare hands. You need to watch for contamination with datura, poison ivy, and other dangerous plants. Some of those are particularly nasty if inhaled, so don't go sniffing around, either, trying to pinpoint a scent that may seem peculiar to you."

"Good to know, brother."

"I'll be there in about forty minutes," he said.

Ella joined Justine. "My brother's coming to take a look."

"As soon as we can, we should talk to Truman," Justine said, taking photos of the drypainting from different angles. "He's Navajo, a social studies teacher, teaches Navajo culture, and he's probably a skilled researcher as well. He may be our man."

"I agree. The teacher's been out of work for months, yet

still seems to be prospering. If he's found a way to make some extra money, like working an illegal dig and selling the artifacts to O'Donnell, he might have decided to use fear to keep others away from his site."

"But then why not take credit and let people think he's a skinwalker?" Justine asked.

"Remember what happened to his grandfather? He probably wants to make sure he stays in control—in other words, undiscovered. He doesn't want to end up dead."

"One thing—there's no way our friend came across this drypainting," Justine said, avoiding Harry's name now that they were so close to where he'd died. "It rained Tuesday, the day he was killed, and Wednesday it was windy and dusty. Like the other things we've seen recently, even the tracks at the crime scene, this display was created at least a day or two *after* the murder."

Ella studied it and nodded. "If our friend was killed by a skinwalker protecting an illegal dig that would tie in to Billy O'Donnell, too, the man marketing the artifacts. Billy must have put things together when our friend turned up dead, but figured it was to his advantage to keep his mouth shut. Then when we caught Billy with the illegal pots and stuff, he knew the only way to avoid jail time was to identify his source. The skinwalker knew that, too, so he killed Billy, the only person who could identify him."

"I'm also thinking along those lines, partner," Justine said.

"The problem is that in order to prove any of this, we need more than a theory. My gut tells me that our best bet is to identify the mystery 'hooker' who picked up our friend at that bar," Ella said. "She's tied to the killer. Otherwise, the timing of that 'date,' the missing laptop, and H's murder are way too coincidental."

"We looked into Alice Cisco's background, but ruled her out despite her resemblance to the woman in the sketch," Justine said.

"Yes, but we never considered Eileen, who's older and appears to be a die-hard New Traditionalist. Would she do whatever Truman asked without question? We need to get Eileen's prints, not Alice's, and compare those with the ones on the belt buckle."

Justine nodded. "A wig and makeup can make for an amazing transformation. Give her a halter top and a push-up bra, and most men wouldn't spend much time looking at her face."

"Once my brother gets a chance to check things out here, we'll turn the scene over to other officers. They can continue the search. You and I need to go over to Teeny's and use his special software."

TWENTY

✕ ✕ ✕

Since Benny and Joe were still busy at E. Atcitty Construction, Ella recruited Victoria Bitsillie and asked her to provide a team to search the area for signs of a dig.

Ella called Teeny next and described what she needed. He assured her he'd have something for her by the time she arrived at his compound.

Ella didn't have to wait long for the first of the search team to arrive. Though it was her off-duty day, Victoria came within twenty minutes of Ella's call. Four other officers also arrived on scene minutes later.

Victoria fastened a small medicine pouch to her belt, then put on two sets of gloves. "My ad hoc team will search for signs of a dig, but tell me again about the evidence of evil you found."

"There's an ash drypainting around that hollowed-out rock," Ella said, and pointed.

"Okay." Victoria glanced down at the pouch on Ella's

waist. "When you called, you mentioned that your brother was on his way?"

Ella nodded. "He should be here anytime now," she said, then warned her about Frenzy Witchcraft plants.

"I'll tell everyone. My team will also need special protection. Maybe your brother could provide the officers with medicine pouches? Under the circumstances, I'm sure the department would compensate him."

"If I know my brother, he'll be bringing extra medicine pouches with him for whoever needs one."

"Good." Victoria glanced around, studying the area. "How far out do you want us to search?"

Ella told her the areas she and Justine had already searched, then described the plant her mother had identified. "If you find any of those plants, search the adjacent areas very carefully. Beyond that, use whatever strategy works for the team."

"I'm acquainted with blackbrush. My *shimasání* used to call it useless brush," Victoria said with a smile. "She's a Plant Watcher, too."

"Maybe she knows my mom," Ella said.

Victoria shook her head. *"Bi adin doo holo da—bi,"* she said.

"I'm sorry," Ella said, understanding from her words that Victoria's grandmother had passed away. There was no direct way in Navajo to say that a person had died. The word *adin,* which was used to describe death, meant the absence of everything. Translated, what Victoria had said was that her grandmother didn't exist anymore.

"My *shimasání* sounds a lot like your mother. She knew the land and lived in harmony with it," Victoria said, then walked away to join her team.

Hearing the familiar sound of her brother's big truck, Ella turned her head. Like a giant ATV, it could go practically anywhere on the Navajo Nation, even places where roads were scarce.

Clifford, wearing the white headband that identified him as a *hataalii*, climbed out of the four-wheel-drive vehicle and looked around.

"Sister," he said, coming over carrying a small cardboard box. "I've brought some medicine pouches for anyone who might need them."

"Good. I've already been asked about that," she said, then waved at Victoria.

"I know her," Clifford said, and smiled. "Her great-uncle taught me to be a *hataalii*."

"She never mentioned that," Ella said.

"Uncle," Victoria said, walking up and greeting Clifford. "It's good to see you here." She looked down at the box. "Are those for our officers?"

"Yes, feel free to hand them out."

"Thank you, uncle. Four of my people are unprepared for this kind of danger."

"Have you already seen the drypainting my sister found?" he asked, handing her the box.

Victoria shook her head. "This time I have a different job."

As Victoria walked away with the medicine bags, Ella looked at her brother. "What did she mean by 'this time'? Have you worked with her before?"

"It was ten or twelve years ago, I think. Her great-uncle over by Teece Nos Pos asked for my help. Three skinwalkers had staked out their territory, and people were being witched. When I arrived, I saw he'd brought her along to help."

"Why? That's no place for a kid, and she must have been my daughter's age back then."

"It surprised me, too, until I saw her work. That woman has a very special gift." He gazed at Victoria, then looked back at Ella. "I'm a *hataalii*, a Singer, and my power comes from the Songs and the knowledge I've acquired through the years. Hers is a divine gift. She's a stargazer."

"You mean a diagnostician, like a hand-trembler?"

"No, not like that. She has the ability to gaze into a rock crystal and find things that are missing." He paused. "Her abilities are . . . remarkable."

Her brother never handed out praise easily, so his words surprised her. "Does she work as a stargazer when she's off duty?"

He shook his head. "According to my teacher, to develop her talent, she would have had to apprentice with one who's like her. Unfortunately, like many of our young people, she won't even acknowledge that the gift is hers."

"Why?"

"I'm not sure, but I do know her older brother is a pastor at a very conservative Christian church in Farmington. He preaches that her gift is a mark of the devil. Maybe that has something to do with the choices she's made."

Ella watched Victoria, a consummate professional, direct the officer in a methodical search pattern. Ella had a feeling that little escaped her careful gaze.

"It looks to me like she's reconciled who she is with the ways of the future and the needs of our tribe. I admire her for that."

Ella led Clifford to the drypainting and watched as her brother crouched down and studied it closely.

"Some of the details of the drypainting aren't quite right, but the one who made this may have been in a hurry," he said.

Ella showed him the horned toad pouch, the hair, and the nail clippings.

Clifford looked at the evidence, then gazed at Victoria for a few seconds before going over to talk to her. Ella followed.

"I need to ask you a question," Clifford told Victoria. "Are those the only places the evil one marked?" he said, pointing with his lips to where the drypainting and the other items lay.

"Uncle, I don't know. I'm only here to search for signs of a dig."

"Look within yourself," he insisted. "Are those the only places?"

Victoria stared at the stretch band bracelet on her wrist. It was made of small rock crystals strung together.

"I believe so," she said at last. "The drypainting alone must have taken a lot of time, and he wouldn't have wanted to linger out here in the open any longer that absolutely necessary. This one likes being invisible."

Victoria looked at Ella quickly. "That's just cultural knowledge and logic, nothing more."

As Victoria returned to her work, Clifford walked away, shaking his head. "She may want to believe that, but deep down she knows the truth."

Splitting up, Ella continued the search while Clifford spoke to each of the officers, offering encouragement and, when needed, reciting prayers of protection. After about an hour, he went back to his truck.

"I'm leaving now," he told Ella as she came over. "I have patients I need to see."

"Let me know if you hear of this kind of activity anywhere else on the Rez."

"Of course."

As he drove off, Justine came up, cell phone in hand. "I just spoke to Benny. He and Joe are back at the station. They brought Big Ed's brother in for questioning, no arrest or cuffs, and Elroy drove himself. Benny found the missing county property at the construction company's site. Elroy claims he didn't know the merchandise was stolen, and he does have at least something to back up his claim. Someone glued on metal tags with phony serial numbers over the originals, and you couldn't tell without scraping them loose."

"This is still going to weigh heavily on Big Ed. No matter how you get around it, the stuff *was* stolen. Is the press or media on to the story yet?" Ella asked.

"Joe said no, but Benny thinks it's just a matter of time. He's got that Los Angeles big-city perspective when it comes to bad publicity and news cycles."

"This isn't L.A., but I agree with Benny," Ella said in a heavy voice. "Bad news travels a lot faster than good. Let's get over to Teeny's before it all hits the fan. We'll leave the scene to Victoria and her crew."

By the time they arrived at Teeny's doorstep, he already had what they needed. "I took the sketch county had circulated and altered it by minimizing the woman's make-up and adding long hair to the image. Come see what I've got."

Ella followed Teeny inside, and as she did, the rich aroma of cinnamon and baking bread filled her senses.

"I made cinnamon rolls. They're cooling right now," Teeny said. "Once you take a look at this new sketch, come try some."

"You really should open your own restaurant," Ella said with a happy sigh. "You'd be a millionaire in no time."

"Cooking is something I do because I enjoy it. I don't want it to ever become a business for me. I love to eat, in case you can't tell, and if others like what I cook, too, that's just a plus."

Moments later, Ella sat in front of Teeny's computer and studied the image on the monitor. "That could be Eileen Tahoe, but I'm not one hundred percent sure. Can we find a photo of Eileen and work backwards, giving her short hair and heavy makeup, and see what we come up with?"

"Is she from this area?" Teeny asked.

"She went to Chinle High," Justine said. "I did a quick background search on her, and their Web site has tons of alumni photos. She's got to have at least one photo online."

It didn't take Teeny long to find a suitable photo. "Okay, here we go. Let's give Eileen more pronounced eye makeup, then go with short, close-cropped hair like in the sketch," he said.

After several minutes, he waved Ella toward the screen. "Here's what I got—close, but not identical."

Ella studied the altered photo. "Let's take this to the Horny Toad and show it to the bartenders and waitresses."

"Right now?" Justine asked.

"*After* we have one of Teeny's rolls," Ella said with a smile.

"Good call," Teeny said, chuckling. "You'll still catch some of the lunch crowd."

Ella and Justine left thirty minutes later. It was nearly one in the afternoon.

"I'm going to call Dan, that's his jurisdiction," Ella said.

"And you'd love a chance to see him."

"Cousin, it's *business*," Ella said.

"Yeah, yeah, but admit it. The man's pure eye candy. I was invited to the county's gym a few weeks back. Sergeant Emily Marquez, my old roommate, stopped by and asked me to go with her. When we got there, we ran into Dan, who was busy working the heavy bag. He was hot and sweaty, stripped to the waist with his six-pack on display, and whooee!"

Ella laughed. "So you've been checking out my boyfriend?"

"What can I say? You can't blame a girl for looking. That guy's ripped—hot."

"That he is, partner." Ella said, smiling.

By the time Justine pulled into the parking lot in front of the tavern, Dan was already there, standing beside his pickup. He wore dark slacks and a Western shirt, with a light Western-cut jacket that covered his badge and gun.

They met at the entrance. "There's still a good lunch crowd inside, judging from the nearly full parking lot," Dan said. "Do you have the sketch you told me about on the phone?"

Ella handed a copy to him. "The similarity is there, but I'm still not convinced we've got the same person."

"Let's see what kind of reaction we get," Dan said.

They went inside and spoke to as many patrons as they could, but no one could help. Seeing a bartender he knew, Dan went with Ella to talk to him. Meanwhile, Justine decided to question several women wearing ID badges from a nearby company. All were seated at a corner table.

The bartender looked at the image for several seconds. "I'm almost certain I've served her before. I was working a split shift the last night Harry was here, and she may have been the one with him, but I can't say for sure."

Disappointed, Ella and Dan joined Justine. "I've got nothing," Justine said in a sour voice.

"What we got is inconclusive. We need to check this out with the regular evening staff and clientele," Ella said. "We also need to find a way to get Eileen's fingerprints without letting her know what we're doing. She's not on file anywhere. Justine checked."

"You'd like a match to the partials on the belt buckle?" Dan asked.

"Yeah, exactly," Ella said, then added, "I know where Eileen works. If we could get something she's handled—"

"Where *does* she work?" Dan asked.

"The Little Bear Café in Beclabito," she said.

"That's your jurisdiction, not mine," Dan said. "But she's met you, right?"

Ella nodded, "And Justine, too."

"Sheriff Taylor will loan me out to your department for this, no problem. I'm already dressed in civilian clothes, so I'll drive up there and find a way to get her prints."

"Sounds good to me," Ella said, "but do you think you can do it without tipping her off?"

"Oh yeah," he said easily. "I'll make it happen."

"Thanks. We appreciate it," Ella said.

He nodded once, then walked off.

Ella watched him for a second longer, then heard Justine laugh.

"You're checking out his butt," Justine said.

"You're crazy."

"Yeah, maybe, but I'm also right," Justine said, getting back into the SUV. "And for what it's worth, so was I."

"Head to the station. I want you to fast-track the DNA on the hair and nail samples we found at the skinwalker site," Ella said. "If that person is the next target . . ."

Justine nodded. "I'll ask Blalock to process them at the FBI lab in Albuquerque. The New Mexico State crime lab is always backed up and will take weeks. I'll let you know when we can expect results."

Ella returned to her office a short time later. Carolyn's postmortem report on Harry Ute's death was on her desk, but it held little she didn't already know.

Ella leaned back in her chair and took a deep breath. Harry's death had hit her a lot harder than she'd expected. It wasn't just the manner of his death, but the randomness of it that bothered her. Harry had woken up one morning, gone to work, and never returned to those he loved.

She thought of her daughter and her family. They were more important to her than anything else in the world. Yet everything was changing at home, and before she knew it, Dawn would be going off to college. If she wanted to spend more time with her family while they were all still together, it was now or never.

Ella shook free of her musings and forced her mind

back on work. She was busy filling out reports when her cell phone rang. Hearing Dan's voice, she smiled. She didn't even have to ask if he'd succeeded. His upbeat tone as he'd greeted her had said it all.

"Done deal," he said, "and she never caught on. I pocketed a water glass she handled, then processed it in my truck. No one saw me. I'm sending the print photo over to you now."

"Send it directly to Justine. She's in her lab and will process it right away. Are you coming in?"

"Yeah, I've been asked by Sheriff Taylor to brief Big Ed."

"See you then," Ella said, then hung up.

Big Ed walked inside her office a second later. "Jaime Beyale of the *Diné Times* just called. They found out what happened to my brother, and so did most of the regional media. A camera crew from one of the television stations is coming over, too. I'll have to issue a statement."

"You can't be held responsible for what your brother does or doesn't do," Ella said.

"Not legally, no, but the media is always looking for some way to stir things up, and this will play right into the hands of my . . . enemies," he said, sounding tired. "Circumstantially, the case against Elroy is strong—his wife has cancer, and he's been hit with a lot of overwhelming bills. It'll be easy to argue that he knowingly purchased stolen merchandise in order to cut corners."

"The DA will still have to prove that," Ella said.

"Yes, but in the interim, Elroy will have legal fees to deal with on top of the growing stack of bills on his desk. He'll also have to return the merchandise he purchased. That means he'll forfeit the money he laid out at the same time that he'll lose the machine itself. Worst of all, this is going to damage his company's reputation when he can least afford to lose clients."

"Is there anything I can do to help?" Ella asked, hating feeling helpless.

"No, it's better if you stand back. If you tell reporters that my brother isn't getting any special treatment, they'll jump on that idea and hint that maybe the exact opposite is true."

"Yeah, I know how the media sometimes 'creates' the news," she said softly.

"Just give them a blank expression and a 'no comment.' They won't like it, but they can't put a spin on a nonanswer."

As Ella watched her boss walk back out into the hall, a heavy feeling fell over her. Big Ed had worked hard for the tribe all his life, but there was really no way for him to fight and win a situation like this. The whole thing stank.

She hadn't been working at her computer for long when Dan knocked and came in. "Have you been able to match that fingerprint yet?"

Ella looked up at the clock and realized that forty minutes had passed since she last spoke to him. "No, but Justine should have finished running it by now. Let's see what she's got," she said, and led the way down the hall.

As they entered the small lab/office, they found Justine sitting by her computer at the far side of the room, staring at the screen.

"Partner, what's going on?" Ella said.

Justine jumped, startled. "I didn't even hear you come in!"

"You must have really been concentrating," Ella said.

Justine rubbed her forehead with her forefinger, then met Ella's gaze. "Sit down. I have something I need to tell you."

"About the fingerprint on our friend's belt?" Ella asked, curious about Justine's reaction.

Justine shook her head. "Sorry, I didn't get to it yet. I got sidetracked by something more important—at least to me. I was going to go to your office just as soon as I found a way to . . ."

"To what?" Ella pressed, losing patience.

"I was studying the hair and nail clippings we found at the skinwalker's site. Since DNA takes a long time, even when the FBI gives it top priority, I decided to identify the nail polish and see where that might lead. It was Peach Surprise."

Ella felt her chest tighten. That was her daughter's favorite color. "Go on."

"Next I looked at the hair. The color told me nothing. Black's too common. So I followed my gut," she said, and swallowed hard. "I had a strand of Dawn's hair cataloged in the computer. Remember when she was working on her science project last year and I showed her all the ways hair can be classified—pigmentation, cross section, et cetera?"

"What are you telling me?" Ella said, almost losing her voice.

"I don't have the DNA results yet, but I'm almost ready to conclude that the nail clippings and the hair belong to Dawn."

TWENTY-ONE
——— ✖ ✖ ✖ ———

Anger rose inside Ella until she couldn't stop shaking. "That SOB is targeting my kid?" Her jaw clenched. "It wasn't enough to threaten me and my home. He now wants me to know that he's got my kid in his sights."

"The question you need answered quickly, is how he got that stuff," Dan said.

"It must have happened the day he snuck over to my house to put that calcified animal jaw in my truck. While he was there, I bet he decided to help himself to our trash. I remember Mom had told Dawn to clean her bathroom and that means emptying the trash, too." Ella's hands balled into fists. "No matter what it takes, this piece of walking garbage is going down."

"I've got your back on this—whatever you need," Dan said.

"Me, too," Justine said. "Do you want me to pass this along to the rest of our team?"

"Yes. I'm also going to talk to Big Ed," Ella said, then turned to look at Dan. "Can you stick around for a few minutes?"

"You bet."

Ella walked down the hall and knocked on Big Ed's open office door. He waved her in and wordlessly invited her to take a seat as he finished a telephone conversation. While she was waiting, she texted Dawn, at her friend's house, and told her to avoid strangers. Dawn got the message, because she texted Ella back with "im safe luv u."

Placing the phone down after a moment, Big Ed focused on Ella, who'd just put away her phone. "I got a heads-up from Jaime at the *Diné Times.* Reporters will be here shortly."

"Do you want me with you when you make your statement?"

He shook his head. "I'll handle it. Besides, we come across as more professional when our investigators are actively investigating, not fielding questions from the press. Now, tell me, what brings you to my office?"

She told him what Justine had found. "I want to request that an officer be sent to protect my family in addition to the ones already patrolling the area."

He nodded. "It'll have to be officers willing to work during their off-hours. Right now we're strained to the limit. With all the cutbacks, we've lost too many patrolmen, and the ones who are left are working overtime in this latest crisis."

"I know," Ella said, and cleared her throat. "If the department can't provide what I need, then I'll hire Bruce Little's people."

"*No,*" Big Ed said. "You're one of ours, and we handle threats to our own. I'll get what you need even if I have to call officers back from vacation. You'll have someone at your home within the hour, and I'll have my secretary set up a schedule, starting with volunteers first."

"My daughter's at her friend's house. Can someone pick her up there and take her home?"

"Yes. Give me the address," he responded, sliding a piece of memo paper across the desk.

"Thanks, boss," Ella said, writing it down, then standing.

"Don't let this skinwalker business distract you, Shorty. I think that's precisely what he's trying to do. If he'd really wanted to harm your family, he would have done so already. He's trying to keep you busy looking over your shoulder instead of hunting him down."

"I don't fear him. The guy is just annoying."

"That also works against you. Once he clouds your thinking, he wins."

"You're right. Thanks, Chief."

Ella returned to her office and found Dan waiting.

"Did you get the additional protection for your family?" Dan asked.

"Yeah, but with all the cutbacks in personnel, it'll be hard finding enough officers."

"Once word gets out, you'll have no end of volunteers. Cops take care of their own," Dan said. "County deputies, too," he added.

She nodded, knowing it was true. "If I ever see this skin-walker scumbag around my place, I may shoot first and worry about it later."

"If he's wearing an animal skin, no one would convict

you, not here on our land. He may not realize it, but he's made himself some dangerous enemies by going after an officer's kid."

"Yeah, I hear you," she said. "When he left that animal jaw in my truck, he was threatening *me*. I didn't like the fact that he got close to my home, but I was clearly his target. Now, since I haven't backed off, I guess he decided to move things up a notch and threaten my kid." She paused, trying hard to stay calm. "Big mistake."

"Are you going to tell Dawn about this?"

"I've got no other choice. I've already texted her to be alert, and someone is going to escort her home from her friend's house. I'm going to have to restrict her to the house, which means I'll have to give her the reason."

"Do you think she can handle it?"

"Probably better than me. We've been through these kinds of things before. My mother and brother will help her, too—and Herman. He was there for me even before we were family."

Hearing a light knock at the door, she looked behind Dan and saw Victoria standing there.

"What's going on?" Ella said, nodding for her to come inside.

"Big Ed told everyone in the bullpen what happened. Most of the officers have already volunteered to be part of the protection detail whenever they're off duty, including me. I'll be at your house tomorrow morning. Four-hour shifts are being set up through the chief's office. One person will be inside the house at all times and another on the grounds, watching the perimeter. We'll keep it up until you arrest the suspect."

Ella hadn't expected support to come so quickly and found herself almost speechless. "Thank you," she managed at last.

Victoria shook her head. "No thanks are necessary. When something like this happens, we all stand together—as a tribe and a department."

After Victoria left, Dan stood and gave Ella a smile. "She's right on both counts. I'll be volunteering my time, too. In fact, I intend to stop by your house once I leave here and stick around until I'm relieved. I'll call Sheriff Taylor and fill him in."

"Thanks. I really appreciate it." This was what she'd miss most once she retired. Police officers were a brotherhood, particularly here, where their culture, as well as the badge they wore, united them. If one was threatened, they all were.

Just then Ella's phone rang. Seeing on the display that it was Joe Neskahi, she picked it up, waving her hand for Dan to stick around. The first thing she heard were gunshots in the background. "What's happening, Joe?" she asked quickly.

"Benny and I are taking rifle fire from what appears to be a single gunman," he said, his voice low. A few more seconds went by, accompanied by heavy breathing.

"Had to change positions," Joe said. "We're still okay."

"Roger that. Report on the situation."

"We were working the other side of the hill, north of the skinwalker drypainting, when we saw a sedan parked on the road about fifty yards to our left. We decided to go talk to the driver, but before we got there, he jumped out holding a rifle and started shooting. We took cover."

There was another gunshot. Two more followed, and those sounded much louder. Return fire, Ella guessed.

"Our vehicle was just put out of commission—took one to the radiator, and it's spraying antifreeze like a steam engine—so we're not going anywhere," Joe said. "The shooter has taken cover on the roadbed beside his vehicle, but he's trapped, too. Even if he manages to get back in the car, he can't drive off without crossing open ground. If he tries, his vehicle will be shot full of holes, and he knows it."

"Wait him out. Is backup on the way?" Ella asked.

"Negative. None available."

"We'll be there in fifteen," Ella said. "I'll call when we're close." She looked over at Dan, who'd been listening intently. "Shots fired—Joe and Benny need backup and I can use some help. Do you have a vest in your car?"

He nodded. "I'll be right behind you."

Ella gathered up Justine from the lab, then brushed past two reporters in the parking lot, ignoring their questions. Five minutes later, they sped by Shiprock High and the Phil, the concert hall just to the west. After that, Highway 64 stretched out before them.

Dan remained right behind, his county cruiser easily keeping pace with their big Chevy Suburban. Once Justine turned south onto the dirt road, Dan allowed the distance between them to grow so he could avoid the spray of gravel they left in their wake.

Ella decided not to use the radio to contact Joe and Benny, suspecting the disabled unit had been turned off, and the radio wouldn't be powered up. Instead, she called

Neskahi on the cell phone. "We're closing in from the highway," she said as soon as Joe answered. "You two okay?"

"Yeah. He's stopped firing for the moment. Maybe he's out of ammo."

"Don't count on it. Stay put. He may be waiting for you to break cover. We're coming in two vehicles and will split up before we reach you. Stay on the line, and we'll come up with a plan on the fly."

Five minutes later, she spotted the disabled white department vehicle, and Neskahi's stocky shape behind the engine block, shotgun in hand.

Ella looked around for Benny. Seeing him lying prone a few feet to Joe's left, her heart nearly froze. Then she saw movement as Benny turned back to look.

"We'll go a hundred yards past Joe's vehicle and take up firing positions," she told Dan via the radio. "I want you to stop about fifty yards short of his unit, then get set up to give us some cover fire. We'll flank the shooter, force him to reveal his location, then make our move, pinning him down while others advance."

" '-four," Dan said.

"Hear that, Joe?" Ella said over her cell phone.

"Copy," he replied.

Justine raced past Benny and Joe's position, then stopped abruptly, raising a cloud of dust. She slid out, then covered Ella as she jumped out the same side and retrieved the assault rifle from behind the seat.

Ella took a firing position over the hood as Justine took the assault rifle and dropped down prone beside the rear tire.

With Justine in firing position, Ella crouched low and inched around to the front of the SUV.

"You get a location on the shooter?" Ella asked Joe via cell phone.

"Yeah. While you were exiting the SUV, he ran into the brush. He's now about a hundred yards west of his vehicle. I think there's an arroyo over there—like a trench network running roughly north and south. He shifts positions after each shot. There's another person with him now. That subject was already in the arroyo area, and he joined him or her. So far, though, we've seen only one gun, and there hasn't been any cover fire from that location."

"React like there are two weapons, just in case. I'm going to circle around the south flank while Dan takes the north. Justine will provide cover fire. How you doing on ammo?"

"Shotgun is topped off and we've both got a full magazine, so when he starts shooting again, we can help pin him down. The shooter has a rifle—bolt action, I think. Benny said he heard him working the bolt. That gives him five shots before he needs to reload. If he's got only one box of reloads, he can't have more than ten rounds left."

Ella contacted Dan and relayed the information, then moved forward in a crouch, zigzagging, pistol out, and using the brush to screen herself. Dan was also on the move, but no shots were fired.

Three minutes later, she discovered a four-foot-deep arroyo at the base of a slope. It ran northeast-southwest—a trench, of sorts, as Neskahi had predicted.

Ella jumped in and stayed low, checking for tracks. While she searched, Dan's voice came in over her handheld radio.

"No tracks in my direction. I can see the arroyo to my left. Nobody in sight," he said.

"Keep watch. I'm down inside. I plan to follow the arroyo south, in your general direction. If anyone's head pops up, let me know."

Ella worked her way along the natural ditch, carefully checking around each curve and blind spot before moving on. Finally she saw fresh tracks in the damp earth ahead. The side of the bank had caved in slightly, suggesting this was where the gunman and his companion had either entered or exited the arroyo.

As she got closer, she saw a small shovel, one of the folding ex-GI designs, on the ground beside a hole about a foot deep. Scattered nearby on the ground were several brass rifle casings, along with a maze of tracks. To her left, a fork in the arroyo led west. There were two sets of tracks leading off in that direction.

"I'm rising up to take a look. Hold your fire," Ella said over the radio, then her cell phone. She paused a few seconds, then stood and took a look west. The suspects had run in that direction, sticking to the arroyo.

A second look at the tracks revealed one set was larger than the other—a man and a woman's, probably. Beyond the casings, in Dan's direction, there were no footprints at all.

Crouching down again, Ella spoke to Neskahi first. "The second subject must have been here when you arrived, digging up something. From the looks of the hole, it wasn't buried too deep, nor was it bigger than, say, a basketball. They left the shovel here and took off west down a fork in the arroyo. I'm going to follow from within the arroyo. Advance in this direction, but do it in stages with someone keeping watch in case they try to circle or stand up to take a long shot."

She contacted Dan and Justine next. Dan moved west from his position, guarding her flanks, while Justine kept watch with her assault rifle scope. Ten minutes later, Ella came to the end of the trail. The tracks disappeared as the arroyo opened up onto a gravel-littered wash at least fifty feet wide.

Ahead was higher ground punctuated by deep arroyos originating below a broad mesa, then beyond were the piñon- and juniper-covered foothills. Above that were steep canyons leading up the mountains and into Arizona.

Ella hurried back to the others, meeting them at the junction in the arroyo. "From their tracks, we've probably got a man and woman. I lost their trail in the rocks, but it looks like they're heading west. There are two routes leading toward that last mesa just before the foothills, but unless we figure out which one, we could lose them for hours."

"What we need now is a helicopter—or an old school Indian tracker," Justine said.

"Well, we can forget the helicopter, but my brother's still the best tracker around, and the tribe has used him before. Let me get permission to call Clifford in." Ella dialed Big Ed and gave him a quick update of the situation.

"I'll call your brother and make the request myself," Big Ed said. "He's already been contacted about the threat to your family, so he's already up to speed on some of this. In the meantime, I'm pulling in officers from the Arizona side to watch the road junctions in case they manage to find transportation. Let's box these suspects in before it gets dark and they disappear completely."

Ella hung up and updated Justine. "Judging from the size of the footprints, I'm guessing that we're chasing down Truman and Eileen."

"Maybe she made me after all," Dan said, joining them.

"Let me call the Little Bear Café. If she's still there, we may be looking for the wrong pair." Ella stepped away to make the call, then returned. "She took off about two hours ago, probably to warn Truman. It must have been right after you were there, Dan. My guess is they decided we were getting too close, but before making a run for it, stopped to dig up something they considered important. When Benny and Joe made them, they must have panicked."

"I wonder what was so important that they'd risk coming back here for it," Justine said.

"Money? Our friend's weapon? Who knows?" Ella said. Hearing her phone ring, she looked at the display. It was Ralph Tache.

"The dentist is finished with me. I'm ready to come back to work," he said, his words slurred. "Where do you need me?"

"You sure you're up to this?"

"Yeah. I can't drink water without drooling on myself, but I'm clearheaded."

"Okay, get a warrant to search Truman John's residence and property. Then meet Joe at Truman's. He'll need backup. Search the place for Native American artifacts, anything connected to the county thefts and Billy O'Donnell, or our friend's murder. We still haven't recovered his gun, notebook, or cell phone."

"On it."

"If you want me to go over there," Joe said, having overheard, "I'll need the keys to your SUV. My vehicle is shot—literally."

"I can't afford to be stranded," Ella said, then looked at Dan. "Can Joe catch a ride with you?"

"Sure. I'll drop him by the station, or stick with him, whatever's needed."

"Sounds like a plan," Joe said. "Anything else?"

"Yeah, make sure you wait for the warrant before you go inside. Do everything by the book. We don't want this getting thrown out of court," Ella said. "And, Dan, thanks for the backup."

"Gotcha. Keep me in the loop."

As Neskahi and Dan headed back to the road, Benny stepped up.

"Where do you need me, Ella?" Benny asked.

"You're the best tracker here, and there's no sense in wasting daylight. Let's start from where I lost them. Maybe you can pick up something I missed."

"Let me walk ahead of you, then. Give me a good thirty feet. I'll work across the wash, back and forth, and search for their trail."

Ella nodded and watched Benny move out ahead of them. "Stop often and randomly, and look around, Benny. I'd rather risk losing their trail than walk into an ambush."

"For sure," Benny said, moving up the wash.

Five minutes later, he stopped and pointed to a long ridge of sandstone bedrock along the center of the shallow wash.

Ella stood rock-still, waiting, then hearing a faint noise to her left, slowly lowered her hand to her weapon.

"Relax, it's me," Clifford said, his voice barely audible as he jumped down into the wash and into full view. "Your boss told me all I needed to know."

Ella and Justine followed Clifford as he walked toward Benny, deer rifle slung over his right shoulder. Her brother was wearing a greenish brown jacket and tan slacks—his hunting clothes, minus the bright orange vest. As usual, she hadn't heard him approach until the last second. He could be as silent as Wind when he wanted to be.

Benny greeted Clifford with a nod as Clifford walked ahead of him for several feet, searching the ground and brush along the perimeter of the wash. After a minute, Clifford stopped.

"We're going in the right direction?" Benny asked.

"Yes, you are," Clifford said, "but they left the wash. They stepped into the middle of those bushes to hide their tracks, but they pick up again over by the tree," he said, pointing Navajo style by pursing his lips. "They're moving southwest."

"Stay in the lead, brother," Ella said. "Benny, stay focused on possible hiding places and look for signs of ambush. Justine, hang back and cover our six. I'll keep an eye on our flanks."

They set out again. After several minutes, the footprints led them west through a maze of rock formations ranging from house-sized outcrops to weathered sandstone towers fifty feet high or more. Though massive, these were mere infants compared to those east of the Cortez Highway or the towering giants of Monument Valley.

Despite the difficulty of tracking anyone over hard ground, Clifford never lost the trail, finding scuffs or recently overturned rocks still slightly darkened on one side due to moisture differences.

Soon they came across an old ceremonial hogan standing about twenty-five yards from a single-wide trailer home. From there, a rutted pair of tire tracks led downslope toward a dirt road about a quarter mile away.

Among a stand of junipers was a log corral made of rel-atively straight lengths of cottonwood. Inside were two well-muscled, shaggy horses and a half dozen churro sheep browsing for any errant plant debris or blade of grass.

A sturdy-looking loafing shed provided shelter for a stack of dry-looking hay just past the enclosure and out of the extended reach of the horses.

"There's an old man in the shade over there," Benny said, pointing with his chin.

"He's got a rifle," Ella said.

"He's not our man," Clifford said. "Wrong shoes and too short for the stride of the tallest . . . what do you call him, subject?"

"More like killer," Justine said, her hand on her pistol.

"This man must have seen our suspects," Ella said. "Scatter and keep alert while I go ask."

"Wait, sister. Let him make the first move."

Ella nodded. Judging by the presence of a hogan and the lack of a television antenna or a telephone line, this man was probably a Traditionalist. She stood still, looking in the man's general direction, but not making eye contact.

The man soon waved, motioning her forward.

Ella approached, brushing her jacket aside casually to reveal her badge. "Good afternoon, uncle," she said, greet-ing him with appropriate respect.

The man nodded, propped his Winchester against a fence rail, then waved her closer. She was almost to his per-sonal space when he held up his hand. She stopped, still not making eye contact.

"The *yee naaldlooshii* and his woman walked down that trail," he whispered, pursing his lips toward the path.

Ella recognized the term for "skinwalker." Literally, it meant someone who walks on four feet. The stories about Truman had traveled all the way out here.

"His grandfather was evil, and now him. That family's got bad blood. Need an extra gun?" he asked.

"Thank you, uncle, but no. Stay here and protect your home," Ella said. "How long ago did they pass?"

"No more than five minutes ago."

"Did they see you, uncle?"

He shook his head. "It's good that you brought the *hataalii* and extra protection," he said, looking down at the medicine pouch on her belt.

"What's down that trail?" Ella asked.

"My brother and his wife make their home just beyond that rise. His son and family are visiting today, so I've warned them to be careful. My brother has his rifle loaded and ready in case they get close to his home or try to steal one of their trucks," he said. "The trail the evil ones took means they'll have to walk two miles before they get there, but there's a shorter way. Through there." He pointed to a narrow passage between the rocks. "If you hurry, you can get there first."

"Thanks, uncle," Ella said. "Keep watch in case they turn back. Okay?"

He picked up his rifle again. "If they come near my home or truck, it'll be the last thing they ever do."

Ella told the rest of her team what she'd learned as they headed toward the cutoff. "They're close, so let's split up. Benny and Justine, stay on their trail in case they decide to backtrack. Clifford and I will try to outflank them. Be sharp, and if you spot anyone, use your radio and call in."

Ella turned to her brother. She'd already decided that Clifford needed to stick with her from this point on. She knew him better than the others did, which made tactical sense. Besides that, with him being a civilian, she also knew it was her job as leader to take responsibility for his actions. "We may have a gun battle on our hands after we catch up to them. Are you up to this?"

Clifford removed the rifle from his shoulder and switched off the safety with a flick of his thumb. "Lead the way, sister."

They were family, and she hadn't really expected anything less from him. By threatening Dawn, Clifford's only niece, the skinwalker had made yet another dangerous enemy.

Clifford found the trail quickly, a narrow path worn to a soft dust by foot traffic. The ground muffled their steps, so she picked up the pace to a jog.

It didn't take long to get the lay of the coming terrain. Their shortcut rose up a steep hill, while Justine and Benny's made a more leisurely circle, an easier hike but considerably longer. Beyond was another low mesa, and from the gentle curl of smoke rising from the far side of a grove of fruit trees, the home of the old man's brother and his wife.

For a second, she wondered how exactly the old man had warned his brother of approaching danger. There were no phones lines that she could see.

Figuring that would be answered later, Ella concentrated on her breathing, covering ground quickly. It was possible that once Truman and Eileen realized they were trapped, they'd try taking hostages. The possibility sent a chill through her and remained in the back of her mind as she pressed on.

Ella went to a prone position as she drew closer to the top of the ridge and looked down on the single-wide trailer below. Clifford crawled up beside her, well aware of the need to avoid being seen.

Nobody was in sight, but there were two pickups parked in front of the hogan. On a wooden table beneath a shaded porch, she could see a satellite telephone receiver. That explained how the old man warned his brother. Neither was quite so traditional after all.

"Why didn't the family just drive off once they knew?" Ella whispered.

"Some people refuse to leave their home when danger is close," Clifford whispered back.

Ella nodded. "Good point. Who's that behind the pickup?" From that position, the people there were hidden from anyone coming up the other trail.

Clifford raised his rifle, looking through the scope. "Looks like we're too late. There's a girl, maybe sixteen. Crouched down beside her is a woman in her twenties or early thirties, wearing some kind of waitress uniform. Farther to the right, there's a man with a rifle."

"Let me take a look." Ella shifted her position slightly and Clifford flipped on the safety before handing her the weapon. A quick look was all Ella needed. Though she couldn't see the face of the man with the rifle, she knew who it had to be. Eileen was the waitress, and she had the girl by the arm, refusing to let her go, though the teen was struggling.

"They've got a hostage, but where's the rest of the girl's family?" Ella asked, straining to see. Nothing was more powerful than a mother's need to protect her child. So where was this girl's mom? Not knowing meant big trouble.

Clifford crawled to another position, then stared intently for a moment. "A man is just inside the trailer. He has a rifle aimed at the pickup through the open door. It looks like a standoff," he whispered.

"We've got to act now before things get worse," Ella said, verifying what he'd seen using the scope. "If we go around the trailer, we can catch the perps from behind. That'll also give Benny and Justine time to close in from the other side." She switched on the radio and updated Justine quickly. "Watch yourselves," she said at last.

Ella handed Clifford his rifle, and, covering each other, they circled left and inched silently down the hill, using the terrain to screen themselves from below. Ella moved quietly, yet in comparison to her brother, she sounded like a herd of stampeding elephants.

Behind the trailer were several peach trees, low and heavy with green, immature fruit. Their approach from that direction would be well screened by branches.

They were at a critical point, moving from cover to cover, knowing that if the hostage-takers happened to turn around and look up onto the hillside, they could be spotted. Suddenly there was a shout.

"Stay where you are—or I'll kill the girl," a man said, looking up the trail Justine and Benny had taken.

"Truman John," Ella confirmed in a whisper, crouching low. Following Truman's gaze, she saw Justine duck behind a boulder about the size of a dishwasher. Benny would be close by.

"Time to move, sister," Clifford said.

Slipping downhill while Truman remained focused on the others, they reached the ceremonial hogan to the right of the trailer. The six-sided structure was made of stucco and construction-grade timbers rather than the traditional notched logs. Tactically speaking, she would have preferred thick logs right now.

She held up her hand and stopped. Clifford got down on one knee a few yards away. Justine was yelling at Truman, ordering him to release the girl and put down his weapon.

Clifford got Ella's attention. "Our cousin knows we're here now. The officer with her saw us circling around. He nodded when I looked through the scope at him."

"Okay, then. Let's take advantage of the diversion and close in. Stay low. I'll take him out the first opportunity I get. Switch weapons with me," she said, bringing out her pistol.

Clifford nodded. "I'm not so good with a pistol, but if you're going to target the man, the rifle is more accurate. You sure you want to do this?"

"It's my responsibility. I can live with it, brother."

"And the fact that he's threatened your daughter isn't going to weigh on your decisions at all?"

"I'm here to do a job, and my first priority is the hostage."

Truman had threatened her child, and she wouldn't mourn his death if it came to that, but neither anger nor revenge could play a part in what she had to do. The weight of the badge at her waist helped her focus. Rational thought and training had to prevail now, not emotion.

She handed him her pistol, butt first. "Just aim and squeeze the trigger. You've got fifteen rounds."

He thumbed on the safety, then handed her the rifle, a bolt-action Remington .30-.06 with a Weaver scope. "It's dead on at two hundred yards."

Ella switched off the safety. "Let's go."

Justine kept up a steady one-way dialogue. Truman hadn't responded yet, but the distraction kept him focused on her. Where Eileen was looking was anyone's guess, but hopefully she wouldn't glance back over her shoulder.

They crept to within thirty yards of the pickup, and from there, Ella finally had a clear shot. She took a kneeling position beside the trunk of a peach tree and raised the rifle. She used the scope to find Truman and placed the crosshairs on the right side of his head. He was standing, his hunting rifle resting on the hood and aimed up the trail. A pistol was tucked into his belt, and it looked like the same model and caliber as Harry's missing weapon. Maybe that was what they'd dug up in the arroyo. She could also see a revolver on the running board. It looked like a Smith & Wesson, probably the .38 used to kill O'Donnell.

Moving the scope, she checked out Eileen, who was sitting on the running board of the pickup, her hand gripping the forearm of the teenager—their prisoner. Truman's girlfriend didn't appear to be armed. All things considered, deciding who looked more terrified, Eileen or the girl, was a tough call.

Truman was the real threat. If she took Truman out, that would solve the immediate problem and probably end the hostage situation. The man was a multiple murderer, and innocent lives were at stake.

The easy answer was to just squeeze the trigger. Yet, as tempted as she was to use lethal force, there was the chance, however slim, that Justine could talk him into giving up. Her job was to protect—not to judge. If they brought Truman in alive, they'd also be able to get answers that they might never find otherwise.

As she was trying to decide what her next move should be, she heard someone calling out from the top of the hillside to her right.

"Let the girl go, or I'll kill you where you stand."

Ella turned her head and saw that it was the old man who'd given them directions here. He'd obviously come up the same trail as she and Clifford. He was now down on one knee, his rifle aimed in the direction of the pickup.

Ella quickly considered her options. Even if he was an expert shot, from his position, and over open sights, the old man could easily end up hitting the hostage. She had to act now. Ella focused, her finger on the trigger, crosshairs of the scope on Truman's head.

"You can't get away, Mr. John, and there's no reason for you to die out here today," Justine called out to him. "Nobody will shoot if you put down your weapon, and there's no death penalty in this state. If you let the hostage go, you'll also keep Eileen from getting hurt. She's stood by you all this time. Are you really willing to risk her life?"

Truman looked back at Eileen. "Go!" he yelled at her.

Eileen stood there frozen for several seconds, finally nodded, then took the young girl's hand.

"The women are coming out. Don't shoot!" Truman yelled, looking up at the old man with the rifle, then back toward Justine and Benny.

Eileen led the girl out, then gently pushed her away from her and toward the trailer. The girl raced to the door, was grabbed by someone there, and quickly pulled inside.

Eileen put her hands up.

"Walk toward me!" Justine called out.

Eileen walked across the yard toward the sound of Justine's voice.

While Eileen was still walking, Truman backed away from the pickup, turned, and ran straight toward Ella.

"Stop! Down on the ground!" Ella yelled at Truman, taking aim.

Seeing her and Clifford for the first time, Truman reached for the pistol at his belt.

"No, don't do it!" Ella called out to him.

Truman smiled, then moved his hand away from the butt of the gun.

"Okay, Clah. You win—this time. I give up."

Ella stepped away from the tree trunk, rifle still aimed at Truman's chest. "Hands out, away from your body. Get down on your knees," she said just as the badger fetish at her throat became scalding hot.

In a lightning draw, Truman grabbed the pistol from his belt and shot from the hip.

Though punched hard in the chest, Ella fired, then staggered back, nearly dropping the rifle.

Truman stared at her, shock in his eyes as he reached down with his free hand, groping toward the two bullet holes only inches from each other. Blood quickly turned his shirt crimson, and life faded from his eyes as he pitched forward onto the ground.

Realizing that her brother had fired as well, she turned

to look at Clifford. He was staring blankly at the skinwalk-er's body. After a moment, he slowly lowered the pistol to his side.

"You okay?" she called out to him, still struggling to breathe.

"Yes," came the one-word response.

Pain shot through her, dulling her other senses. The round Truman fired had been stopped by her vest, but it still felt as if she'd been kicked by a horse. She focused on breathing, but could do so only in short gasps.

Clifford rushed to her side as she dropped to her knees. "Are you hit?"

"Vest," she managed. "Hurts."

"You'll be fine," he said, and smiled, realizing the bullet hadn't penetrated.

"Give me a hand up," she said. Her ribs felt like they were on fire, but she'd live, which was more than could be said for Truman.

"If you don't need me here anymore, I'm going back," Clifford said.

"You'll have to give us a statement," Ella said.

"I'll meet you at the station later."

"I'll need my pistol back, and I'll also have to keep your rifle for a while. The lab . . . ," she said, and had to fight for air again.

"Take it easy," he said, and waited. Once she nodded, signaling that she was okay, he gave her back her pistol. "Take care of yourself," he said, then walked back toward the trail.

She understood his hurry. He didn't want to linger around the body a second longer than was necessary. The

chindi of a man like Truman would be particularly dangerous. Although she was going against procedure by letting
Clifford leave, she doubted she'd be disciplined for it. Clifford would honor his word and come to the station to wrap
things up later today.

Justine arrived just then, and looked at her with con-
cern. "I saw you take a hit. You okay?"

"Yeah, vest stopped it," she said.

"Eileen went a little crazy when she saw Truman go
down, but she's not resisting now," Justine said. "Benny's
going to turn her over to the first patrol officer to arrive and
let him take her to the station for booking."

"And the hostage? The girl?"

"Apparently she's fine—terrified but okay. The family's
already packing up. They refuse to stay here, until a *hataalii*
can come out to do a blessing."

"They can't go until we take their statements," Ella said
firmly. "I trust my brother to go to the station later, but there
was a hostage situation here, and we need to get the details
of what happened from the new residents. What we can do
is offer to take them to the station and question them there."

"I told them essentially the same thing," Justine said.
"I don't know if you've noticed yet, but the gun the suspect
had looks just like our friend's old Glock. It even has the
same grips. I'll double-check ballistics when I'm back in the
lab and run the serial number, but I think it's the same one."

Soon they began working the area, taking photos and
carefully documenting all the evidence. Since Ralph and Joe
were at Truman's, looking for more evidence, the job at this
crime scene fell to Justine, Ella, and Benny.

The ME arrived forty minutes later after almost getting

stuck in the sand. Ella, who'd been helping interview the witnesses and victim, excused herself and went to talk to Carolyn, who climbed out of her vehicle, still shaking her head.

"It should be open and shut this time," Ella said.

Carolyn walked over to the body and crouched beside it. "Two bullets to the chest. That's your COD right there."

Ella waited while Carolyn conducted her preliminary examination.

After several minutes, Carolyn finally looked up. "Both rounds penetrated his heart, one almost dead center."

Ella remained silent. For now, she wouldn't ask which round had done that, her brother's or her own.

Just then her radio crackled. "It's Joe," Neskahi's voice came over clearly. "I think you better get over here. Ralph's found something you're going to want to see."

"Copy that." Ella saw Justine talking to the family, and hurried over. "I'm needed at the suspect's residence," she said, avoiding the use of names.

"Go. A patrol car is on the way. I'll catch a ride back to the station with them," Justine said, gesturing to the family, then tossing Ella the SUV's keys.

Fortunately, the old man who'd directed them to their current location volunteered to give Ella a ride back to where the Suburban was parked.

Forty minutes later, when Ella arrived at Truman's, she saw Joe searching the grounds. She was just getting out of the SUV when another large SUV pulled up.

Ella waited, ready to run interference in case it was a civilian. To her surprise, Victoria Bitsillie emerged a second later.

She hurried over and joined Ella. "Dan Nez is at your house right now. I was going to relieve him, but I heard from dispatch that the man who threatened your family is now dead, and you were en route to search the subject's home. I figured I would be of more use to you here."

"Thanks. I'd like you to focus on anything that might lead us to a hidden dig site, and the location of more Native American artifacts," Ella said.

Joe came over and smiled at both of them. "We've found a few things that you'll both find interesting. Ralph's already inside. Come join us."

"Lead the way," Ella said.

TWENTY-TWO

—— ✖ ✖ ✖ ——

Joe, wearing a single pair of gloves, opened the flaps of a large cardboard box containing very old pottery, carefully packed in straw, foam peanuts, and Bubble Wrap. "The pots have traces of that purple fountain grass Truman used to landscape some of his yard. That tells me that he either packed this up outside or the dig's really close by."

"Why would he bring those back here from another location, then pack them up outside the house? That doesn't make sense," Ella said. "The dig's got to be here somewhere."

"If there's a dig around here, we haven't found any sign of it," Ralph said. "The house is constructed on a concrete slab and the crawl space is just that, barely. There's a landscaped backyard, a horse corral, a loafing shed full of straw bales, a vegetable garden, and the fence."

Ella gave Victoria a speculative glance.

"Uh-uh," Victoria said. "I know what you're thinking,

and you're way off base. People think I'm some kind of seer, but I'm just a trained cop with an eye for detail."

Unsure, Ella said nothing. When she was Victoria's age, she'd also dismissed anything she couldn't prove, often labeling it superstition. Yet her many years on the Rez had shown her a different truth.

Ralph cleared his throat. "Let's go back outside and search again. We can consider this building ground zero and work outward."

"Sounds like a plan," Ella said.

After thirty minutes, Justine and the others who'd worked the earlier crime scene came to join the search at Truman's. Another ninety minutes passed, and although they found two shallow holes that had been freshly dug, those appeared to be the result of someone taking fill dirt to place elsewhere. The dig site, if it really was close by, still remained a mystery.

Justine came up to Ella, who was looking around the front yard one last time before leaving for the station to question Eileen.

"You really need to push Eileen, Ella. She's been living with the guy. She must know the location of the dig," Justine said.

Victoria, who'd been looking around the driveway, joined them. "For what it's worth, ladies, I think what we're looking for is right here on the property somewhere. We're just overlooking it."

"Gut feeling?" Ella asked.

"Yeah, but it's one based on the evidence we have, like the purple fountain grass we found inside the boxed Anasazi pots. That plant isn't native to our area."

Ella nodded. "Yeah, makes sense."

"You're leaving to question the girlfriend?" Victoria asked.

"Yeah. Blalock will probably take the lead and I'll follow up."

"I took a training course in reading body language and learned to spot small tells. I may be of use to you there," Victoria said.

"Good. Follow us back to the station," Ella said.

Ella and Justine arrived just ahead of Victoria. As they went inside, Ella saw Blalock standing in the hallway next to the one-way glass, watching the suspect inside the interrogation room.

Seeing Ella, he greeted her with a wave. "Hey, Supergirl. Heard you deflected another bullet today."

"Good thing for Kevlar and instinctive body-mass shots. How's our girl reacting to captivity?"

"She's nervous and way out of her element, so I think she can be pushed," Blalock said. "If we let her know that she's going to serve hard time as an accomplice to murder, I think she'll cooperate."

"Don't underestimate her." Victoria, who'd come up behind Ella, spoke as she watched the woman. "She's more composed than she appears to be. Look at her more closely. Yes, her eyes are darting around and she's hugging herself, but she's handling her fear. She's not pacing, she's just waiting, knowing she's probably being watched. That's a woman with a plan. She's made up her mind what she's going to do next, and now she's biding her time."

"Dwayne, let me go in alone, at least at first," Ella said.

"We need to establish a line of communication, and for that to happen, she has to lower her guard. The fact that she and I are both Navajo, and women, may help me loosen her up."

"Then go for it," Blalock said.

Ella went inside, and instead of sitting across the desk, she sat on the empty chair beside the prisoner. "I'm going to give it to you straight, Eileen," Ella said. "As it stands now, the evidence says you're an accomplice to murder, but I've got a feeling that you just followed Truman's lead. At first you looked the other way, then things escalated and one day you realized you were in way over your head."

Eileen nodded. "That's exactly what happened," she said, almost eagerly. "I fell in love with Truman. We moved in together, and at first things were great. Then he lost his teaching job and everything changed. He was angry all the time and started fighting with Norman and Mrs. Yazzie. He really hated them."

"How did the skinwalker thing get started?"

"The Yazzies kept provoking Truman, cutting across his land, letting sheep get into my garden, and creating ruts with tire tracks that turned into ditches every time it rained," Eileen said. "That's when Truman got the idea. I warned him that it was dangerous, but Truman said he'd stay in control and wouldn't let it get out of hand."

"So what went wrong?"

"Norman found out. He came over one day and said that unless we moved out, he'd tell everyone that Truman was a skinwalker. Truman refused to leave, so things got worse after that," she said, then in a whisper-thin voice added, "Truman never figured out how Norman knew it was him."

"But you did, because you were the one who told Norman," Ella said, taking a guess.

"Yeah, but it was an accident, I swear. Norman got angry with me at the café one day when I got some lunch orders mixed up. He really lit into me, so I told him to back off or I'd tell the skinwalker to witch him. I never actually said it was Truman, but after that, he knew."

"So things went even further downhill," Ella said, and saw her nod. "Tell me about today. Start with why you left work early."

"When that good-looking Navajo guy came into the diner, I saw the badge on his belt. He wasn't tribal because it was a star, like the deputies wear, so I didn't worry about it," she said. "I served him and because he was nice to look at, I watched him through the little window in the kitchen door. That's when I saw him switching water glasses and putting the one I'd touched into his jacket pocket. I'd seen that on *CSI*, so I knew what he was doing. I called Truman right away, and he told me to come home as soon as I could."

"Truman used you to do his dirty work, so you knew that the net would close in on both of you once we had your fingerprints." Ella's voice was soft as she pressed Eileen.

"No, that's not really true. I'm still not sure why you needed my fingerprints."

"We lifted a partial from Harry Ute's silver belt buckle, the big rodeo one. Truman got you involved, sure, but you're now in this up to your eyeballs. You've got to give me something so I can help you, Eileen. Without that, you're going to be an old woman before you're ever out of prison."

Ella had placed no particular inflection on her words, and maybe that's what ended up scaring Eileen most.

She sat up in the chair and stared at Ella, wide-eyed. "But that's crazy! I never hurt anyone! Even when we were on the run, he kept all three guns."

"I'll need more than that, Eileen. Give me something substantial, then we can make a deal."

"I don't know what to tell you," she said, almost in tears. "Truman killed the private investigator. Did you know that?"

"And you had no part in that?"

"I told you, I never hurt anyone!"

"Tell me what you know," Ella said.

"The day the PI was killed, Billy O'Donnell came over. I heard him warn Truman that the Navajo ex-cop they'd spoken about before was closing in on their operation. Truman decided to check out O'Donnell's story and found the PI staking out the road leading to the house. I went to work after that. It wasn't until I got home that evening that I found out what happened," she said, and shuddered.

Ella gave her a moment to compose herself. "And?"

"It was horrible. Truman told me that he'd gone back with his rifle and shot the PI. He said he gave him time to bleed out, and once he was dead, he took all the man's things, including his gun. He also did things to him . . . with a knife and bolt cutters. He wanted to make it look like the work of a skinwalker." Eileen's hands began to tremble and she clasped them together so tightly, her knuckles turned white.

"You weren't there?"

Eileen shook her head. "No, I told you. I was at work. That'll prove I had nothing to do with that," she said. "Truman also told me that he'd used the man's keys to get into his apartment and steal his computer and flash drives. He wanted to make sure there was nothing that could lead back to him."

"So what happened to the things he stole, including the laptop computer and drives?"

"Truman destroyed them as much as he could with a hammer, then threw the pieces into the river."

"The gun, too?"

"No, Truman thought he might need that someday, so we drove over to that arroyo, put it in two layers of plastic bags along with an extra magazine of bullets, and he buried them. That's what I was digging up today when those two cops showed up. Truman had gone back to the car, so I hid in the arroyo when the shooting started. When you showed up, he ran over to where I was. We didn't know what was going down, but we figured we better make a run for it."

"You still haven't given me any proof," Ella said. "I'm trying to help you, Eileen, but you've got to give me something I can take to the DA."

She considered it for a moment. "I've got videos on my phone that show some of Truman's meetings with O'Donnell," she said at last. "I also recorded Truman telling me about the PI's death, though he didn't know I was doing that. The phone was in my purse at the time, so the words are muffled. But I can fill in a lot of the details."

"Why did you videotape and record all that?" Ella asked. "Were you trying to get back at him for something?"

"No, but I was afraid he'd leave me, and I wanted something that would force him to stay. I'd always thought I could make him fall in love with me again, but when he asked me to sleep with that detective, I realized I was just fooling myself. No man would ever tell the woman he loved to have sex with another guy."

"Why did he want you to hook up with Harry?" Ella asked.

"I was supposed to find out how much he knew. But I didn't get anywhere. I tried to get him to lower his guard and mess around—that's how my prints got on his belt buckle—but he wasn't interested. I don't think he trusted me."

Ella bit back a smile. That was Harry. When he was working a case, nothing else was allowed to interfere, no matter how tempting, and he always had good instincts about people.

"So where has Truman been getting all the Anasazi stuff? Digging it up? Buying it from someone?"

Eileen stayed very still and stared at the floor. "I don't know. He wouldn't tell me. I followed him one time, but he saw me and got really mad. That was the only time he threatened to hit me."

Ella knew she was lying and was about to confront her when Justine came in and whispered in Ella's ear.

"We found her phone. There's nothing there," Justine said.

Ella glared at Eileen as Justine left the room. "You've lied to me, so I'm finished with you. My team checked your phone, and there's nothing in the memory. Good luck in prison."

"Wait. I wasn't talking about the one in my purse," she said quickly. "To make sure Truman never found out what I was doing, I had two identical phones. Truman snooped through my phone from time to time to see who I talked to and what I was doing, so I hid the one with the stuff I needed."

"Where's that phone?"

"It's in my locker at the Little Bear Café. Check it out. You'll see."

"You still haven't told me why Truman killed O'Donnell with that revolver," Ella said, letting Eileen assume she already knew that's what had happened. "Did O'Donnell figure out that Truman had killed the PI?"

"Yeah, and he was using that to pressure Truman into giving him a better deal on the Anasazi stuff," Eileen said. "It was a standoff until Truman spoke to one of Billy's cashiers, Cassie something. She told him that Billy was in trouble with the police."

"Truman was worried that Billy would sell him out," Ella suggested.

"Oh, yeah. He drove to Billy's house to find out what was going on. Billy said he was going to cut off his ankle bracelet, get rid of the evidence, then turn himself in. He promised to keep Truman out of it, but Truman wanted his pots back. Billy said that they'd all been sold, but Truman didn't believe him. He followed Billy to his stash and shot him. Before he could search the place, you guys showed up, so he had to take off."

Ella said nothing for several long moments, then spoke slowly and deliberately. "You know exactly where the dig is, Eileen." Ella stood and, with one hand on the back of Eileen's chair, leaned over, invading her personal space. "So why are you still playing games with me, mixing in lies with the truth?"

Eileen remained rock-still. "I've cooperated completely and told you everything I know. Now I want a tribal lawyer. I'm not saying another word."

Ella met Victoria out in the hall. "What do you think?"

"She remained calm when you got in her face. That much control tells me she's holding back," Victoria said. "She knows exactly where the dig is."

Ella stared at the floor for a second, gathering her thoughts, then looked directly at Victoria. "My brother said that you have a remarkable gift."

Victoria quickly held up one hand. "Don't go there, Ella. I'm a good observer, and my police training is a real asset to any investigation. If you're willing to accept my help on that basis, I'll go back to Truman John's home and help you find that dig site."

"All right. Let's do it."

Blalock, standing by the coffee machine, waved them over. "There's nothing more we can do here until the tribal attorney arrives. Coffee, my treat?"

"Instead of coffee, why don't you join us at Truman's home and help us search? I'm convinced the dig is there," Ella said, then looked at Justine, who was jogging over.

"Got some good news," Justine said. "The patrolman we sent to the Little Bear Café found a phone in Eileen's locker. He's bringing it in along with the rest of the locker contents, including a red wig and some sexy clothes. His words, not mine."

"No surprise. Stay here and check out the phone, Justine. We need to know if Eileen was lying about the recording and the video. As soon as you know, call me," Ella said.

By the time they arrived at the site, they were running out of daylight. With luck, they'd have another hour, maybe a little more, before they'd need floodlights.

"Okay, everyone. Search the ground for new vegetation or plants that are different from the ones growing in the surrounding area. Keep your eyes open and trust your instincts."

"It's not here," Blalock said after thirty minutes. "I think this is one secret Truman may take to his grave."

Victoria shook her head. "It's here." She stood completely still, facing away from the house.

As Ella waited, she saw Victoria playing absently with something in her hand. Curious, Ella watched for a second longer and caught a glimpse of the rock crystal bracelet that was now in Victoria's palm. She wasn't gazing at it; she was just holding it, as an Anglo might a good luck charm.

Victoria smiled slowly, then turned to look at the property. "There's one place we haven't looked. I bet it's there."

Ella glanced around. "What are you talking about? We've looked everywhere."

"No, not really." Victoria pointed to the sixty or more bales of straw that had been stacked on large wooden pallets inside the loafing shed. "He doesn't have animals that might use the straw for bedding, and his landscaping barely makes use of one bale. Although he's used straw for packing before, that amounts to maybe one more bale. So why does he have a stack that size, and why use pallets to keep them off the ground? They're on a high spot, so it's not a drainage issue."

"Maybe he intends on reselling them off-season and making a little profit," Blalock said.

"Alfalfa, maybe; straw, I don't think so," Victoria said. "I'm guessing those bales are there to cover up something."

"Doesn't make much sense to me," Blalock said. "Each time he wanted to excavate and search for artifacts, he would have had to move those bales. That's a lot of hard work. Those pallets aren't on rollers, and he doesn't have a forklift to shuffle them around."

"Okay, if we assume he's hiding something below the pallets, here's another idea. What if he's booby-trapped the bales?" Ella said. "This guy was a game player—for keeps."

"We'll keep an eye out, just in case, but there's no way we're moving those fifty-plus bales without some extra muscle. Call in reinforcements," Blalock said.

Ella put out the call, then got hold of Big Ed and updated him. Once she hung up, she turned to the others. "Before we waste more energy on speculation, let's take a closer look at the bales and the area around them. Maybe we can find something that'll tell us if we're on the right track. And keep a sharp eye out for anything that doesn't look right, like a trip wire or a pressure plate. I suggest we start with the corner pallet least visible from the road, then check every corner pallet before working toward the center of the stack. If it were me hiding something I needed easy access to, I'd put it around the perimeter of the stack."

It wasn't long before Philip and Michael Cloud, who'd been off duty, arrived to help out. Ella worked alongside them while Tache, their explosives expert, checked out each bale on the corner pallet before they removed it. Several of the officers had horses of their own and were used to handling bales of alfalfa or grass. They found these straw bales lighter than expected and easier to move, which led to them breaking a few open to look inside, just in case.

When they got down to the last two bales on the first pallet, Ella saw the wooden platform wobble slightly.

"Hold it, guys," she said.

Working together, Blalock and Ella carefully lifted the two remaining bales and tipped the pallet on end.

"It scraped something solid underneath," Ella said, reaching down. After brushing away a layer of straw and sand, she exposed a thick sheet of plywood coated with sand-colored deck sealer.

They set the empty pallet completely aside, then lifted away the sheet of plywood, which had been reinforced on the bottom with rails of sealed pine. Beneath it was a space about four feet deep resembling a basement. It was supported on top with an intricate wooden framework that also shored up the other pallets. A battery-powered lamp lay inside close by, and when Ella dropped down and turned it on, she saw a ladder leading into a vertical shaft.

Victoria jumped down beside Ella. "This is the dig site. My guess is that when he and Eileen were setting up her garden, they stumbled on a real treasure trove."

"So they constructed the loafing shed over the spot, and worked their way down, maybe covering the hole with that tarp at first," Blalock said, joining them and pointing to a large, dusty canvas tarp rolled up against one side of the earthen enclosure. "Putting a roof over everything, then covering it with the bales, kept everything out of sight and safe."

"The problem is, those artifacts were never theirs. They belong to the tribe," Victoria said.

"To make sure this discovery remains safely in the hands of the People, let's clear more of the pallets away, take the tarp topside, and use it to cover and protect whatever remains below," Ella said.

As soon as they were back on the surface, Ella pulled her cell phone out. "I'll call the anthropology department at the tribal community college and have some of their experts assist our crime scene people. They'll know the best way to preserve the site. We'll also need to leave a couple of officers out here tonight." Before she could say more, Ella saw the plume of dust rising in the air.

"There's Big Ed now," Blalock said. "I got a text message saying he was on his way. The local reporters for the TV affiliates won't be far behind."

"Reporters? How do they know about this place already?" Ella asked.

"Get with the program, Clah. The new tribal police motto is—never miss a photo op," Blalock said. "Department Head Bidtah was in the office when you called the chief, and Big Ed told him what was going down."

Ella groaned.

"Cheer up," Victoria said with a smile. "It's not that bad. The tribal police should share its successes with the public. It generates trust and confidence."

Ella saw the tribal public safety director's special SUV following closely behind Big Ed's. This wasn't about sharing a victory; it was about taking credit—the wave of the future.

TWENTY-THREE
—— ✖ ✖ ✖ ——

It was close to nine that night when Big Ed took Ella aside, away from the gathered crowd of reporters just outside the fenced-in enclosure. All the bales and pallets had been removed and stacked against one length of fence, exposing the entire dig, which was now illuminated by floodlights on stands. Bidtah was speaking to the members of the college anthropology staff and the reporters gathered there.

"I know you hate this kind of grandstanding and so do I, but this is his game now," Big Ed said.

"You're still the chief," Ella said.

"Not for long, so watch your back, Shorty," Big Ed whispered in the dark.

"You're retiring?" she asked, not surprised, but not happy to hear the news, either.

"I go on vacation starting tomorrow, then my retirement kicks in at the end of the month," he said with a nod. "Bidtah made me an offer and I took it. The DA won't press charges against my brother for the purchase of stolen county property—providing full restitution is made. Basically, it's a done deal, except for the paperwork. All parties have agreed to the terms, so this is my last official function."

"Why did you let them force your hand like that? They didn't have that much of a case against Elroy. Proving that he'd actually known the merchandise was stolen would have been nearly impossible."

"I know, but I didn't want to drag my brother's name through the mud. His wife's cancer has progressed, and the guy needs a break." He paused, then added, "I've been in this game long enough and made my mark, for what it's worth. It's time for me to move on."

Ella nodded slowly. "Has Bidtah selected a new chief yet?"

"Yeah. Nelson Natani will be taking over tomorrow morning."

"Crap." Ella's stomach sank. Today had been a roller coaster ride of emotions and events, and she felt back at the bottom again. Her eyes were suddenly moist, but the tears were for her old boss, not because of her new one. Ella wiped them away, glancing over at Big Ed, who was also having eye problems at the moment.

Gerald Bidtah waved at them and called out. "Come over, team. Let's get a photo of all who worked so hard to bring justice to the People."

Big Ed forced a smile. "Come on, Shorty. One last time."

Sunlight played on Ella's pillow, nudging her awake. Judging from the stillness in the house and the high position of the sun outside, she'd overslept, but it didn't matter. She'd worked almost all night, wrapping up the case.

Hearing her cell phone ring, Ella picked it up with a groan and saw it was Justine calling.

"You better get over here, partner," Justine said. "Things are happening fast. The new boss showed up early and has already hand-delivered letters and marching orders to every officer at the station. The biggest impact on us is, quote, 'outdated and no longer cost effective' and is the reason we're being eliminated. We're all being reassigned. Benny and I are the only ones from the team who'll be staying here in Shiprock as detectives, working homicide, burglary, or wherever we're needed. We'll answer directly to Natani."

"And Ralph?" Ella asked, knowing he, too, was close to retirement.

"I don't know, he won't say, but he wants to talk to you as soon as you come into the station."

"I'll be there in thirty," Ella said, already heading toward the shower. She'd made her own career decision on the drive home last night. She knew what she had to do. For her, the hard part was over.

Ella met her mother in the kitchen fifteen minutes later. "Just coffee this morning, Mom."

Rose studied her face. "Anything you want to tell me, daughter?"

Ella smiled, suspecting her mother already knew what she'd decided. "I have to get going, Mom, but we'll all talk tonight. I promise." Ella gave her a quick hug, then hurried outside to her pickup.

———

When Ella walked through the front doors of the station, she could feel the tension in the air. It was a tangible presence evidenced in the hushed voices and the flat, emotionless cop stares—a sure sign that emotions were deliberately being kept in check.

Tache met her in the hall, nodded with the trace of a smile, and walked with her to her office. Once there, he waited for her to go behind her desk before sitting down.

"What's going on, Ralph? Does it have something to do with the fact that you're not wearing your badge?" she asked, taking a seat.

"I knew that wouldn't escape you," he said, then paused for a moment. "It's like this. Natani, the new chief, suggested I take my retirement now. The new benefits package coming out in January will have more restrictive health coverage and reduced retirement benefits. There's no grandfathering in, so if I stay on past December, I'll be switched over to the new plan. That's a big cut for me."

"So basically they've found a way to force you out, too," Ella said, shaking her head slowly.

"You're still in the game, Ella. Word is that they want you in Window Rock." Ralph stood. "Good luck. It's been a pleasure working alongside you all these years."

"Walk in beauty, Officer Tache." Ella stood there for a moment, awkwardly, then reached out. They hugged each other for about a minute, neither saying a word, then let go.

Ralph nodded, gave her a big smile, then turned and left.

They'd all served the tribe, and now it was time for her to move on, too. Ella took a deep breath, then with a heavy heart began loading her personal items into an empty printer paper box.

As she removed a framed photo of her original team from where it hung on the wall for years, she stared at each face, one at a time. Harry's smile was broad and his eyes sparkled. Justine looked even younger than Ella remembered, as did Joe Neskahi. Jimmy Frank had died of cancer years back, but in the photo, he looked ready to tackle the world. Ralph had changed the most, the bomb blast that almost took his life had aged him beyond his years. But his spirit was still strong, and his recovery complete.

She placed the photo into the box. Time had slipped by, bringing with it too many unwelcome changes. Although a part of her hated saying good-bye to the department, she no longer wanted to be a tribal officer.

After she'd gathered her things, Ella sat in front of her computer and finished the resignation letter she'd written in her head late last night. It was short and to the point. There was no reason to belabor things.

She signed below the single paragraph, placed it in an envelope, and strode down the hall to what had been Big Ed's office. To her surprise, the name on the door had already been changed.

She took a moment to prepare herself, knocked on the open door, and went inside as soon as Natani waved an invitation.

He stood and smiled as she came in. "Just the person I wanted to see, Investigator Clah. Sit down and make yourself comfortable," he said, then regarded her from behind the massive desk. "As you've undoubtedly heard by now, I'm here to move the department forward, to modernize the way we've been doing things. That means a brand-new opportunity for you, Ella. The tribe needs an officer with your experience and expertise to train a new generation of officers. Director Bidtah has instructed me to offer you a well-deserved promotion. Your new package will include a twenty percent pay raise, transportation to and from Window Rock, and a generous housing allowance."

She listened carefully, then placed the envelope before him. "I appreciate the offer, but I think it's time for the department to greet the future unencumbered by the past. I resign."

His eyebrows shot up. "You sure about this? The department needs your experience."

"You've got some good people here. Treat them right, and they won't let you down."

"No way I can change your mind?" Natani replied.

She shook her head and placed her badge on his desk.

"Well, then . . . good luck, Ella," he said.

Ella turned and walked out of his office. There was no sense in looking back, because it was the path ahead that called to her now, and it was one filled with endless possibilities.

Justine, who was coming out of her lab, stopped, then looked down at Ella's waist. "You turned in your badge," she whispered.

It wasn't a question. "Yeah, but I'll be around, and you always know where to find me. We're family."

"I don't know what to say . . . ," Justine said, her voice trailing off. "I'm not sure I can even talk right now."

Ella didn't want her cousin to cry, that would only make things more difficult, and a hug right now would lead to that, for sure. They were that close. Ella needed to leave the station free of doubt and with her head held high. "It's not the end, Justine." She smiled. "Just a new beginning."

A few minutes later, Ella walked out the department doors carrying the cardboard box that held mementos of her seventeen years as a tribal officer. She stopped on the front step, turned to look at Ship Rock, forever a reminder of her past and her future, and took a breath of fresh air.

Life never closed a door without opening another. What lay ahead was still unknown to her, but that's exactly what would make it the best of all adventures.